Devya's Children Book 5: Dustin's Decision

By Julie C. Gilbert

Aletheia Pyralis Publishers

Questions and comments email: devyaschildren@gmail.com

http://www.juliecgilbert.com/

Other Fiction:

Scratched Off
Beyond Broken Pencils
Heartfelt Cases
Megan Luchek Books 1-10
Guardian Angel Files
Aeris Legends
Redeemer Chronicles
Anotech Chronicles

Nonfiction:

5 Steps to Better Blurbs
5 Steps to Better Audiobooks
5 Steps to Better Dialogue
5 Steps to Surviving Chemistry
5 Steps to School Success

Dedication:

To series fans who made it this far (and brave souls jumping in now). It's been quite a journey.

Devya's Children Series in order:
Ashlynn's Dreams Shorts (prequel)
The Dark Side of Science (prequel)
Ashlynn's Dreams
Nadia's Tears
Malia's Miracles
Varick's Quest
Dustin's Decision

Important People:

(Warning: may contain spoilers)

Dr. Carla M. Wittier – Jillian's old shrink lady
Dr. Stephanie Sokolowski (a.k.a. Dr. S.) – Jillian's new shrink lady

Dr. Dean Devya – researcher, creator of Devya's Children
Dr. Evelyn Carnasis – researcher, former associate of Dr. Devya, mother to Jillian, Benjamin Connelly, and Aiden
Cora – former associate of Dr. Devya, mother to Brenton, Dustin, and Anastasia
Dr. Karita Robinson – former associate of Dr. Devya, mother to Malia and Michio
Dr. Jessica Paladon – former associate of Dr. Devya, mother to Varick and Nadia
Danielle Matheson – Jillian's friend; Varick's girlfriend
Dr. Calvin Mulligan – admirer of Dr. Paladon's work

Devya's Children:
Brenton – soldier; deceased
Varick – soldier
Nadia – minder, Queen Elena, Naidine, Nadie
Ashlynn – dreamer, Jillian Blairington
Malia – empath
Dustin – Devya's telepathist
Reeve – second dreamer, Benjamin Connelly
Michio – first nanomachine controller
Aiden – second nanomachine controller
Anastasia – meant to be second minder, project sabotaged

Table of Contents:

Summary: ITEM 1-231:

(Warning: definitely contains spoilers)

Ashlynn's Dreams includes the first 72 items which detail how Jillian Marie Antel Blairington comes to know she has the unique ability to shape dreams. During those adventures, she forges a strong friendship with her babysitter, Danielle Matheson, who gets kidnapped as a means of controlling Jillian's behavior during the Dream Shaper training.

Nadia's Tears covers items 73 through 130 which follow Jillian's efforts to awaken Nadia from a coma and Danielle's efforts to keep Christy Roman safe and out of trouble. In Nadia's dreams, Jillian meets her sister at various stages of life, including the emotionally wounded Nadie, the fierce Naidine, and the wise Queen Elena. After helping Jillian get to Nadia, Danielle tries to concentrate on school but gets drawn into Christy's troubles. Jillian succeeds in waking Nadia in time to rescue Danielle and Christy.

Malia's Miracles contains items 131-178 which recount the healing efforts to save Susan Kilpatrick, mother of Christy and Dominique Roman. The matter becomes complicated by the government's efforts to capture Jillian and her genetically Gifted siblings. They successfully elude capture, but the bold move convinces Dr. Devya to transfer Nadia to a more secure facility.

Varick's Quest encompasses items 179-231 which involves Jillian and Danielle being kidnapped by Dr. Lanier and Nadia and Dr. Carnasis falling into the hands of opportunists looking to sell the Minder to the highest bidder. Varick faces a really tough decision about who to rescue first. Things work out but there are consequences. Jillian discovers she can't go home. Reluctantly, she agrees to travel with Nadia and Dr. Devya back to the new secret lab.

Prologue:

"There's never enough time unless you create it." ~Dr. Devya

ITEM 232: Carla Wittier's ninth letter
Item Source: Dr. Carla M. Wittier

To Dr. Stephanie Sokolowski:

Sorry these entries are out of order. I took the liberty of retyping and printing this one because the original is quite unsightly. In addition to shredding the hand-written version, I spilled coffee over most of it.

I sincerely hope the troubles facing Jillian will soon return to this level of chaos.

Have you heard from her or Nadia lately? Since the move to the new facility, communication with them has been intermittent at best. I am trying not to worry, but I cannot shake the foreboding sense that things will once again get worse before righting themselves.

Kind regards,
Carla M. Wittier, Ph.D.

***

ITEM 233 (formerly ITEM 4): Jillian's third pre-kidnapping journal entry
Item Source: Dr. Carla M. Wittier

The short version of my name is Jillian, but the version Momma shouts when she gets riled, is Jillian Marie Antel Blairington. Momma says I'm a handful, but she never tells me a handful of what. My Old Daddy's full name was Jason Alexander Antel, but he wasn't no good for Momma, so she fixed him with some papers and told him not to come back. Nana said that was a bonny blessing of a good day if she ever saw one.

My New Daddy's full name is—great galoots! I don't know what my New Daddy's full name is. He's always been Mr. Blairington to me. Honest. Now, afore you go scolding me for forgetting my New Daddy's name, I'd just like to say that he's only been my New Daddy for about a month. I'll have to ask him when he gets back from that Yankee state he went to see on business. I think it was New Jersey. He says it's a real good place for buying and selling houses. That's probably why the puny state looks like a money sign symbol on the map.

Anyways, my New Daddy's been gone for a whole two days, and he'll be gone another three some more at least. The first night he called Momma, I answered the phone and asked him what he wanted.

He said, "I want to hear your beautiful voice, Sweet Cake."

Nana calls me Pudding Cake so I guess my New Daddy wanted a cake of his own to call me, but he ain't that inventive. I told him he was full of overdone baloney. He just laughed, so I turned him over to Momma. She took the phone to the TV room, and they talked and talked for near forever. I don't know what he was telling Momma but even from my room with the door closed I could hear her giggling. But that's not what I meant to be telling y'all.

One thing they don't tell ya about having a New Daddy is that there's lots more laundry. See, it'd been just Momma and me for quite a while before Momma and Mr. Blairington got hitched. About a week after Momma brought my New Daddy home from the honeymoon, the old drier called in all its quit cards at once. Daddy and a friend of his, Mr. Little, who ain't actually small, hauled the old drier off for a fitting burial for a faithful old machine, as Mr. Little put it. He talks like Nana. I wonder if he knows her.

After the drier quit, Momma let the laundry pile up some, I think she was hoping my New Daddy would buy her a new drier before she had to face the mounting mountain of soiled second skins. I'd say that Nana was being overly dramatic in describing our laundry pile, but I get around so I know that sometimes my clothes come back to Momma nasty as toe fungus with a matching smell to boot. Momma waited as long as she could, but when I told her I was wearing the same pair of underwear for the third day in a row, she rolled up her sleeves, tied back her long hair, and went to war with the laundry pile.

It was a Saturday. I remember 'cause soon after Momma started on the laundry I hiked down to the crick to dig up bait worms to use over at the river behind Jimmy Denson's place. Jimmy's my best friend in the whole world. Nana said one day if I have any sense at all, I'd "get hitched to that fine, handsome youngin'." Nana's sure got some crazy notions. She meant Jimmy before the day Nicholas VanUrp went insane during recess. That's a sad story. I can't tell ya about it now, but I will one day.

I never made it to Jimmy's that day 'cause I had to talk to the police for a long time. I'd just finished collecting the bait, when Momma and a skinny stranger came tearing towards me like Hades' hounds were licking their heels. Momma was screaming something fierce in a loud screeching tone I hadn't heard since my Old Daddy left.

"Get back here, you bleep thief!" Momma shouted. "Help!"

I couldn't believe my ears. Momma had used the "d" word. It's not fair. If I'd said that, I'd have a burning backside to remind me of my manners. I was so caught up in the fact that Momma used one of the bad words that got the Old Daddy in such a heap of trouble that I hardly realized the lanky fellow and Momma were barreling towards me.

He gestured wildly and screamed. It took me a full second to understand what he was saying and by that time he was only three steps away.

"Move! Move! Move!"

I stood my ground and measured him like my Old Daddy taught me. The young man wanted to get away, and Momma wanted him to come back. No one—besides me—disobeys my Momma. The fellow lowered his shoulder and braced to shove me aside, but I didn't give him the chance. With a scream that woulda stopped a train cold if it could, I threw my whole bucket of worms and dirt right in the man's face. He pulled up short and squealed, so I smacked him in the back of the knees with the bucket.

"Momma told you to stop!"

He dropped and sputtered like he'd swallowed a worm.

By this time, Momma arrived and grabbed a handful of the young man's hair. Her other hand snatched back a pair of my new daddy's jeans. "That'll teach ya to not steal from decent folk! What do you have to say for yourself?"

"Sorry, ma'am," mumbled the boy. "I didn't mean no harm." His tone was smooth and well-designed to get one's way.

"Get out of here!" Momma ordered the young fellow, just before taking my arm rougher than necessary and yanking me towards the house.

I probably shoulda let that stand but I couldn't help saying, "You leave our laundry alone, you clothes-stealing wretch, or I'll feed ya a whole crick full of fish!"

Momma looked real disapproving and yanked my sore arm some more, but she didn't yell or nothing so it was a good day.

Chapter 1:
Real Bad News

ITEM 234: Jillian's 115th post-kidnapping journal entry
Item Source: Jillian Blairington

Normally, Nadia would wake me around 7:00 so I could take care of the necessaries before heading to the mess hall for breakfast, but when I woke on my own well after 7:30, I knew something was wrong. I wanted to force myself back to sleep so I could access my gifts and check on her, but I figured Maisha would know where to find Nadia anyway.

I considered skipping teeth brushing, but a mental image of Nana's frown of deep disapproval made me include the morning chore. Figuring I needed all my wits wide awake, I also threw cold water on my face. I didn't care when my shirt got all wet 'cause I needed to change into day clothes anyway. Eager to find my sister, I threw on the first shirt and pair of jeans I could find. Not entirely sure they was completely clean, but they passed the sniff test.

I'd been at the lab long enough to be comfortable enough with the compound's layout to make it from the room I shared with Nadia over to the mess hall. From inside, it's kinda hard to tell directions, but if ya looked from above, the eastern half held mostly living quarters and the western half held labs, training rooms, classrooms, and offices. The mess hall and a few larger training rooms sat in the middle, separating the work and life halves of the compound.

My sense of unease got worse when I found a covered plate of food, a glass of water, and a note from Maisha saying I could find her and Nadia in the gardens when I finished eating. I'd never heard of gardens since it wasn't part of my initial tour, but the notion of there being some here didn't surprise me much. The compound had been built underground back when the government thought nuclear war would wipe out surface life.

Removing the cover, I found a giant egg and sausage casserole with two fresh biscuits. As with everything Maisha makes, the egg concoction was delicious, but I couldn't really enjoy it 'cause I was busy belting it down at unsafe speeds. My curiosity grew by the second until it stirred my stomach something fierce. That's not a great feeling at the best of times. It's worse after an egg casserole. The mess hall had never been this empty either.

As soon as my brain decided I was full, I felt the urge to get up and move toward the south hallway. Recognizing it as an impulse sent by Nadia, I quickly rushed the tray over to the proper cleanup spot and followed the gut instinct. Didn't know Nadia could do such a thing, but I decided a long time ago it ain't worth wasting brainpower being shocked by new tricks she comes up with.

It wasn't exactly like having a map in one's head, but every time I reached a place with options, I got a distinct feeling about which way to turn. Sure hope there's a reverse sense of direction thing, or I'm likely to get good and lost in here. Guess that's a problem later me will have to face. Finally, the weird sense of direction led me to a plain white door. It musta had some kind of sensor on it 'cause as I stop the door got sucked into the frame.

Maisha swept me into a huge hug practically before I crossed over into the room.

"Miss Nadia's jus' had some real bad news. Do whatcha can ta help her, honey. I needs ta get back an' feed my boys and princesses, but then I be back with somethin' fer Miss Nadia."

She rushed off before I could ask any questions.

I didn't see Nadia right away, but I heard her crying. Like Dr. Devya's other lab, the gardens had been carefully laid out to make a relaxing setting. Mighta been my imagination, but the air felt fresher out here even though we were probably still underground. I found my sister sitting on the edge of a small fountain. The sight made me think of Malia 'cause she used to sit on the fountain at the other lab. Not sure what to say, I sat next to Nadia. She threw her arms around me and continued her cry.

A dozen questions ached to bust outta me, but I kept shut 'cause I figured she couldn't answer anyway. I held her until she finished with the sobbing part. When she finally pulled away, I got a look at her face. Tears still leaked from her eyes, but she caught 'em with her sleeve and drew several deep breaths.

"Andrew is dead," said Nadia. Somehow her British accent made that short statement sadder. The speed the words came out at was entirely too slow for normal Nadia standards. That too made it sadder.

Before I could ask about Andrew, an image of the young scientist popped into my mind, giving me a good shot of guilt. Andrew was one of the first people whose dreams I entered and changed. I'd stumbled across a dream of him kissing Nadia and turned the image of her into a giant rat. That's how Dr. Devya found out about their relationship, and he had the man beaten for it. I'd not really given the matter much thought since Andrew left soon after that incident. Given my sister's gifts and how much I don't know about her, I guess they coulda kept in touch.

Fixing her gaze on the fountain water, Nadia continued her speech at something a little closer to normal speed.

"We ended our relationship soon after he left with my mother, but I checked in when I could."

"What happened to him?" I asked. She woulda told me anyway, but I didn't like sitting there doing nothing. The usual things one says to somebody hurting like that didn't seem good enough.

An article appeared in my head. I closed my eyes to concentrate enough to read it, but Nadia flooded me with the details before I could get much past the first sentence. The article talked about a murder-suicide and an apartment fire with three casualties, a woman and her two grown sons.

"Do you believe the article?" I asked, reaching the portion where it said one of the sons shot his mother, brother, and set the fire before committing suicide.

"No, and neither do the officials," said Nadia. "I have not had a chance to check every mind related to the investigation, but so far, nobody will speak of it. The order to bury the case came from very high up." The way she looked at me said she had more to say but wasn't sure she wanted to burden me with the extra knowledge.

"That ain't all that's got you worried," I said, changing position so I could face her more directly. "What else is wrong?"

"I may not be able to keep my promise to teach you." Her words took on the slow, scary pace again. Nadia's lips twitched, like she wanted to smile but couldn't quite manage it. She picked up my hand and held it gently between her palms. "I believe the government has finally lost patience with Father."

I didn't catch her meaning right away, but when I did, I gripped her hand pretty hard.

"You've gotta leave." I jumped to my feet pulling her up with me.

"Not me." Breaking free of my hold, Nadia moved her hands to my shoulders. "You, Dustin, and Aiden. You need to hide and help the others break free and get to a safe place. That is the task I have given to Cora and Dr. Carnasis."

"What others?" I asked, not bothering to hide my confusion.

"Dr. Lanier was not the only one who attempted to set up his own program like Father's," said Nadia. She squeezed my shoulders once, then clasped her hands in front of her body. "There are others, but I will only reveal those you need to know when you need that knowledge. To do more would place an unfair burden upon you and needlessly endanger those we aim to aid."

"Sounds like something from one of Varick's video games," I grumbled, giving her my best Evil Eye.

"I believe he is working on a new game to facilitate your training." Nadia tipped her chin up slightly. "You can have a big role or a small one in these affairs, but knowing you as I do, I have asked Varick to factor you into our plans."

The fact that she had plans with Varick surprised me more than it ought to 'cause they have always been close since they have the same mother. The thought made me think of Dr. Jessica Paladon—Nadia and Varick's mother—as well as Dr. Robinson—Malia and Michio's mother.

They probably ain't safe either.

"Right now. Nearly everybody with close ties to us or the programs that created us faces some manner of danger," said Nadia, responding to my thought. "We are moving as quickly as possible to see that they are kept out of harm's way, but we cannot force them to hide while we deal with the troubles to come."

"What do ya need me to do?" I really wanted to knock some sense into her, but I figured I oughta get my assignment first.

"Varick will speak with your parents soon, but it would help tremendously if you spoke with at least one of them before he approaches with details," said Nadia. "You will also need to pack. I have an exit strategy for you to follow, but the timing is very much fluid because it is based on the whims of others."

I gave her a hard look, crossing my arms to let her know I wasn't pleased with her.

"Before I do anything, I wanna know why you ain't planning on going into hiding with everybody else."

Nadia gave me one of those familiar, sad smiles, picked up one of my hands, and directed me to sit on the fountain once more before speaking.

"There is a plan for that, but many things must happen before we reach that point," Nadia said. "I have thought through many scenarios, and this one has the highest probability of the lowest fatalities."

Her last word made me think of Andrew and his family again.

Nadia's thoughts musta drifted there too 'cause her eyes got shiny with new tears.

"I do not know if those deaths were a sign, a warning, or something unrelated to us, but if we do nothing, other deaths will follow," said Nadia.

"Why can't we all stay and face this together?" I asked. "Aiden's young, but he can probably build us a crazy complicated weapon to fight back. I dunno what Dusty can do, but he seemed pretty bent on bargaining for our lives with Dr. Lanier. My Dream

Shaper gift is mostly useless to ya, but I can knock out the first dozen people who try to harm ya." I added a mental picture of bad guys falling over to lighten our dark mood, but if anything, my sister looked more serious.

Her expression said she was once again measuring the worth of revealing something to me.

"Varick and I have long been the public face of Father's program," Nadia explained. "That affords me some protections, but there is one whose safety must be considered first because his gifts are most coveted by those who wish to control us."

I considered my brothers. Aiden and Michio can build stuff and heal through nanomachines. Reeve—Benny Connelly—has Dream Shaper gifts like mine. Varick can fight well and come up with plans like Nadia. Dustin's the only mystery.

She had to mean him.

"What are his gifts anyway?" I asked, knowing Nadia followed my short mental journey to focus on Dustin.

"He knows everything about Father's program," Nadia replied. "Everybody who has ever tried to set up a similar program has failed in some fundamental way because they lacked some important information. Father used to keep notes, but the first time they got stolen, he knew he needed a better way."

"Why not dump everything into a computer program behind a really strong firewall?" I asked. "Ain't he afraid Dustin will just walk off with the information?"

"I am not certain Dustin understands the nature of his Gifts or how to access them," said Nadia. Her gaze turned distant and troubled. "No matter what happens to the rest of us, we must keep the information he bears out of certain hands."

"You're kinda scaring me," I told her. "What's so dangerous about the knowledge he carries?"

"It may be the only thing we can use to purchase our lives," Nadia explained, "yet to let the wrong people have it will mean condemning many more innocents in our place. I cannot do that."

"I'm gonna start by saying I don't like this, and you have a whole heap of explaining to do," I declared. "Then I'm gonna tell ya to give me something to do 'cause you're getting my help whether ya like it or not."

Chapter 2:
Not Going

ITEM 235: Danielle's 68th letter
Item Source: Danielle Matheson

Dear Dr. S.,

Life's good. I feel weird saying that, like I'm tempting fate to drop me into another insane situation. Settling back into college life has been surprisingly easy. It's hard to believe two weeks ago I wasn't sure I'd live to see one more day let alone be headed home after a full week of classes.

How are things with you?

I'm using Malia's thoughts-to-words program as I drive home, so forgive me if the letter is a bit more scattered than usual. This drive is about the first time I've had to relax since I had a lot of catching up to do in the classes I missed due to my second kidnapping. (Or is it the third kidnapping? I guess it's third if you count the incident with Christy's family. You could even call it the fourth kidnapping if you count the run-in Christy and I had with those human traffickers. Let's just go with fourth kidnapping.)

Thankfully, there's not much to report. Some profs are better at communicating than others, but on top of attending normal classes, I've managed to catch up on the reading for English, write an essay for psych, and string together a semi-coherent lab report for bio. At least one professor hinted that more leeway would be given if I gave even a hint of what went on. I get that, but I'd rather take a 0 on a really big assignment than go into details.

Though I'll probably regret my decision by Sunday evening, my game plan for tonight involves absolutely no schoolwork. Not sure if Varick will be free to hang out, but I'm hoping he can. I miss him. Between my class marathons and his check-in duties to make sure my family, Jillian's family, and Anastasia's family remain safe, I've hardly seen him this week. Since I promised Mom and Katy I'd participate in a trip to the mall to get my sister some winter clothes and then agreed to a movie night with Dylan and Dad, I won't be able to see Varick until Sunday after church. If an impromptu date with Varick's off the table, I'd like to catch up on some me time.

Or check on Jillian and Nadia.

I'm sorry. I thought I could go a whole letter without mentioning them, but Jillian hasn't visited my dreams, and Nadia's contact has been sporadic this week. That's never a great sign. I've tried to reason that Nadia is leaving me alone so I could handle the class catchup, but this doesn't feel like that kind of silence. I'll be the first to admit to not being an expert at telepathic communication, but this has the feel of a calm-before-the-storm sort of quiet. Besides, Jillian isn't subtle. She occasionally gets too busy to do her regular dream checks, which is also never a great sign.

I believe I've let my feelings be known before, but the situation warrants another rant. I hate almost everything about this situation with Jillian. Getting to spend more time with her sister, Nadia, is one of the few good points, but having to avoid the family that raised her to keep them safe is heartbreaking and wrong on so many levels. Having to stay in the same place as Devya also rankles. You can blame that word on Nadia, but the point remains: it's not fair.

When I started this letter journey with you many, many months ago, I said as much. Jillian should be worried about school bullies and not falling asleep during tests. She should be home chasing Isaac and Michio around the back yard. Instead, she's hiding in a secret government lab from psychopaths who want to control her and the rest of Devya's children.

Don't know what happened to Lanier. Sure hope he's rotting in a prison cell, but the way life's been going, it wouldn't surprise me if his money let him wriggle free somehow. I don't even know if he could be properly prosecuted without raising exactly the sort of questions we need to avoid right now.

I guess I'm feeling helpless again. How do you keep people from making reckless and dangerous decisions, especially when you half-agree with them?

I'm almost home now, so I guess I'd best wrap this up. Looks like Katy's waiting on the front stoop for me, and she's wearing a frown and hot pink hair. Sorry for the abrupt end. I'll return to my musings post-pink-hair investigation.

The Hair Detective,

Danielle Matheson.

***

ITEM 236: Danielle's 69th letter
Item Source: Danielle Matheson

Dear Dr. S.,

The crisis has been averted. (Thank you, Google and YouTube.) Turns out my sister decided her rebellious act of the week would be dyeing her hair with cherry flavored Kool-Aid. Mom isn't the sort to vent her woes to me, but apparently, at eleven going on thirty, Katy's done being a little kid and is ready to make complicated life decisions like what color her hair should be.

A few weeks ago, she decided to refer to Mom and Dad as Lisa and Craig. I thought it was funny, but that got her grounded until today. Tried to talk Mom into letting the kid keep the strange color until it washed out naturally, but she wasn't exactly in a negotiating mood after cleaning up the mess Katy left in the kitchen.

The current stunt may have jeopardized our scheduled shopping trip, but I think I talked Mom down from that ledge as I prepared the baking soda and vinegar concoction to get the color out. Katy cried when I helped wash her hair with shampoo, but afterward, we had a nice long conversation. Actually, I'm not sure I said six words together during that half-hour. My contributions consisted of many uh-huhs, mmms, and variations of *I see*. Though it makes me feel terribly old, I find myself siding with my mother on most of the grievances Katy aired, but I hid it well enough to maintain my cool-sister status.

Dylan nearly blundered in during the hair washing therapy session, but thankfully, the upstairs hall bathroom is too small to hold three people. He realized the mistake as the door hit me and stopped moving inward, though I'm sure Katy's bloodcurdling scream helped bust through his video-game induced stupor. He must have had to use the facilities seriously enough because he fled to the parents' bathroom without entering a verbal duel with our sister.

This is the sort of chaos I wish upon Jillian's family. Normal chaos.

Dinner chatter was a tad frostier than usual because of the tension between Mom and Katy, but Dad managed to guilt everybody into a family game night. Katy's mood improved once she trounced us at Life and Matheson Family Candyland. That's the altered version of the classic game where in order to move one has to share something from their week or share something nice about one of the other players. It turned dicey when Dylan complimented Katy's hair. The afternoon battle against the Kool-Aid had mostly been successful, but her hair still sported a few patches of fading pink. Once again, Dad saved the day by calling a halt for ice cream sundaes.

After dessert, we declared Katy the Candyland victor because she was the farthest and moved on to other games. Dylan won Yahtzee. Mom won King's Corner and Ticket to Ride. I'm usually better at family game night events, but at least it passed the time. I'm a much more graceful loser than Dylan and Katy anyway, so it helped keep the peace. As we considered another round of Ticket to Ride, Shorty decided we'd had enough family fun and really should pay more attention to her, so she parked her furry backside right on the gameboard. Dylan and Katy tried to get her to move, but she refused to be budged.

I'd give the night a solid 9 out of 10 if it ended there, but it didn't.

As soon as we finally convinced Dylan and Katy to head up to bed, Varick showed up.

Normally, I'd be delighted by the surprise, and I was for

about three seconds. That's the length of time it took me to recognize the cool, business-like expression he wore meant trouble.

"I need to speak with your parents right away," said Varick.

Curiosity helped me conquer the momentary sting of having my boyfriend completely skip pleasantries.

"They're in the kitchen," I said, waving him into the house. By the time I'd relocked the door and entered the kitchen, I only caught the tail end of Mom's greetings and drink offer.

Varick moved to a position behind my usual seat and declined the drink.

Mom set a fresh bottle of water on the table for him anyway

Dad, the more observant parent, picked up on Varick's mood.

"What brings you by at this hour?" asked Dad.

"Your safety," Varick answered.

Mom sucked in sharply but refrained from commenting, choosing to lean against the counter for support.

"Certain incidents have convinced us you ought to take the children on a road trip," said Varick. "You can't tell anybody where. I'm here to deliver money and a basic plan, but nobody should know much more than that. Leaving tonight would be best."

"For how long?" asked Mom.

"What incidents?" Dad demanded at the same time.

My head echoed Dad's question.

"For at least two weeks," Varick answered, addressing Mom's question before moving on to Dad's question. "As for the incidents, my sister, Nadia, can share one of them with you if you wish, but I'll warn you it's not pleasant."

A strange feeling came over me. Recognizing it as Nadia's offer to share the story Varick mentioned, I opened my mind to receive the information. My parents must have too. Mom's left hand flew to her mouth. The reaction unsettled me until I absorbed the details of Andrew Marlton's horrific death along with his mother and brother.

"The fellow used to work for Dr. Devya," Varick

explained. "Other scientists and people with some connection to us have also been killed or disappeared suddenly over the past three weeks. While there's no reason to think anybody would specifically target your family, your daughter has become very important to us. Many of the wrong people already know this."

Dropping her hand from her mouth, Mom shot a hard look at me.

"Pack some stuff, Dani," she ordered. "You're coming with us."

Dad raised his hands in a half-halting, half-beast taming gesture.

"Hang on, Lisa," said Dad. "Let's think about this."

"What's to think about?" Mom's tone dropped the atmosphere at least ten degrees. She drew two shaky breaths before managing more words. "Did you forget the past few weeks? We almost lost her. Again. If a road trip will keep her safe, we're taking a road trip."

"I'm not arguing that point," Dad said, slipping into lawyer mode, "but it's not that easy to just disappear. I'm expected in court on Monday. I'll need to clear it with my bosses, notify my clients, and think of an excuse that won't get me fired."

"Nadia can give you some options," said Varick. "The fewer—"

"I'm not going." I didn't realize I'd even spoken until all attention fixed firmly on me. I bounced my gaze between my parents. "If some nutcase is going to come after me again, the last place I want to be is near you two, Katy, and Dylan."

After considering my logic, Varick nodded once.

"That's probably for the best, but you should take your own road trip," he said. "I can bring you more money tomorrow. Leave your credit cards, cell phones, and other trackable electronic devices here. Do you have any maps?"

"We have an old GPS," said Dad.

"Too dangerous," Varick said. "I'll bring you a map when I bring the additional money tomorrow, or you can ask my sister to plot a course for you."

Varick stayed a few extra minutes, giving us a crash course in staying untraceable. I'm not sure how much my parents got out of that, but I got nothing. My emotions were too busy railing against the destruction of my peaceful weekend plans.

When my parents huddled to confer with each other, I walked Varick to the front door.

"I'm sorry for the worry this is causing you and your folks," said Varick, drawing me into a hug. "It's just a precaution now, and I hope it's not necessary."

"Let me help." I voiced the plea even though I knew Varick had made his mind up. "There must be something I can do."

"Stay safe," Varick said, placing a kiss on my forehead.

He started pulling away, but I caught his face and kissed his lips.

"You don't get to leave it like that," I said, when we had to pause the kiss to breathe. Fighting frustrated tears, I continued my speech. "And if there's a chance to help you or your siblings, I'm taking it. Nobody gets to come for you without a fight. Got that?"

"That's why we love you." Varick gave me a softer kiss before breaking free.

I watched him go with a weird feeling flitting around in my gut like a bee in a jar. The comparison made me miss Jillian. I felt like I was sending Varick off to war without knowing who or what he would face. That's even more terrifying than knowing.

That's how I came to be packing for a trip of unknown length at 2:38 in the morning.

The Would-be Refugee,

Danielle Matheson.

Chapter 3:
Partings

ITEM 237: Jillian's 116th post-kidnapping journal entry
Item Source: Jillian Blairington

Between her training sessions, Nadia walked me through her plans for getting Aiden, Dustin, and me away from the lab sometime next week, but it didn't matter. I'd turned in early so I could check on Momma, my New Daddy, and Danielle. Even if I couldn't find one of 'em asleep, odds were decent I'd find somebody's dreams to enter. I'd just tracked down the dreams of Danielle's black Lab, Shorty, when a blast of cold brought me awake instantly. I tensed, ready to fight the fiend who woke me.

Nadia caught my shoulders as I launched to a sitting position.

"I am sorry, Jillian, but you were not responding to gentle measures to awaken you," said Nadia. "I needed to give you some new programs I prepared for a situation like this. They will explain themselves later as necessary. Please get dressed. We must see Father right away."

I musta really been tired 'cause I didn't notice the two security men standing behind my sister until one shifted. Questions crowded my head until Nadia spoke again.

"Dustin is gone."

My sister backed up enough for me to exit the bed and find clothes. She ushered the security men out so I could dress in peace.

"Why are there security men with ya?" I asked, once Nadia

shut the door to our room.

"Father fears that since I helped Dustin leave, I mean to follow him," said Nadia. "I do not like that Dustin is deviating from the plan, but it is just as well he is away."

"Did ya tell Dr. Devya why Dustin had to leave?" I wondered, pulling a green shirt over my head before wriggling out of the other one.

"He is aware of the problems facing us," said Nadia.

Deciding the pair of jeans I'd worn all day hadn't gotten too dirty, I tugged 'em back on before finishing the other parts of getting dressed.

I had to jog to keep up with Nadia and the security men as we flew through the hallways to Dr. Devya's office. Once there, Nadia and I sat in the two oversized chairs set before the big desk. The scene reminded me of sitting before Dr. Lanier's desk with Danielle before he told us of the pending move from the mansion.

"I have an assignment for you, Ashlynn," said Dr. Devya.

Dunno what I was expecting, but that made me sit up straight real quick.

"Nadia tells me she has made arrangements for you to go to a safehouse." Dr. Devya raised a hand to cut off a denial I was about to voice. "I'm fine with this, but while you're there, I want you to find Dustin."

"Can't Nadia find him?" I asked.

"I will try," said Nadia, "but he has been actively blocking me in recent days. Since you work while people are sleeping, their mental defenses tend to be lower."

Figured that would be the end of the conversation, but Nadia reached out and picked up my right hand.

"When you find Dustin, tell him he has never been alone in this, and he never will be. I would also like to speak with him, but he must reach out to me."

I promised to pass the message along.

"Good. Mr. Brady and Mr. Russell will escort you to the rendezvous," said Dr. Devya. "Keep Nadia apprised of your progress." He turned his attention to some stuff on his desk.

"Can Nadia go with me?"

I knew his answer before he voiced it.

"No. She still has work to do," said Dr. Devya, not bothering to look at me.

"But it ain't safe," I argued, "and she could work from anywhere."

"The compound has adequate security," said Dr. Devya, finally looking at me, "and if Nadia is correct about government overseers coming, they need to find somebody here or they will search for you."

Nadia stood and used our clasped hands to pull me into a hug.

"Be brave, Jillian, and come visit my dreams." Nadia said it lightly, but I knew she meant business. Something about the way she looked at me said that much.

Though curious why she didn't speak with me privately like she usually does, I had enough sense to keep shut on the issue.

The two men who'd first arrived in my room with Nadia shifted position enough for me to understand they must be Mr. Brady and Mr. Russell. I released Nadia and nodded to Dr. Devya before following my escorts through the massive compound to the underground garage. We walked past three black SUVs. I kept expecting Nadia to tell me which security guy was which, but again, she was strangely silent. One of the men opened the back door of the fourth SUV and waited for me to climb in.

To my surprise, I found Aiden and Maisha already there.

"Ash!"

I had about a quarter-second to prepare before my little brother barreled into me like a linebacker keen on sacking a quarterback. I grunted at the impact and returned his hug while my lungs recovered from the blow.

"Didn't expect I'd have company on this trip," I said.

"Dr. Dean and Miss Nadia said it was important ta hide the little un away, so that's jus what we's gonna do," said Maisha.

"Are we headed to the same place?" I wondered, still holding Aiden.

"Can't. Nadia said to hide with Maisha and call her Nana," said Aiden, pulling back and shaking his head.

For some reason, I found my little brother's statement sad.

"Don't worry, Miss Jillian. I's gonna take good care of

him," Maisha promised.

I believed her. Given that Maisha and Aiden both had dark skin, it made sense for her to play the part of his nana, even though he and I have the same momma and all the scientists whose genes got used in the experiments have light skin. Still, I felt guilty that Maisha got caught up in our messy lives. She could be doing anything, but instead, she sat right beside me headed to a safe house 'cause trouble is headed our way again.

I tried my best to keep up with Aiden's chatter and talk to Maisha, but the worry kept me quiet most of the journey. I don't even know how long we were driving or which direction we headed in. Spent every second of the trip clinging to Aiden's hot little body. Still not sure why he always runs a very high body temperature, but I guess it's a side effect of his Gift, like Varick's shifting eye color.

It's a good thing the security man driving didn't crash 'cause I'd never bothered putting on a seat belt or strapping Aiden in. He slept in my arms. Maisha napped some too. I coulda joined 'em, but I felt better holding my brother.

Finally, we stopped, and a security guy opened the door and helped Maisha down. I had to wake Aiden. Parting was painful, even though I tried to brace for it. I wanted to get out and give 'em both proper hugs, but as soon as Aiden cleared the door, the man slammed it shut. The tinted windows didn't let me even see if anybody met 'em.

More time passed, though I couldn't say how much for sure 'cause Nadia still wasn't talking to me, and I didn't have a watch or a phone. Normally, I could read the time off the dashboard clock, but the SUV had a tinted piece of plastic separating the front from the back. It kinda surprised me that its presence didn't bother me when Aiden and Maisha were with me. I wanted to sleep so I could at least get some answers, but I was too worried I'd miss something.

When the SUV stopped, the driver got out and opened my door. I climbed out and thanked him. He merely nodded, tossed me a light jacket, got back in his seat, and drove off, leaving me standing on a lonely road with big empty fields in every direction.

I didn't waste any time getting that jacket on. Thought

maybe my hands and face would still be cold, but somehow, the jacket kept the cold at bay.

"This way, Jillian," called a woman's voice.

I turned in time to see a figure walking away. There wasn't much time to hesitate 'cause the other option was stand there in the middle of nowhere, so I followed her. My feet hurt by the time the lady stopped. I thought she'd lost her way until she leaned down and pushed something aside. When I got closer, I realized it was a wooden board covered in grass and dirt like somebody's mobile garden. Wheels on the bottom helped the lady with her task. Soon, she'd uncovered a hole with a ladder going down into the ground.

"You won't be underground for long but there's a fresh set of clothes for you down there," said the lady.

Reluctantly, I started climbing down.

"When you get to the bottom, change and run the blue lightbar over as much of your body as you can," instructed the lady. "Leave your old clothes in the shielded box, then come on back up. I'll take you to the safe house."

My head decided to unhelpfully imagine several horrible scenarios where I ended up trapped underground as I climbed down that long ladder. It musta had twenty-five steps. Anyways, I reached the bottom without breaking my neck and changed as ordered. The ground was lit by a few dozen yellow and green glowsticks. The light showed me the new shirt was black. The outfit came with a black leather jacket too. The jeans were normal color just like the ones I already wore. Though tempted to cheat and not change the jeans, I reminded myself the cryptic instructions probably came from Nadia.

After some creative folding, I finally got my old clothes to fit in the small gray box sitting next to the pile of glowsticks. I really hated to leave the neat jacket behind, but I didn't have many options if I wanted to avoid possible microtrackers from Dr. Devya's labs.

Took me a minute to figure out how to work the blue light thingy the lady had talked about. It tingled the skin closest to the light regardless of whether or not there was cloth in the way. I spared a thought for hoping the light wasn't harmful 'cause I usually rely on Nadia to explain such things. I couldn't reach some parts of my back well, but I did several sweeps with both hands.

When I made it back to the top, the lady held out a black helmet for me. She already wore one and sat atop a motorcycle.

"Where'd ya get that?" I asked, meaning the bike even as I took the helmet.

"Some friends left it for us," replied the lady.

"Don't suppose you're gonna tell me where we're going," I said, climbing on behind her.

"You'll know if you need the knowledge," said the lady, "but we've got a ways to go. Our time would be better spent on the road. Hang on tight. It'll be a little bumpy until we get back to the paved road."

"Can I at least know your name?"

"Emma."

She fired up the motorcycle's engines, filling the night with enough noise to draw everybody withing fifty miles to our location.

I nearly fell off the motorcycle as Nadia's voice spoke in my head.

Chapter 4:
The Third Silence

ITEM 238: Nadia's third letter to Jillian
Item Source: Jillian Blairington

To My Dear Sister, Jillian:

Once again, I find myself having to explain why I must cause you pain. Unlike my previous two lengthy silences, this one is my choice. If you need to hear these words again think the phrase *repeat Nadia's explanation and apology for the third silence.*

Though I have no proof yet, I suspect there is at least one other Minder tracking my thoughts. I do not yet understand the extent of his or her Gifts, so I am keeping contact between us to a minimum to prevent this other person from tracking you easily. The other Minder may already know how to track your thoughts, but when you were near me, I shielded you as best I could. You should be well away from me by the time this message activates.

I am sorry for the many elaborate precautions being taken to see you to safety. The blue light should have suppressed the nanomachine tracking devices placed in you. Please do not be alarmed. They are relatively harmless and can only pinpoint your location to within a few miles. The change of clothes was for much the same reason in case there were other types of tracking devices I had not anticipated.

Your company during the first phase is Emma Carter. To

my knowledge, she is not related to Dr. Elizabeth Cliella, who became my public face during several formative years, allowing me to attend college classes only offered in person. You will recall that Dr. Cliella chose to become Grace Carter, what you may not know is that it was also her grandmother's maiden name. Nevertheless, Emma's family has a long history of helping us. You can trust her. She will take you to her grandfather, Leonard Murphy.

Stay with Mr. Murphy as long as you can. I suspect those who seek us will do everything possible to convince you to leave the refuge or betray its location. Varick has carried the warning cry to your family and Danielle's family, but there is always the chance the warning will fail in some way. I have alerted Malia and Michio to the possible trouble. Michio confirmed that Varick's warning was at least delivered.

Please check in often. I will have Naidine and Elena maintain the throne room. The lock will be back in place, but you should have no problems conquering it as you did before. That should be a safe place within my mind to leave messages. I could be worrying for nothing, but I have learned to trust my instincts.

One way or another, our troubles will come to a head soon, especially if Dustin allies himself with our enemies. I hope he does not, but I sense he longs for an end to the dangers and threats as much as the rest of us.

Do not take unnecessary risks. I promise to be cautious as well. You should be free to check on Malia, Aiden, and Michio's dreams.

Your loving sister,
Nadia Elena Ayers

***

ITEM 239: Jillian's 117th post-kidnapping journal entry
Item Source: Jillian Blairington

Even if it didn't tell me much, I made that letter repeat about a dozen times, partly 'cause I wanted to hear Nadia's voice. The letter made me wanna hug her and tell her to quit taking on every problem known to mankind. Had to concentrate on being mad at my sister so I wouldn't cry 'cause the helmet made it impossible to wipe the tears away.

I passed some of the riding time by thinking about Emma. Nadia's brief introduction didn't tell me much. I wondered how somebody came to the dangerous role of protecting us. To even get that far, the person had to know about us and our Gifts. Good guys and bad guys combined, the number of people aware of what my siblings and I can do can't be more than a few hundred. I guess the number goes up if Nadia's right about there being other programs like ours.

The motorcycle's vibrations and loud droning noise lulled me into a relaxed state, almost to the point where I fell asleep, but the cold countered some of the effects. By the time we stopped, my arms ached a lot. Had to think about how to move again. My legs were shaky after dismounting, but a man steadied me.

"Easy does it. You'll have your walking legs back soon," said an even, pleasant male voice.

Before I could even thank Emma, she waved to the man and drove off.

"Don't know how she can stand to ride that thing for hours on end," said the man, dropping his hold on my arm. His stance said he was ready to catch me if my legs quit. "Call me Murphy or Mr. Murphy as you like. Do you have a preference on how I address you?"

"Jillian," I said without hesitation. He probably already knew my Gift and project name, but if I had to trust him as a friend, I might as well be addressed as one.

"You've probably got a lot of questions, but you should sleep first."

Not having a better suggestion, I let the man lead me into a modest farmhouse. He showed me to a room and pointed out where I could find night clothes.

"They're all ancient but clean and functional," said Murphy. "Emma's outgrown them." He started to withdraw from the room but stopped. "She stocked the bathroom with toiletries based on Nadia's suggestions. If you're missing anything, let me know tomorrow, and I'll see about getting it. I'm the last room at the end of this hallway. If you sense any trouble, let me know, but be careful when wandering the house at night. I keep a few loaded guns handy."

Too tired to shower, I sat on the bed and wrestled off the boots. My feet complained a bit 'cause they're not used to boots, but at least Emma got the right size.

Nana woulda scolded me for not doing the nightly turn in activities, but I needed to do my check ins and reassure myself everybody got where they was supposed to go.

Aiden's dreams felt normal. Can't say I've been in enough of Maisha's dreams to know normal for her, but at least nothing seemed unusual or scary. I had trouble finding Nadia's dreams. That made me nervous, but given the tense situation I'd left, Nadia might still be up working. I moved on to Danielle, but once again, found no dream to enter. Though annoying, that worried me less than not finding Nadia. Danielle keeps some odd hours, especially on weekends. Momma and my New Daddy weren't dreaming, but Isaac and Michio had calm dreams.

Baby dreams are confusing, so I didn't stay with Isaac long.

Curious, I ducked into Michio's dream and found myself inside a miniature town made entirely of matchsticks. He musta gotten the idea for the model from an old Western movie 'cause there was a main street with a General Store, a Saloon, a Bank, a Sherriff's Office, and a place for carriage rentals. Michio had made people, horses, and cows for his stick town. Shaking my avatar's head, I exited my brother's dream.

Since my head was bent on keeping me in work mode, I worked through some of the mental exercises Nadia had described throughout the week. Like the task of getting in and out of dreams, the exercises were tedious, but what I needed at the time.

In the first exercise, I imagined a giant translucent shield around me in the blank mind space. Then, I remembered the beautiful place where I'd met Nadia and Malia and spaceships borrowed from one of Aiden's early dreams. I let the scene play out like it had at the time but changed small details like the color of our shirts or the flavor tea we had while the ships blasted at each other. The lesson—working through distraction—was pretty easy 'cause I'd spent some time at home with Isaac and Michio, and baby boys and little boys are really big distractions in tiny bodies.

The next exercise took me to a carnival. Not sure whose

dream it was originally since Nadia provided the memory. In this one, she wanted me to stop all movement in the dream. I thought it'd be easy, but the dream fought me quite a bit. If I concentrated on a section, it would freeze as expected, but Nadia musta woven instructions throughout the dream 'cause as soon as I got a handle on one part, another would misbehave. I only won by multiplying my avatar and having each version concentrate on a different aspect of the dream. It worked but strained my Gift enough to give me a headache.

The third exercise about scared a few years off my life until I remembered my Gifts. It consisted of a series of quick situations that in normal circumstances would be deadly. My poor avatar found herself caught in a riptide, tied up in a burning building, dropped into a war zone, stuck in outer space without a suit, and buried beneath an avalanche. I had to freeze dream time just to buy enough time to think of an adequate fix for her in each scenario. By the third crisis, I was calmer, but the first two caused enough panic to kick me up a few levels of sleep.

Before the fourth exercise could begin, I put a mental marker on it and brought myself down into a restful, non-working sleep. I didn't know how much real time had passed, but I figured I needed a clear head to wrestle with the problems facing me and my siblings.

Chapter 5:
Bizarre Scene

ITEM 240: Danielle's 70th letter
Item Source: Danielle Matheson
Dear Dr. S.,

Given the past few years of my life, it takes a lot to shock or horrify me. Ethan managed to do both in the span of twenty minutes. Yes, that Ethan. Dr. Lanier's psychotic soldier-boy who's supposed to be tucked up tight in Devya's new lab, receiving therapy and something to detox him from growth hormones. He swears he's working for the United States government on a matter of national security this time. Not sure I completely believe him, but he came with a suited sunglass-wearer who quietly directed the half-dozen black-clad thugs they brought as a show of force.

I should be flattered to warrant that kind of caution, but I know it was merely their nod to the possibility of having to tangle with Varick.

Guess I should back up and start my fifth-ish kidnapping tale from the beginning. I really, really wish I was kidding, but I'm not. Wish I was alone in this too, but I'm not. It's strange to not solely be the leverage piece this time. They haven't explained their wants and demands, but so far, I'm getting the impression that there's a massive operation in play.

Anyway, by the time I finished my frantic road trip packing, I collapsed onto my bed and fell asleep. The sound of my mother's voice brought me back to consciousness in increments.

"Dani. Wake up. Please."

At first, I didn't have enough working brain cells to pick up on her nervous tone, but eventually, I forced my eyes open. The overhead light made my eyes water, so I blinked rapidly and squinted toward my mother. Upon realizing she was flanked by two tall figures, I sat bolt upright. The sudden movement sent my suitcase crashing to the floor, but I didn't have time to worry about that. A male voice spoke from the other side of my bed.

"She's fine, and she'll stay fine as long as you cooperate."

I nearly got whiplash turning toward the voice. My brain identified the voice as Ethan's a split-second before my eyes settled on his face. His light brown hair hung longer than I remembered, but he still gave off a boy-next-door vibe. He didn't carry a weapon, but like Varick, something about the way he held his body said he could handle almost any situation without a weapon.

"Get up," said Ethan. "We're going to meet the rest of your family in the game room."

It didn't even occur to me at the time to wonder how he knew we referred to the family/entertainment room as a game room.

The question *why* fired through my head, but I had the sense to hold it in. My head tracked left again to check on my mother, but she'd already left—or been led away from—the post by my door. Needing answers, I hauled myself off my bed and moved toward the two blackclad men blocking my doorway. They parted enough to let me pass and fell into step behind me. Trying to ignore their presence, I dashed down the hallway and flew down the stairs.

The bizarre scene in the game room brought me to an abrupt halt in the threshold dividing the room from the kitchen. A brief shove forced me into the game room. My feet sank into the thick beige carpet.

Dad sat on the couch holding Katy. My normally energetic, independent sister rested her head on our father's shoulder. She wasn't currently crying, but telltale streaks marked her face. Looking dazed, Dylan sat on the middle couch cushion maintaining a death grip on Mom's arm. Mom had the seat next to Dylan. The set of Dad's jaw and the horror in Mom's eyes said they'd probably been instructed not to speak.

Two men stood on the left side of the room near Dad, and two more men stood off to the right side of the room. The two men who shadowed me from my bedroom brought the general thug total to six. A seventh man stood in front of the coffee table, which had been moved away from the couch and pushed close to Dad's reading chair. The odd man out wore a dark suit, but he didn't seem interested in wresting control of the situation away from Ethan, who brought the number of home invaders to eight. The six general thugs each wore a black facemask. Only the sunglasses guy and Ethan remained unmasked.

Shorty—our black lab—lay a few feet to Mom's left. The sight of our drugged dog upset me more than the strained expressions on my parents' faces. Maybe you can help me reason through that one later. I would have gone to Shorty if Ethan didn't step up beside me and place a hand on my right elbow. I jerked my arm away, but then, I wasn't sure what to do with my hands. Crossing my arms helped quell the urge to punch Ethan, so I went with that, inching left to put a little distance between us.

Ethan held his hands out in a calming gesture.

"We're going to leave soon, so I need you to make a decision quickly," said Ethan.

I leveled a make-your-point glare at him.

"You're coming with us because I have a task for you," he continued, tipping his chin up defensively. "Most of your family will go on a road trip with some of my people, but I'll need one person to travel with us as a more immediate hostage. Who should come with us?"

Dylan sat up straighter. Mom practically tackled him to keep him from volunteering. Dad tightened his hold on Katy. Something about Ethan's body language presented the situation like a test question.

"You already made up your mind," I said, flying by instinct.

Surprise flitted across Ethan's face, but he covered it well.

"I got a recommendation from a Minder," he admitted,

"but I'll still consider your opinion."

Tearing my gaze from Ethan, I focused on my family. Katy clung to Dad. Dylan shifted to free himself from Mom. Dad glared at Ethan. Mom divided her attention between subduing Dylan and channeling a message at me. I couldn't turn it into actual words, but I got the gist. She'd never forgive me if I took one of my siblings down with me.

My breaths quickened. Adrenaline made my muscles shake. My ears started ringing.

About two seconds before I thought I'd faint, my head cleared, and Nadia spoke within my mind.

Choose your mother.

Did you know about this?

Ethan will take her anyway. His team has been instructed to be rougher if you pick the wrong person.

Anger shot through me, warming my whole body.

That's crazy. Why?

This is a test to see if our lines of communication are open. You may let Ethan know I am aware of the situation and will negotiate as best I can, but I do not have any authority over my siblings or the situations they find themselves in.

Why can't you talk to him directly?

Because he has taken a drug that blocks most Minders. It would take more time and effort than we have right now to work around the effects. Please convey the message.

My throat tried its level best to close, but I managed to choke out my choice and the essence of Nadia's message.

If I truly thought that would ease the tension, I was dead wrong.

Katy yelped and launched herself at Mom. Dylan kind of growled, wrenched free of Mom's grip, balled his fists, and stood in front of her. Dad started to rise, but two men rushed in and reached for his arms. Throwing his weight right, he drove his shoulder into the first guy.

Noise blended as people shouted over each other.

The remaining men converged on Mom, Dylan, and Katy. Their coordinated movements told me they each had an assigned target.

I didn't get to watch much more because my next view was a closeup of the carpet. My breath left and refused to come back while something heavy pressed into my back. As suddenly as the pressure appeared, it disappeared, and hands pulled me up to a kneeling position.

"Stop resisting, or we'll hurt them." Ethan's threat wasn't loud, but somehow, it managed to bring movement in the room to a complete standstill.

Since the thought of resisting hadn't even moved through my brain yet, I guess he was talking to my father.

As the idea started having some appeal, Ethan bound my hands behind me with plastic flex cuffs.

A glance at Dad showed him in a similar position, kneeling with his hands secured behind his back.

Ethan yanked me to my feet.

Katy sobbed until her guard let her return to our father and plaster herself to his side.

A pair of guards loomed over my mother and brother.

Mom had Dylan trapped in a bear hug, but he jerked his shoulders left and right to break free. I couldn't hear what she whispered to him, but soon, he stopped thrashing.

The guards pried Dylan out of Mom's arms before giving her the flex cuff treatment. The surreal moment etched itself in my mind with startling clarity. It's one thing to experience danger and another beast entirely to watch masked men systematically subdue your entire family.

"You don't need to do this." My statement surprised me, and I hardly recognized the hoarse voice as my own. Thankfully, the words nudged some sense into my aching head. "I'll help any way I can, and I'll work better knowing you haven't harmed my family."

"Should we bring them all?" asked Ethan, sounding amused.

"No!" The reflex response burst out of me and my parents.

"We're on a schedule," said the suited man, sounding impatient.

"It won't work," said Dad. "You can't just make an entire family disappear."

"Actually, we can," said the government suit.

"You've officially won a family bonding contest," Ethan announced. "This includes an all-expenses paid six-week tour of the United States in your brand-new trailer."

I twisted my head around to give Ethan a dubious look.

"Your boss has already approved the leave of absence, Mr. Matheson," said Suit.

The man's statement pulled my skeptical glance his way. Dad's boss has always struck me as the workaholic, vacations-are-for-the-weak sort who expects employees to eat, breathe, and dream about their cases.

If the news shocked Dad, he hid it well, but he still looked frustrated.

Agent Paul Rydell.

I liked Suit for him better but silently thanked Nadia for the information anyway.

They have compromising paperwork concerning Mr. Jameson's personal finances and personal relationship with a former assistant.

"Your boss approved too, Mrs. Matheson," Suit added.

That didn't surprise me. Mom doesn't work so much as volunteer to help Mrs. Vance run the library a few days a week so it can stay open on a shoestring budget that keeps getting slashed every year.

Thinking about Mrs. Vance distracted me enough to miss a bit of my parents' desperate attempt to reason with Ethan and company. I refocused as my mother spoke.

"What about Dani's college?" she asked. "Her professors are going to wonder if she misses more classes."

"They probably don't know her name," Rydell said, shrugging. "But I'll have somebody make appropriate excuses."

"She has a roommate," said Ethan. "They don't communicate constantly, but they have exchanged quite a few text messages. We should have Danielle confirm the cover story with her."

Ethan sent one of the men to retrieve my phone from my room while I tried to recover from the shock. The blatant invasion of privacy really shouldn't have surprised me. I mean if these people dove deep enough to dig up dirt on my father's boss to blackmail him, reading private messages wouldn't faze them.

Would you like me to let Karen know your situation?

I considered that but rejected the idea quickly. It'd be nice if somebody knew the truth, but I didn't want to involve Karen in this mess. I didn't even need to officially think my thought. As soon as I reached a decision, Nadia knew it. Even with all the rampant privacy invasions, I drew comfort from Nadia's presence.

Mom and Dad tried a few more arguments, but Rydell and Ethan shut those down in short order. The six guards herded Dad, Katy, and Dylan out of the room.

Rydell and the remaining guard flanked Mom.

Ethan suddenly cut through my zip tie, releasing my hands. Next, he shoved my phone into my hands.

"Check in with your roommate and grab your mother's car keys," he instructed.

When I didn't move quickly enough, Rydell tightened his grip on Mom's arm.

Nadia sent me enough calming images to obey the orders without indulging in counterproductive acts of violence.

That's how I ended up driving my mother's Corolla with Ethan riding shotgun and Mom and Suit in the back. At least, they agreed to rebind Mom's hands in front, so she'll be more comfortable. Poor Mom.

The Reluctant Chauffer,
Danielle Matheson.

Chapter 6:
I Spoke Too Soon

ITEM 241: Allison's sixth letter to Dr. Sokolowski
Item Source: Allison and Jeffrey Blairington

Dear Dr. S.,

I have always expected this day would come, but I thought we'd have more time.

Varick arrived late last night to deliver some money and instructions to leave. He even agreed to drop TJ off for a long visit with Pastor Carl and his family. His wife, Tammy, has been ill. I'm hoping TJ will be a good sort of distraction for their two children.

Jeffrey had warned his boss he might have to take a sudden leave of absence. I did the same. Not sure if either of us will have a job if we return, but today, I'm just praying we live long enough to have such a problem.

Malia explained how I could communicate with you and said I shouldn't discuss anything about our travel plans. It's not exactly easy to travel any length of time with two children under five. That holds doubly true when they're as active as Isaac and Michio.

Jillian's in trouble again. Varick didn't say nothing about it, but I can tell things are different this time. It kills me that I can't help Jillian directly, but I can keep Michio hidden away for now.

Jeffrey and I are not qualified to teach Michio much, but

we can love him. I don't like running, but I will do it until the end of my days if it'll keep that child safe.

I also don't like having to trust people, but every step of this journey can involve others.

The hardest part about disappearing is the guilt of leaving friends and family suddenly. Nadia said she'd speak with Momma and get her hidden if necessary, but her initial proposal was rebuffed. That made me laugh 'cause I can picture how that scene went down, even if the girl spoke with Momma directly.

Jeffrey's been a good sport about all this, but he's quieter than usual. And sadder. I want to help him, really I do, but I am just barely holding myself together.

Sorry I don't have better news. We're safe for the moment, but life couldn't be more uncertain. If you're the praying sort, lift us up. We can definitely use the extra help.

Sincerely,

Allison and Jeffrey Blairington

***

ITEM 242: Allison's seventh letter to Dr. Sokolowski
Item Source: Allison Blairington

Dear Dr. S.,

I guess I spoke too soon. Life is more uncertain now than at the close of my last letter.

Didn't expect to check in this soon, but I need somebody to talk to. Nadia understands, but she's dealing with a lot right now. I don't want to add to her burden, and I suspect she'll know soon anyway.

Is it possible to love and hate someone so thoroughly ya get physically ill thinking of 'em or what they've done? I understand why, and part of me would do the same if my heart wasn't so thoroughly divided on the issue.

I probably ain't making much sense.

At the time of signing off, I was fixing to crawl into bed in a plain but clean-looking hotel room, when a soft knock sounded.

"Don't answer it!" I called.

Ignoring me, Jeffrey strode to the door, took off the security latch, and swung the door open.

Three men wearing dark suits entered. The last one in shut

the door. The first man stopped in front of Jeffrey and handed him a thick envelope.

Isaac was already asleep. Michio climbed over Isaac and watched the men carefully.

The other two men spread out, one moving toward the lounge chair set in the corner and the other moving toward the boys.

I instinctively moved in front of Michio, blocking the third man.

"Take your kid and go," said the first man, addressing Jeffrey.

"What about my wife?" Jeffrey demanded. "You said we'd all get safe passage."

"And you will," assured the first man, "but your wife is part of my contract. Not a large part, but enough that I am invested in delivering her safely. As far as I'm concerned, you fulfilled your side, and I've fulfilled mine." He gestured to the envelope still in Jeffrey's hands. "What happens next is up to you."

Only then did I realize all three men held handguns. I spread my arms and moved even closer to the boys, but the guns weren't pointed our way. They focused on Jeffrey.

Questions and denials crowded my head, making it buzz with pain.

"The deal was for Michio, that's it." Jeffrey's hard tone spoke of his soaring frustration. "You never said anything about Allison. She's coming with us or we're not going." His gaze flicked my way before returning to the speaker.

"I go?" asked Michio.

"Stay behind me, baby." My breaths came in wheezing little gasps as the panic choked me.

Michio's tiny hand landed on my back, and my breathing evened out. I don't know what he did, but it was nothing short of a miracle. I curled my right arm behind my back to embrace the boy. He wrapped his arms around my neck.

"It's okay, Momma," said Michio.

That about broke my heart.

"Perhaps I wasn't clear before," said the first man, addressing Jeffrey. "Allow me to explain your options. You get your kid and walk away, or I shoot you and him and the cleaning crew gets a nasty surprise tomorrow."

Understanding the situation faster than I could, Michio released my neck.

I turned in time to watch Michio throw his body across Isaac, waking my son. Following the lead, I climbed onto the bed and curled my body around both boys. Not sure when I started crying, but suddenly, I couldn't see a blessed thing.

Something sharp pricked my left arm, making me feel lightheaded. My limbs felt heavy, like they were filling with quick-hardening cement. Isaac and Michio's cries reached me dimly. I sort of feared I'd crush the boys, but hands pulled me back and laid me flat on the bed.

Jeffrey's concerned face floated before me briefly. He said something, but I couldn't understand any of the words.

I watched helplessly as he picked up Isaac and left.

Jeffrey didn't have a choice, least not in that moment. I know that, but we might not have been in such a position if he'd not given the men our location. Even knowing he wanted to spare Isaac and me, I don't understand how he could sell Michio for our safety. The tyke's been with us for months. We might not share blood, but I thought we'd started to be a real family.

I love Jeffrey and don't see that changing anytime soon, but I'm having a real hard time squaring the man I fell in love with and the man who'd hand an innocent little boy over to dangerous people on command. Part of me understands he probably had no choice, but I have no way to know what order things happened in. I only know my husband took my son and left me and Michio with the suited men.

I have no idea where we're going, but I'm told the more thoughts I share with ya, the better chance we'll be found eventually. Dunno how that will work, but I've learned not to question Nadia and Malia. If they say they can accomplish something, they can.

I need to sleep now. Maybe my heart will hurt less later. At the very least, some sleep should give me enough strength to hold Michio. Isaac will be safe with Jeffrey. Far as I can tell, Michio's only got me. They drugged him soon after me, and there wasn't a thing I could do to help him. I can't even entertain the idea of the men separating us.

If ya hear from Jillian, please let me know. Dangerous things are happening, and I know she's involved.

Sincerely,

Allison Blairington

Chapter 7:
Recruiting Pitch

ITEM 243: Jillian's 118th post-kidnapping journal entry
Item Source: Jillian Blairington

I shoulda known I wasn't gonna get much sleep, even if I used my Gift on myself. Some time back, I left marks on each of my siblings so I could find 'em easily. It's the closest I've come to tapping into one of Nadia's Gifts. It doesn't tell me much, but the mark lets my siblings reach out to me and form a strong enough connection that I can draw 'em into one of my dreams or get sucked into one of their dreams.

Way long ago I likened some aspects of my Dream Shaper Gifts to fishing. Well, this is like cheating by tracking the fish with a GPS marker before casting a line in the water.

Malia has always been good at storing and reassembling memories for me, but that wasn't necessary since I got drawn to her this time. I already knew she was way east of me, but it helped that Nadia made me update and expand the mental maps Dr. Das started a few years ago.

As with most of these kinds of dreams, I spent the first few seconds trying to orient myself to the place and the people. Only this time felt mighty different 'cause I recognized Malia's new room and got the impression she was physically alone but as tense as if a dozen armed men stood around her.

Thank you for coming. Please help your sister with her

assignment. We can chat later.

The strong presence showed up in my mind long enough to deliver that message and disappear. The voice quality sounded youthful and male but not like a child. Once it vanished, Malia's shoulders relaxed a little. She sat with her legs crossed in the center of her bed wearing a huge frown.

I formed an avatar and placed her next to Malia's bed to make communicating easier.

"What assignment was he yammering about?" I demanded. I'm comfortable enough speaking with Nadia in my head, but I didn't like the boy's tone or his attitude.

Malia's expression turned neutral enough to let me know her Gifts enhanced her calm.

"I'm supposed to get up, go outside, and wait for someone to pick me up," Malia answered.

"That doesn't sound too bad," I said, knowing there had to be more.

Malia might be controlling her emotions to project calm, but she wasn't hiding her frustration.

"What do ya need me for?" I wondered.

"I'll need you, if I choose to run away without explaining myself," Malia answered. "It's only my parents and Marina since Nick started working a night shift, but Marina's a light sleeper. You could keep them asleep until I'm safely away."

I didn't answer Malia right away, though it struck me again how very Nadia-like she could sound. She wasn't really asking anyway. I could do it, but I'd never used the Gift that way before. I'd knocked out bad guys for a few seconds, but it sounded like Malia meant a whole heap longer than a few seconds. I made my avatar shrug.

"Wasn't what I wanted to do tonight, but I can handle that," I said, trying for a cheerful tone.

"No." Malia shook her head to reinforce the word. "I need to tell them."

My avatar's expression musta demanded a better explanation.

"And I wouldn't put it past the government to try and track you through the work," Malia added. "I assume Nadia succeeded in getting you to a safe house."

I didn't need to confirm anything. My sister could read my emotions well enough even from an avatar. Besides, I don't have her Gift for hiding my emotions. They usually show up on my face. The knowledge lessened her frown.

"The longer you can stay free, the better for everybody," said Malia.

"You say that like they've already got you," I noted. "Let your Second Momma and Daddy know. They'll protect you."

To my surprise, Malia nodded once like she agreed.

"I need to let them know I'm leaving," said Malia.

My avatar's hands flew up.

"If you're safe in that house, why would ya leave?" I let a glare fling the question a second time, but Malia's sense of calm never wavered. "I don't understand. Are you going willingly or are they forcing ya?"

"I promised to lend what aid I can because Kay—the Minder who spoke to you before—was right about one thing. Before you arrived, he said that the longer I stay with these people, the more danger they'll face. I can protect them best by leaving."

"You don't believe that," I said, not needing to read her expression or tone. The fact that she hadn't left yet declared her doubts. "If ya did, you'd already be standing out on that curb. What's holding you back?"

"I'm trying to compose a compelling argument for why they should let me go," Malia admitted. "I'm not as good at the task as Nadia would be."

"Why can't ya just sneak out?" I asked. "I can watch Marina and keep her asleep if necessary."

"Thank you, but you should go. There's—"

It's me again. Sorry. Change of plan. Malia, you need to bring Mrs. Davidson with you.

"There's no reason to involve my family," Malia argued. "I already promised to help."

Her last statement made me give her a questioning look.

I'm only a messenger. I don't make the decisions.

To his credit, the voice sounded sorry.

"Then tell the decision-makers that I'm not leaving this

house or helping the cause until you people acknowledge my family is off limits." Malia spoke evenly, but anybody watching her could tell she meant business. She'd closed her eyes to aid conversing with the Minder. "Furthermore, I'm prepared to release a lot of evidence exposing the sins of several government entities, including the programs responsible for making us."

You're bluffing. That would put your family in more danger. Besides, this is to protect her. Que found a partial plan that could mean people are coming for her.

"It would change the nature of the danger," Malia clarified, "and I don't believe you."

I can send you his notes, but you'll still have to trust me since you don't have time to verify the source.

"I definitely missed something," I muttered. "If Mrs. Davidson's in trouble, why aren't ya worried about the rest of the family?"

I addressed this comment to the air 'cause there wasn't a figure to focus on.

Show her the picture.

Malia plucked something off her bed and held it up so my avatar could see. Her iPad held a picture of an aerial shot of a neighborhood. One house had crosshairs over it. My expression musta told Malia the picture wasn't helping much.

"Que is one of Kay's brothers," Malia explained. "He has some training in cyber security and stalking. I am worried about the rest of the family, but the only accounts that have been monitored lately have belonged to Mom."

That's the house Malia's currently in. Que found it because somebody had placed a tracer on Mrs. Davidson's phone.

"Guess ya better try to get her somewhere safe then," I said to Malia, before turning to Kay. "What do ya need Malia's help with?"

We need everybody's help. We're going after Katharos. They already have our guardian, and if Que's findings are right, they're headed for a lot of people your side cares for too.

"This isn't about sides, Kay," Malia said, tossing her iPad back onto her bed.

The figure of a boy appeared on the other side of Malia's bed, directly opposite my avatar. He looked real enough but a faint, blue-white aura surrounded him. Nadia once explained that sort of glow was standard procedure so trainers could tell avatars from real people. It didn't take much brainpower to guess this was Kay. He had reddish brown hair, dark eyes, and a confident stance.

Malia opened her eyes and gestured to the boy.

"Kay, meet Jillian. Jillian, this is Kay. I can tell you more about how we know Kay and his siblings later, but for now, Nadia wants me to extend an invitation to you both. She's calling a Council of War to discuss the alarming events of the past few days."

"How do I know this isn't a mental trap?" asked Kay.

His question earned an impatient glance from Malia and me.

"Because we don't work like that," Malia replied. "You are free to skip the meeting. Nadia or I can update you later, but we're eventually going to have to trust each other or this relationship will fail."

"When's the meeting?" I wondered, trying to get them back on track.

"Right now, if you like." Malia swiveled her head in my direction. "That's up to you. You can host the meeting now, or Nadia will do so in a few hours when everybody's awake."

"How many people are coming?" I asked. "I need to know to figure out how much space we need."

"The standard conference room should suffice," Malia answered.

"Give me a few minutes to set it up," I said.

Without waiting for a response, I let my avatar disappear and started fixing a suitable place in my mind for Nadia's Council of War.

Chapter 8:
Strange Position

ITEM 244: Danielle's 71st letter
Item Source: Danielle Matheson

Dear Dr. S.,

I apologize in advance if this is messier than usual. I am using another of Malia's highly illegal programs to chronicle the latest adventure. And by *adventure*, I mean terrifying series of events I hope to live through. I really, really wish I was exaggerating.

Not sure how this program works, but I think it combs through emails and text messages from any device in range and uses words from them to compile and secretly send my message through to you.

I can't use the normal thoughts-to-words program because my iPad and phone likely won't remain in range for long. This program is sneakier. I have no clue how it really works, but somehow, it follows me, temporarily storing my thought packets in any nearby electronic devices. In theory, this should allow you live updates. Hence, my warning this might be messy. If it works correctly, you should also eventually receive an encrypted email containing these thoughts.

Mom is handling this better than I anticipated, though I can't say I have given much prior thought to her ever being in such a situation. In hindsight, I admit that was willful ignorance on my part. In fact, Mom hasn't said anything. She's not a huge fan of small talk, but I'm guessing the silence also had to do with tall, dark, and threatening sharing the back seat with her. I checked the rearview mirror a few times, but she mostly slept. I'd forgotten she gets motion sick in the back of a car because she's usually driving or in the front passenger seat.

Her presence comforts me, but I also feel guilty. I'm worried about Dad, Katy, and Dylan, too. It's one thing to keep running headlong into crazy situations because of my connection to Jillian, and a gigantic other issue altogether to drag my entire family down with me. Dad's usually level-headed, but I'm not sure if he'll resign himself to the model captive role while any sort of threat exists against my siblings. Katy's better at adjusting to serious situations, but Dylan has reached the age where he does not like being told what to do.

This is a strange position for me to be in. These past few years I've always played the part of leverage. I'd grown accustomed to it. People threatened me to control Jillian. Never thought I'd completely understand the haunted expression of guilt that often crosses her face.

What could they possibly want from me? I talk regularly with Nadia, but that's a testament to her Gift, not mine. I like to think I'm important to Jillian and Varick, but the way Devya's children are wired, they will always choose a noble path. Hostages don't need to reach a special level of closeness to be effective.

Who are these people? The operation went down like a government job, but I'm not sure how Ethan fits in. Kidnapping my family and getting therapy seem mutually exclusive. Is he a willing participant or under duress? What or who could possibly control him? I don't know enough about him to even predict his favorite food, let alone anybody he's close enough to commit several felonies for.

With these thoughts and more filling my head, I drove for several hours before Rydell directed me to a house seemingly in the middle of the Pennsylvania woods.

"Give me the keys, and get out," Ethan ordered.

I obeyed, but my mother couldn't until Ethan cut the zip tie off of her wrists. I felt bad for not insisting they free her hands sooner. They'd had to free my hands so I could drive. If we're going to be stuck in this mess together, I'm going to have to be better about seeing she's treated well.

Instinctively, I moved toward my mother, but Rydell grabbed my arm and redirected me to the cabin.

Once inside, we were allowed to use the restroom to freshen up. At my insistence, Mom went first. I spent the wait time taking in the place. It held several sleeping bags and a worn, ugly yellow rug, a few mismatched chairs, a primitive kitchen setup (hotplate and coffee maker), and not much else. A metal bar ran from one side of the room to the other at perfect tripping height.

When my turn with the amenities came, I found travel toothpaste and new toothbrushes. Too tired to even conjure a sarcastic thought, I brushed my teeth, washed my face with the tepid water, and took care of other *necessaries* as Jillian calls them.

Upon emerging from the bathroom, I once again took stock of the cabin's main room. I blame sleep deprivation for not picking up on the purpose of the metal bar right away. The realization smacked into me with enough force to wake me up a bit. On another level, it also made me slightly ill. This cabin had held other prisoners at some point.

"That's not necessary," I said. "There's nowhere to go, and we're not leaving while your people have the rest of our family."

"It's protocol," said Ethan.

"Who's going to know?" I argued.

"It's not a debatable point," Rydell said, nudging my mother toward the stack of sleeping bags. "Pick a color. Any color."

Mom just pointed to the nearest one.

The gesture stirred up another realization.

"Why isn't she speaking?" I looked to Ethan for an answer. "Did you threaten her?" I wouldn't put such a move past Ethan or the government guy.

Rydell's smile gave me the creeps.

"Not her. You," he said. "I find it more peaceful this way."

Fatigue made me work hard to untangle the logic. He had threatened to harm me to ensure my mother obeyed every command. I was aware they probably said something while we were at the house, but it surprised me they would insist on no speaking now.

"Consider the reverse also true. Any more comments or complaints get her smacked around a bit, and if you annoy me too much, I do worse," said Rydell. "Any more questions?" His dark eyes dared me to test him on the claim.

I mutely shook my head. At that point, I could have slept standing. Within five minutes, Mom and I were settled on opposite sides of the metal bar with one wrist and one ankle zip tied to the bar.

Even though it wasn't very comfortable, I turned on my side, so I could face my mother. She gave me a strained smile and moved her free hand to brush some hair away from my face. The simple gesture broke through the emotional barrier, letting tears flow.

Fear entered her eyes, and she glanced over my left shoulder. I had seen Ethan taking up a post on a wooden chair near the little kitchen area. Rydell had slipped outside.

Mom placed a finger across my lips to indicate I should be quiet. Then, she gently brushed the tears off my cheeks before moving her thumb to the bottom of my chin. Softly pinching my chin between her thumb and pointer finger, Mom tipped my chin upward. She hadn't done that to me in years, but I caught the meaning: *Be brave. I love you.* She used to say that every time she left me with a babysitter when I was a kid.

Gripping my free hand, my mother closed her eyes and leaned her head on the ground. We stared sadly at each other for a few minutes. Though I can't guarantee our thoughts ran along the same lines, I know I feared this might be the last time I saw my mother.

The One Who's Scared to Sleep,
Danielle Matheson.

Chapter 9: The Wall

ITEM 245: Jillian's 119th post-kidnapping journal entry
Item Source: Jillian Blairington

Turns out, I didn't have to do much to set up the Council of War. As soon as I'd cleared a space in my mind to begin imagining a proper conference room, a small, blue box appeared before me. Since Kay's question about mental traps was still fresh in my mind, I stared at the box suspiciously.

You may safely open the box, Jillian. It merely contains the room we have worked in before. Expanding from there may be easier than starting from nothing.

Opening the box let Nadia's conference room form around me. That suited me fine 'cause the last conference room I'd seen with any detail was a cramped one in a hospital, and I'd rather forget that room and the memories associated with it. Malia and Danielle almost died in there. Besides, this one had way better decorations. In keeping with the military theme, Nadia had expanded the collection of large portraits and paintings of famous battles throughout history.

Nadia, Queen Elena, and Naidine appeared at the same time. They stood in front of the one wall without any pictures or paintings. This wall held thick red curtains like you'd see in a theater meant for putting on plays. Each version of my sister wore an outfit that suited her personality. Nadia had on jeans and a purple long-sleeved T-shirt. I'm tempted to think that's a uniform for her. Queen Elena wore a fancy gown with an intricate, gold pattern on the top and a plain, deep red skirt that flowed right to the floor. Naidine wore dark blue jeans, a white shirt, and a black leather jacket.

"What happened to not talking to me?" I asked, forming an avatar within the room. Making quick rounds, I hugged each version of Nadia.

"We should still take precautions, but the unknown Minder I was concerned about turned out to be Kay." Nadia returned my hug fiercely, but then moved to draw the curtain aside.

"Since Malia reported he would be joining us shortly, that is at least one threat we can lay to rest," said Naidine, folding her arms.

Queen Elena studied the long conference table. With a wave, she added glasses of water on coasters that had strange symbols on them. Curious, I peeked at the two types of coasters. One symbol kinda looked like a ram climbing a mountain. The other showed a tiny version of Earth with a lightning bolt coming out of it and a snake wrapping itself around the bolt. The second symbol looked familiar, but it took a few seconds to recognize where I'd seen the shape before. Dr. Carnasis—my Second Momma—always wore a necklace with that on it. Never paid it much mind.

"They are symbols for Adynatos Industries and Votive, Incorporated," Queen Elena explained, catching my curiosity before I could voice the question. "Kay and his siblings come from Adynatos. We come from Votive. Several other companies conducted similar research, but most have even fewer success stories."

"Most are also better kept secrets," said Naidine, "but we are mobilizing to protect them as best we can."

"Jillian, please have Malia join us," said Nadia. "I will project Kay from here to protect your location."

By the time I dropped Malia into the proper level of sleep to draw her into my dream, Nadia formed an avatar for Kay. At first, it kinda surprised me that he wore the same clothes he had in Malia's dream, but then I remembered who I was dealing with and shrugged it off.

Kay nodded a greeting to the various Nadias. Malia made the rounds giving hugs, ending with me before taking her seat at the table. I hadn't noticed the little nameplates that appeared or that Queen Elena had modified the conference table. Instead of being a normal table, it was about half as wide, twice as long, and curved. From my perspective, it looked like a giant letter "c." I didn't feel like sitting, but I figured it'd be the quickest way to get Nadia talking.

"Do you want me to bring Varick, Aiden, and Michio in?" I asked, tugging on my assigned chair. The big black chair rolled back with surprising ease. I sat down to Malia's right before returning my attention to Nadia.

Kay sat to my right.

"Varick will try to make it," said Queen Elena, "but he is currently occupied with seeing to Anastasia's family." She gestured to the wall by Nadia, which now held a giant map of the United States. Different colored dots populated the map.

A portrait of Varick appeared next to a green dot in the eastern section of Pennsylvania. Danielle and her Momma also showed up in Pennsylvania, but they had blinking orange dots located well north of Varick's dot.

Varick Ayers: ACTIVE MISSION.

Dee: ACTIVE MISSION. The blond woman in the picture looked to be in her mid-thirties, but the stats next to her picture set her age at twenty-one.

Danielle Matheson: CAPTURED.

Lisa Matheson: CAPTURED.

Dustin Ayers: LOCATION UNKNOWN.

The names and statuses overwhelmed me for a moment.

Poor Danielle. Poor Mrs. Matheson. Why's somebody gotta involve them?

"Have you found AK yet?" Kay's question gave me something to focus on besides the worry building up fast.

"Not yet, but we are working with Que to narrow down the locations," said Naidine.

"I can't feel her, so she's probably unconscious," said Kay.

"Jillian and Malia might be able to help with that later, but first, let us look at the larger picture." Nadia waved and more colored dots lit up on the map.

Most of the new ones were gray and had portraits tagged: DECEASED. I only recognized two of them Andrew and a young Asian woman. As I tried to place the lady, Nadia provided her name since there wasn't a convenient box of stats next to the picture.

Mei Li.

The name helped me remember she was a scientist who'd played the part of Michio's mother for a short time back when Dr. Devya had me kidnapped so I could learn how to shape dreams.

"We do not have only one problem," Nadia announced, "we have many situations that are rapidly spinning out of control. I will not highlight everybody, but it is clear that people connected with our programs are being hunted." She pulled one of the portraits forward, so it hovered over the conference table in front of Malia, Kay, and me.

The portrait showed an older Black man wearing an army dress uniform covered in ribbons and pins. Nana woulda said his black hair tried hard but couldn't quite fight off the gray.

"General Danby provided military support for programs like ours for over fifteen years," said Queen Elena.

"He was forced to retire last year and murdered last week," Naidine explained. "You would be hard-pressed to find the story in the news."

Another framed picture moved forward to sit beside General Danby. This man looked to be about a decade older than the general. The new man wore a spiffy suit and a politician's fake smile. I expected to see he was dead too, but instead, the inscription read: MISSING.

"Nobody has seen Senator Foster for 48 hours," Naidine reported.

Two more portraits appeared, flanking the general's picture. One showed a young woman with her arms folded. Her crossed arms tried for a tough look, but her face had hints of a mischievous smile. The other picture featured a serious, dark-haired man wearing a business suit.

"Senator Santelli and Agent Resnicki went dark 24 hours

ago," said Naidine. "Separate issues, but given their ties to ATLAS, they're likely preparing to move against us."

I wanted to ask about ATLAS 'cause it sounded important, but Kay fired a question that steered the conversation back to the missing lady who concerned him most.

"What's this have to do with AK?"

"Who's AK?" I wondered, looking from Kay to Nadia.

"I will explain shortly," Nadia promised. She beckoned two more portraits to move up between the general and the politician. The general's picture moved left and the politician's picture slid right to make room. I didn't recognize either man.

One of the new portraits said DECEASED and the other said LOCATION UNKNOWN. I couldn't figure the difference between *missing* and *location unknown*, but Nadia sent me a quick clarifying statement in thought form.

Missing indicates that there is a higher chance the person has been kidnapped. Location unknown says more evidence points towards a person actively hiding.

"Dr. Emerson ran Adynatos Industries until Firestorm," said Nadia.

"He was supposedly murdered around the same time as General Danby, but I'm having trouble getting confirmation of that. My guess is he's in hiding," Naidine continued. "The other man you see is Stuart Samson. He was the director of Project Keeper, which was one of the government's first attempts to safeguard and control programs like ours. The initiative eventually turned into the Guardians."

"Agent Nicole Kanter worked for Project Keeper," Nadia explained. "She designed most events of Firestorm but defected near the end of the competition. Firestorm pitted representatives from Votive and Adynatos against each other. That is how we met Kay and his siblings. I have prepared a summary of those events for you to review at your leisure." With a snap of her fingers, Nadia conjured a small orange box and tossed it to me.

I caught it, but as soon as it landed in my hands, the box disappeared. That woulda disturbed me if it hadn't happened before.

"The short version is we discovered that the losing team

was slated for termination," said Naidine. Her expression and clipped tone both said the notion still made her angry. "Agent Kanter helped Kay, Que, Tae, and Dee escape. She has been providing for and protecting them for the past ten-plus years."

"She was taken by Katharos agents yesterday," said Kay. "That's when I reached out to Nadia and Malia."

My eyes lingered on the portraits labeled DECEASED.

"How do you know she's not dead?" I asked.

Kay made a face but answered honestly.

"Got a video threat." He nodded tightly to Nadia.

She turned the map wall into a video screen. The short clip showed an unconscious Asian woman chained to a wall. A voice from outside the screen went on a two-minute rant before finally reaching his demands. The man spoke almost Nadia-level fast and used way more words than he needed to, including some not fit for polite society, but the general message was Kay and his three siblings could surrender or watch Kanter die in the next video. They had three days to make arrangements.

"We have to find her fast," Kay declared.

"You gonna make the trade?" I asked. My tone added my opinion that it was a stupid plan.

"That is a last resort," Nadia assured me. She had the video return to being a smaller portrait of the lady and moved it off to the side.

The map returned to full size.

Two of the smaller faces caught my attention.

I stood up so fast my rolling chair moved several feet back. The room started to shift, but Malia caught my hand and sent waves of calm through me. Even with her help, the surge of fear nearly paralyzed me.

"Where are they?" I didn't need to clarify who I meant, but Nadia pulled up the portraits showing Michio and Momma.

"They reached a hotel in Pennsylvania before things went wrong." Nadia stopped speaking and gave me a compassionate look. "Are you sure you want to know the details."

"No. But I need to know," I answered.

"Katharos agents offered your step-father a deal. He was promised he could walk away with Isaac and your mother if he kept them appraised of the travel plans," Naidine explained, "but when the time came, they took your mother as well."

"What for?" The question exploded out of me. "Momma's got nothing to do with this, and Michio's a kid." My gaze swept over Nadia, Naidine, and Queen Elena. I yanked my hand clear of Malia's grasp. For some reason, I wanted to feel the stabbing fear, like the discomfort would somehow bring me closer to Momma and Michio. I'll have to ask Dr. S. about that someday.

Queen Elena came over and wrapped me in a hug.

"You know the answer to that," she stated. "Let Malia help you so we can finish outlining the situations that need our attention. Then, we can form a plan of action to get them all back and end this."

I didn't like the plan, but she made sense. If I let my emotions act normally, I'd be useless to everybody for the next few hours. Since the effort to walk back and right the chair seemed overwhelming, I imagined myself back to the previous seated position. Malia placed her hand on my left arm, lending me enough calm to focus on the meeting.

Kay's brother, Tae, went after the people who kidnapped Agent Kanter even though he's an Empath like Malia, not a soldier like Dee or Varick. I guess Agent Kanter's not really an agent anymore since she cut ties with the government a long time ago, but since that's the way Kay and Nadia see her, it'll do. Que's still hiding out with Kay. Nadia's still with Dr. Devya in the Wyoming compound. Dee's somewhere in Pennsylvania preparing to go after Danielle and her momma or Michio and my Momma.

Dr. Karita Robinson and Dr. Jessica Paladon both had MISSING labels and orange dots. Cora and Dr. Carnasis were way off to the side in a separate section representing the United Kingdom. Thankfully, both dots representing them were green.

The angry, helpless feeling started creeping in again, despite Malia's help.

"Jillian, I can review these things with you later," said Nadia. "Set the dream to record just in case I cannot fulfill that promise, then you may safely begin the work without missing much."

I tried to concentrate, but once Nadia started discussing the potential bad guys, I took her advice, set the dream to record so I could review it later, and tuned her out. I needed to keep part of my concentration engaged in the dream so it could continue, but I also wanted to start the half-dozen searches. Finding Michio and Momma should be easy enough. I'd looked for them enough to have strong natural marks on their dreams. Danielle too should be easy to track, but I'd never met Agent Kanter. If sedatives kept her unconscious, the search could prove harder than the one I'd done for Benny Connelly. Unfortunately, the deadline to find her was also a whole heap shorter.

Kay's gonna have to give me a lot more information if they want me to find her fast.

I'll give you direct access to my memories if you wish. Nadia suggested it might be faster.

Kay's thought surprised me. He still seemed to be concentrating on Nadia's presentation.

Your thoughts are kind of shouting right now, and I'm a Minder. I don't have as much training as Nadia, but I can at least split my attention in two. Come meet me after the meeting. I'll leave a beacon on the table for you to follow.

Chapter 10:
Just You

ITEM 246: Danielle's 72nd letter
Item Source: Danielle Matheson

Dear Dr. S.,

A crash pulled me out of a light sleep. I craned my neck around to see what was happening and saw Ethan standing over Paul Rydell.

"We're not changing the plan." Ethan's calm tone didn't match the scene.

Rydell showcased more appropriate emotions. Ugly red streaks ran up and down his face. His eyes shone with wild, barely contained anger. I only noticed this because he sat facing me, glaring up at Ethan.

"My employer—"

"You can drop the pretense, agent." Ethan held out a hand to help the man up. "I know you're extremely rich and used to getting your way, but you can't purchase what's not for sale. Your father's power, your sister's power, and your power mean exactly nothing here. We do this my way. Period. Full stop. Am I coming through clearly?"

"You'll regret this," Rydell vowed. He rolled to his feet.

Pain in my neck forced me to change positions to continue watching, making me miss a few movements. I tuned back in as Rydell pulled a handgun and aimed it at Ethan. Next instant, Ethan held the gun, released the magazine, popped a bullet out of the chamber, caught it, and offered the various pieces to a gaping Rydell.

Mom grasped my bound hand with her free one and squeezed hard.

"The only reason you're not dead is that my orders say to accommodate you wherever and whenever I can," said Ethan, "but I think it's best you be on your way. There's a motorcycle in the shed you can take, or you can make your own arrangements."

"My people will kill your hostages," said Rydell.

Ethan made a show of checking the time on his phone.

"At this point, your people are either dead or no longer your people."

It probably goes without saying that I had no idea what either of them were rambling about, but their conversation simultaneously intrigued me and skyrocketed my anxiety.

"Just remember, you don't get a third chance to threaten me or somebody in my custody," said Ethan, handing over the gun, magazine, and lone bullet. He smiled tightly. "The government thanks you for your longstanding, continual support, but stick to what you're good at."

Muttering something I couldn't quite hear, Rydell marched out.

A new pain started in my neck, but I kept my eyes on Ethan. Drawing a small pocketknife out of his left pocket, Ethan snapped it open as he approached.

A faint pop sounded in my back as I shifted to relieve the pressure on my right shoulder.

I tensed as Ethan drew near, but he merely knelt next to me and held out the open pocketknife.

"Release your wrist and go wash up," said Ethan. "There's some money and a phone on the table for you. On the phone, you'll find directions to a diner. Eat something. Then, you'll be given more instructions."

Relief and suspicion tumbled around in my gut. I almost dropped the knife, but after I used it, I managed to pass it over to my mother.

"Just you." Ethan kept his tone gentle, but the hard look in his eyes said the point was non-negotiable.

"I'm not leaving without her," I declared.

Mom used her grip on my hand to gain my attention. Carefully, she pressed the knife handle back into the palm of my free hand, curling her fingers around my wrist. She shook her head briefly, begging me to take the out.

"You have to." Ethan said the words matter-of-factly. "The other option is I shoot your mother. I'm supposed to keep her alive, but there are many non-fatal places to—"

"You've made your point," I said, not bothering to hide my bitterness. I stared at my mother, desperately trying to beat back a wave of panic. Oddly, the anger at Ethan helped balance my emotions.

"I'll be all right, Dani." Mom's assurance came out soft but surprisingly steady. She tightened her hold on my wrist, then let go.

Since Ethan's threat still lingered in the air, I had a hard time believing that.

"When you can get free, do it," Mom said. "Get somewhere safe and stay there."

"Nowhere is safe," Ethan countered. "We'll be tracking the phone and your progress. If you break a rule or miss a deadline, you lose a sibling. My guess is your brother, but I can put in a request if you like. If it happens again, you lose them both. Are you sensing the pattern?"

"I got it." I would have preferred spitting at him, but aside from lacking any moisture whatsoever in my mouth, I'd seen enough of his crazy side to know his threats weren't idle.

"She's got it," Mom echoed a split-second later. "Please. Release my husband and other two children. You only need me."

Ethan didn't bother answering her. Instead, he checked the time again on his phone.

"You're expected at the diner at 7:30," he said, looking directly at me. "The timing's going to be tight, but you can still make it."

Closing the pocketknife, I handed it back to Ethan, then gawked at the impressive welt that had formed on my wrist overnight. After letting Ethan help me up, I dragged my stiff body over to the bathroom to deal with wake-up rituals. I skipped teeth brushing, settling for swirling some toothpaste around my mouth while I rinsed my face. The mirror showed the frightful state of my hair. Since I was expected to go out in public, I took the time to tame some of the tangles with a brush.

My first post-bathroom order of business involved making a beeline to that phone. Ethan called out the simple password, which consisted of my birthday. Sort of horrified these people had that information, I tapped in the password and quickly oriented myself to the phone. It didn't have that many apps loaded, but the ones present seemed important. Satisfied I could work the phone properly, I cast a worried look my mother's way. Ethan had released her hand from the bar and handcuffed her wrists together. At least it let her sit up. He tossed me the keys to Mom's car.

I caught them, then stood dumbly, staring down at them. A strange, cold sense of despair crept over my spirit.

Do I really want to do this?

If it had only been me, there's a solid chance I would have sat at the table and waited for Ethan to shoot me. But it wasn't just me. My entire family would live or die by my actions. I'd known that before, but somehow, holding the car keys made that message sink in a little further. Whoever held Ethan's puppet strings knew entirely too much about us. Either they'd done some very thorough research, or there was a Minder involved.

"It's a little early to fall apart, Ms. Matheson," said Ethan.

A jolt of irritation brought my eyes up from the keys, but I studiously avoided looking at Ethan. Instead, I looked at my mother, silently asking for some direction.

"You do what you must to survive and save your siblings." Mom leveled a fierce gaze at me that reinforced the command.

I managed a weak nod and headed for the door. My first few steps unfolded awkwardly, but the urgency soon had me sprinting to Mom's car. The chilly November air made my breaths come out in clouds. I'd donned a coat before the kidnapping, but unfortunately, I didn't have any gloves with me.

Tears didn't come until I slammed the car door, but I held it together enough to start the car, crank up the heat, and settle the phone into the holder fixed to one of the air vents.

Tossing some incoherent prayers heavenward, I wiped my eyes clear of tears, brought up the map app, and let the cheery, female voice direct me.

A few minutes into the drive, my nerves settled enough to release the flood of questions that had built up behind the dam of shock. Ethan was a foot soldier. I understood that, but he had masters. Who were they? What did they want from me? And why involve my family? Every other psycho to come after me has ultimately been after Jillian or one of her siblings. That conclusion didn't take a great leap of logic, but it did birth a few more questions that broke down into their own sets of baby questions.

I didn't have the time or energy to follow every thread, so I picked one and tackled it. Assuming the true target was one of Devya's children, who was it? Jillian might be the obvious answer, but the coordination and planning to go after my parents and siblings argued for a deeper motive than controlling one genetically altered wonder kid. Nadia has a soft spot for everybody in the world, but anybody after a special connection would have to target her siblings for best effect. Varick might be my boyfriend, but his protective setting covers as much of the world as Nadia's. Despite the events of last year, my connection to Malia is tenuous, and I don't know Dustin or Aiden at all. Anastasia's barely a toddler. I've spent some time with Michio, but not enough to earn any sort of influence.

The possibilities tumbled through my head in frustrating circles until finally, my brain spit out the most logical answer.

All of them.

But for somebody to target Devya's program specifically, they had to know a lot about it first. That narrowed the field of candidates significantly, yet still didn't tell me much.

How does Rydell fit in?

I recalled what I could of his conversation with Ethan. Then, Malia's sneaky program kicked in and played it back for me. I reached the diner midway through the third review of that short, weird conversation.

The phone pinged to let me know I had a text message. It appeared over the map.

Eat. Long drive ahead.

A link appeared below the words.

Curious, I clicked on it. Not sure what I expected, but Philadelphia International Airport still managed to surprise me.

Ticket. Clothes. Further instructions later.

A little plane emoji sat between the words *ticket* and *clothes*. Guess I'd better go eat. Looks like I have a flight to catch. It's going to be a very long day.

The Traveler,

Danielle Matheson.

Chapter 11: The Search for Agent Kanter

ITEM 247: Jillian's 120th post-kidnapping journal entry
Item Source: Jillian Blairington

Most of me wanted to forget everything else and work on the problem of freeing Michio and Momma, but I knew finding Agent Kanter would be important overall. From the little I knew going in, AK's the closest thing Kay and his siblings have to a momma. If we wanted to keep them on our side, we'd have to free her.

I'd paid enough attention during Nadia's council of war to understand that at least two groups were actively collecting people. Of these, rogue sections of the Guardians were probably slightly less dangerous than Katharos, but since we couldn't predict the motives of either group, all threats had to be considered urgent.

Naidine had worked out the assignments to address the dangers. She and Queen Elena would work with Kay, Varick, Dee, and Que to plan the rescue operations. I might be involved in those attacks later, but Naidine said I should concentrate on my task. The job of tagging each location fell to me. Nadia already knew where to find Danielle 'cause she'd left a lot of marks with her, and she had a decent guess at where to find Michio and Momma, assuming they'd been kept together. Malia would warn her parents and try to get them some extra protection. It might be possible to send her folks on a trip, but if that failed, maybe they would agree to a road trip that would keep Malia safe.

Of the MISSING and LOCATION UNKNOWN people, Kanter was deemed most important 'cause of that video threat. Nadia and Kay could help search for her, but they were limited to the knowledge of each kidnapped person and in some cases nearby captors. I guess dealing with dreams is easier 'cause most people don't control what shows up in their dreams. When they're awake, they often guard their thoughts, making Minders' jobs a lot harder.

Having a very tight deadline worried me 'cause that was something I'd never dealt with before. I'd never met Benny Connelly or felt his dreams before searching for him, but his captors were basically curious scientists. Delays on my part weren't gonna get him killed. It always helps to know what I'm supposed to be searching for. Still, it had taken me many weeks to find Nadia and my Second Momma, even though I knew what their dreams felt like. This time, I had both problems. I'd never met Agent Kanter, and we had a credible—that means believable—threat to her with a very short deadline.

Since most of the others had stuff to talk about after Nadia dismissed me to work, I invited Kay to a different space in my mind. Once alone, he wasted no time sharing his memories with me. In the eleven years since Firestorm, the strange little family had shared birthdays, ballgames, cookouts, medical emergencies, and about seven different moves. The early years were kind of rough 'cause they had to build up some trust. The information was useful, but not as in-depth as I needed. It told me a little about the woman and how she thought, but it wasn't a full enough picture to predict her dreams.

For me to get a solid location lock and mark it on the map, I needed to find the dreamer. To do that, I needed to predict their dreams well enough to recognize them. This comes down to a matter of perspective. In theory, Kanter should be easy for me to find because few other people would have dreams involving Kay and his siblings. But unless she was dreaming about all four of them at the same instant I searched, I'd have little hope of distinguishing the dream from any other lady worried about the kids in her care.

Fortunately, part of Kay's training involved searching AK's memories. That helped form a fuller picture of the lady. I learned she has a sister named Shelly and that she grew up in New York. Her favorite food is pineapple pizza, and her favorite flavor of ice cream is strawberry. She got recruited to work for Project Keeper as a college senior. The training process took two years, but her uncanny ability to create elaborate scenarios that tested and stretched a subject's abilities put her on a fast-track.

It wasn't the best profile in the world, but I didn't have a few weeks to compile it. Since Kay told me they currently lived in Wimberley, Texas, I started my search there. In a way, it helped to know that AK might be drugged because most things designed to keep somebody unconscious do some very strange things to the way a person dreams.

Checking a dreamer's identity doesn't take much work, but after the first dozen, it becomes mighty tedious. Knowing how important finding people could be, Nadia had helped me prepare a few mental programs to help gather information, but I still needed to monitor them closely and analyze any data compiled.

The timing wasn't much help. After more than twenty-four hours, they could have taken her anywhere in the world, but I was reasonably certain they would stay somewhere in the United States. The borders with Canada and Mexico might be relatively easy to cross, but I didn't think AK's kidnappers would want to take the additional risks of drawing attention to themselves.

My search proceeded in ever-widening circles using Wimberley as a starting point. At the start of my third hour searching, I found them. At first, I didn't believe it. They'd only moved her a couple of hours away north to Gatesville. When I asked Nadia about it, she said there's a maximum-security women's prison there. A check of my coordinates showed AK wasn't in the prison itself, but in a nearby pharmaceutical company building. Nadia suggested it might be because the townspeople would be used to official vehicles in the area. It's as good an explanation as I'm likely to get.

Even though I was sure of my work, I dove deeper into the dream to check. Anywhere in Texas was a very long way to send Varick on a rescue mission without being absolutely sure.

The short, repetitive dream reminded me of the one Benny's momma had been having in the weeks after his kidnapping. It started with a hand opening a door. The perspective indicated AK's personal experience. The feelings that accompanied the dream—curiosity and a hint of fear—came through clearly, courtesy of something Malia had done to alter my Gifts.

Next instant, the door crashed into AK, breaking the little chain thing and knocking her back a step. She barely cried out before a hand snapped out and jabbed something into her left shoulder. She backpedaled but halted abruptly when someone else grabbed her arm and used it to direct her back into the nearest wall.

"Just relax. It's nothing serious," assured the man who had wielded the syringe. "Just a sedative to help you relax. You know what we're after."

"They're not here." AK tried to say it like she meant it, but to me, she just sounded weary.

"They'll come to us eventually," promised the man. "Meanwhile, your cooperation will determine how the subjects are treated once we acquire them. Allow my men to escort you to the van. That will be a good start."

The view shifted as AK observed each captor briefly. If it had only been the suited man, she might have fought, but the combination of facing three armed men and having just been drugged limited her options. She nodded briefly. The rest of the kidnapping proceeded smoothly. The men helped AK to the van, tucked her into a seat, bound her hands, and put a dark hood over her head. By this time, the drug kicked in enough to make her very sleepy. She tried to reach out to warn Kay, but thinking was kind of difficult. The dream ended when she lost consciousness, but instead of stopping, it looped around to the beginning and repeated.

I watched the scene twice through to see if the details would vary. They did slightly, but not enough to make me think AK missed anything important. For example, the color of the suited man's tie stripes shifted from bright blue to a different shade of blue. I also noticed the man didn't have a weapon, but an empty ID holder was clipped to his waist.

After discussing the situation with Nadia, I gave Malia, Kay, and Que the coordinates too, so they could study the security setup. Nadia said pharmaceutical companies were standard covers for government labs. Many times, real companies existed on part of the facilities, but most scientists and technicians working for them wouldn't have a clue. They'd just think they worked on the mundane stuff instead of the top-secret projects. Extra security measures might cause some curiosity, but the people would be used to consciously minding their own business.

I wanted to continue working while I had a good lead, but Nadia insisted I get a few hours of real sleep, so I could help with some of the other missions later.

Chapter 12: Personal Update

ITEM 248: Nadia's fourth letter to Jillian
Item Source: Jillian Blairington

Dear Jillian,

I have set this letter to delay for a time, so you could complete your task without distraction. Finding Agent Nicole Kanter will be vital in our fight for freedom. I will attempt to flesh out those connections after my personal update. The plans must move forward regardless of what happens here.

If you can get to the throne room, Queen Elena will have a record of these events along with a more thorough set of notes. First, I must assure you that Father and I have not been harmed, but the facility is now controlled by the Guardians. Second, please do not be alarmed if you cannot gain access to the throne room. The Darnell boys are here working with a thought amplifier to control me. I may be able to break the mental shackles they seek to impose, but the thought amplifier gives them a significant advantage. When you get a moment, please help me locate it. That should turn the tide. Third, Naidine is not with us. I have sent her to a safe place. She was not pleased with that, but I cannot risk losing her.

This is a dangerous time, and I am grateful the Guardians believe Father and I are worth protecting. However, it should never have reached this point. The attacks against us and those like us are very well-coordinated. I have not yet reasoned through the motives prompting such attacks.

Perhaps I have underestimated Katharos. Judging by their name meaning, I had assumed their vision for the future meant they embraced only life free of genetic manipulation. Though some of their actions have involved murder, they seem bent on control rather than destruction when it comes to us. Please understand that I am not dismissing or condoning the destruction Katharos has brought to many lives. But if their motives were true to the impression Dr. Parris left us with many months ago, we should be the ones marked for death, not those involved in our creation or care.

The takeover went as peacefully as such things can. The current batch of guards was transferred elsewhere, and new soldiers took their place. I doubt many of them know what this facility houses. Four guards received the assignment to watch over me and another four drew the duty of safeguarding Father. He protested, of course, but the new program director, Dr. Calvin Mulligan, insisted.

You likely do not recognize the name since I doubt you have had a free moment to delve into my Firestorm notes. During those events Dr. Mulligan helped our cause where he could for my mother's sake. He was a great admirer of her work, though he took her change of heart toward us as an afront to the great science being done.

Firestorm's conclusion left Project Keeper with a large power vacuum. Several people tried to step in, but all lacked the vision to guide the programs forward. That is how the organization changed into the Guardians and how even that entity fractured into many poorly coordinated branches.

Dr. Mulligan rose steadily up the ranks as a scientist before crossing over into administration. With the passage of time, he has become even more fanatical in his quest to see programs like ours succeed to their fullest. While that sounds good on the surface, he does not see us as people, so he has no problem playing with our lives. He respects our worth in terms of what the government has invested in us, but if we cause him too much trouble, I have little doubt he would sign off on our deaths while thinking of it as the disposal of defective product.

The director has not asked me to do anything yet, but it is only a matter of time. I will certainly do my best to hamper his efforts to collect you and any of our siblings, but my brief conversation with him was disconcerting.

I tracked his progress throughout the facility from the cafeteria where I was cleaning some of the breakfast dishes. Janine Paoli has stepped in as the new cook since I sent Maisha away with Aiden, but she is not quite used to the scale. After sending Janine out the back door, I folded the dish towel and stepped out of the kitchen to greet our uninvited guests.

The director marched in with six soldiers flanking him. Behind the soldiers came two people, a man and a woman, wearing business suits and holding clipboards. I could not sense much about them because somebody was shielding their minds. Once aware of that fact, I could identify the shielding presence as Koresh Darnell. Director Mulligan halted the party a few paces from me and stared for a second.

I patiently waited for him to initiate pleasantries.

"This one is the Minder," Dr. Mulligan said, tilting his head to address the two people with clipboards. "She's very clever."

Though I wanted to speak, I refrained because I gathered the exchange would constitute a test and wanted to evaluate the probable rules first.

"How many languages does she speak?" asked the woman.

Dr. Mulligan sent a questioning look my way.

"Sixty-two," I answered. I could have been more specific, but the woman's stiff, clinical attitude made me curious.

"Is she stable?" asked the man. "Devya's notes mentioned multiple personalities."

That question made me smile.

The director gave me another pointed stare to indicate that I should explain.

"They are projections of my personality at different points in my life, some past, some future."

"What can you tell us about ourselves?" inquired the woman.

"You are currently being shielded by another Minder," I answered.

"Could you break through the shield?" The man's tone tried to be casual, but a gleam in his eyes contradicted it.

"If you have access to my father's notes, you know I can," I replied.

"Why have you not done so already?" wondered Dr. Mulligan.

"I have not had a reason to do so," I answered.

"Aren't you the least bit curious?" asked the woman.

A scan of Dr. Mulligan's thoughts revealed their names as Dr. Kayla Burrel and Dr. Francis DeLuca. Surface thoughts are generally exempt from mental shields because people subconsciously draw them out from behind the shields.

"I find asking questions to be easier, Dr. Burrel."

"We're going to have some good conversations in the next few days," she noted, "but if you're going to be of any use to us, we'll have to adjust some of your programming." She paused a beat to see if I would react to the last word before bowing out of the conversation.

Two soldiers fell into step behind her.

"Do you know where any of the other projects are located?" asked Dr. Mulligan.

"Yes," I admitted, for he certainly already knew that much.

"Will you tell us where to find them?" inquired Dr. DeLuca.

"If I deem it necessary," I said carefully.

"You will," Dr. Mulligan promised.

A wave from the director prompted the remaining four soldiers to step forward.

"Escort the Minder to her room and keep her there until I'm ready to question her," said Dr. Mulligan. He kept his eyes on me even as he addressed the soldiers. "That won't be for a few hours. I need to speak with Devya first. Do you have him yet?"

One of the soldiers spoke quietly to someone not present, nodded, and conveyed the answer, but I did not need the confirmation. Father and Malia had helped me tap into the security cameras around the facility, so I got to witness the confrontation.

I did not resist the soldiers' directions. Instead, I used the time to scan each person's surface thoughts and categorized them by rank, state of origin, height, weight, aptitude scores, latest physical fitness test scores, religious beliefs, favorite animal, and several other preferences. Most of the information will be useless, but I have learned that knowing more about a person can aid with predicting behavior. That is essentially how we reached Agent Kanter.

As part of Firestorm, Agent Kanter had arranged for her brother-in-law to be assassinated, but Varick and I refused to complete the mission. Her outrage against him was justified, but I could not let Varick become the instrument of death. I would never encourage such a thing now, and he was only six at the time. We found a different way to obtain justice. Our actions helped change Agent Kanter's heart so much so that she eventually helped Kay and his siblings escape.

I am not certain whether the Guardians, Katharos, or some other group has her, but she is very important to Kay, Dee, Que, and Tae. They could be fierce allies or bitter enemies. In a way, I feel responsible for them. If we can help them, we must do so.

Aside from unraveling the mystery of who or what seeks to destroy us, Agent Kanter represents the many good men and women who have sacrificed much to aid us. We cannot abandon her. You are our best hope of finding her in time. Meanwhile, I will continue to monitor the situation with Michio and your mother as well as Danielle and her family.

Please stay out of harm's way as long as possible.

Your loving sister,

Nadia Elena Ayers

Chapter 13:
A Strange Hotel in Vegas

ITEM 249: Danielle's 73rd letter
Item Source: Danielle Matheson
Dear Dr. S.,

I ordered scrambled eggs and white bread toast with butter and managed to eat most of it, but I don't think I tasted anything. I ate so fast the waitress hovered nearby, casting anxious looks my way. Pretty sure she thought I'd choke to death. My travel instructions didn't come for another twenty-five minutes, most of which I spent in the restroom near a toilet bowl while my body decided whether to keep breakfast or not. Thankfully, I did not throw up, but it was close for a few minutes.

Guess I could bore you with the details of dashing over to Philadelphia International Airport, jumping through the normal security hoops, and then waiting around for an hour and a half, but I'll skip to the disturbing points. First, the reason my travel instructions took so long to arrive was that they included my driver's license and passport. Second, I didn't even see who dropped the package off. Third, apparently, I have a frequent flier membership with Jetsetters. Fourth, my disturbing care package included one of my own credit cards, which had been used to purchase the plane tickets three days ago.

Why wasn't I contacted by card security? I had even checked the account and credit card balances. It's understandable I didn't see anything post. Those things take time anyway, but I should have seen a pending transaction after a day or so.

During my many hours of waiting, I investigated the mini-mystery via the phone they gave me. A check of the internet app showed a very long history of searches and social media posts. Here's the kicker: as far as I can tell, every single post was sent from one of my real social media accounts. Somehow, they duplicated my profiles, added their own posts and re-routed anything I'd posted during the timeframe they were interested in to a place where they could reply. I may never use any type of social media again. It's one thing to hear of security concerns and quite another to have my identity so thoroughly hijacked. I remember thinking some of the posts should have had more engagement, but I don't post enough to have overwhelming interactions. Anyway, the duplicate profiles had several posts about a planned trip to Nevada, which is why my credit card company thought the plane ticket purchase was on the level.

As I slowly came to grips with the obliteration of my privacy, a series of text messages and pictures came through. The first included a warning that the messages and pictures would automatically delete from the device ten minutes after arrival. I mentally braced. The preparation allowed me to weather the mocking congratulations of reaching the first checkpoint well enough, but I still felt gut-punched when four pictures of my family arrived. Each image featured one of my parents or siblings. Their haunted expressions contrasted with the cheerful holiday frames some sicko had put around the pictures.

It's hard to say which was the hardest to look at. I scrolled left and right through them repeatedly until they disappeared. Mom looked frightened and irritated, which I took as a good sign. Her hair had been neatened, which also struck me as a good sign. Katie's face bore the tell-tale signs of a long cry. The picture showed her sitting on the ground with her arms wrapped around her knees. She held Dylan's hand tightly. My brother's hair stuck out in weird directions. The position of his hands let me see the three zip ties they had applied. That seemed excessive, but if the bad guys posed any threat to our sister, I'm guessing Dylan would show off the berserker side I've only had the misfortune of witnessing twice. Trust me. It's scary. He gets it from Mom. Dad stared sullenly into the camera with enough smoldering anger in his eyes to make me fear for his life.

I almost threw the phone into the nearest garbage, but I refrained because it was the only lifeline connecting us. For about an hour after the messages were deleted, I clung to the phone and stared at the message app, hoping to see a number indicating a new message.

My mind created complicated patterns with the to-do list. *Break free. Rescue family. Take down the bad guys.*

I could not figure out which needed to come first. It seemed like the right order, but how could I break free if they still had my family? Plus, how could I free my family unless I took out some bad guys, and how could I do that while still a captive myself? Nonsensical pieces of several dozen plans formed and went nowhere.

The first leg of the journey brought me to Denver where I got to wait some more. At least they kindly sent another round of temporary photos to remind me why I kept following their strange orders. The second phase carried me to Vegas where I ate a burger and killed another hour. Even though the flight times probably hovered just north of the five-hour mark, I didn't reach a hotel until a quarter to nine at night, local time. The flip from Eastern Standard Time to Pacific Daylight Time also meant it felt like midnight to me.

Not sure how I made it to the hotel because I half-suspect I was sleepwalking at least part of that last leg of the journey. The young desk clerk didn't even ask my name before sliding over a key card and chirping out a room number and directions to the elevator. In keeping with suitable levels of creepiness, I found a duffle bag waiting by the bed with fresh clothes, new sneakers in my size, a bag of food, and a standard battery of toiletries.

Once again, I received a congratulatory text, but this time, I didn't get a round of photos. When I asked about it, I got a snippy order to go to sleep. Instructions would follow in the morning.

My brain and body clearly had different priorities, so I showered and ate the apple slices from my goodie bag. Then, I crawled into bed and spent another few hours writing to you and stewing over the situation. This time, I forced my thoughts away from my family and fixated on Varick, Jillian, Nadia, and the rest of the children.

I'm hoping my brain shuts off soon. I have a feeling tomorrow's going to be another long day.

The Wide Awake One,

Danielle Matheson.

***

ITEM 250: Danielle's 73rd letter continued
Item Source: Danielle Matheson

Yup. Sleep's not going to be much of a thing tonight. Guess I get to regale you with more musings. I know I signed the last letter, which should officially close it, but I don't consider a delay of thirty seconds long enough to be considered a separate entity. You could just think of this as the longest postscript ever.

I don't usually get insomnia, but I can't stop thinking about this strange hotel. Although plenty of signs pointed to something being off, the long day didn't leave me with many nimble brain cells. Thus, it took longer for reality to sink in. I guess the clearest sign, besides there being very few people wandering the halls of a hotel so close to the McCarran International Airport in Las Vegas, is that the door locks from the outside and there's no little security chain on the inside.

While I admit this place has nicer amenities than most of the other prisons I've been in, I don't like the fact that it's huge. I don't know how many rooms each floor holds, if they're all the same size, or even if they're all plush prison cells. Zombie version of me did notice that there's a small gaming room on the first floor, so I'm guessing at least some floors or rooms are legitimate hotel rooms. Still, I don't see the government wasting the effort of converting a single room over to a cell.

To work off some of the agitation energy, I explored the room. The bathroom held an old-fashioned tub that looked like it had seen better days. The toilet and sink also looked worn but functional. The shelves held extra rolls of thin toilet paper and another set of towels. The closet held two empty hangers and a hair dryer. The TV had no remote and turning it on manually only brought up a screen of static fuzz.

The ancient-looking phone had no dial tone. I didn't have

anybody to call anyway, but it would have been nice to have other options besides the kidnappers' cell phone. Speaking of such, one drawer held a charging cable for the phone, which I promptly used. As satisfying as letting the cell phone die might be, I couldn't risk missing something that would get one of my parents or siblings hurt or worse.

The window couldn't be opened, but a small, purely decorative balcony lay outside of it. The heater worked fine but made a disturbing droning noise when cranked all the way up. The walls held not one decoration. The bed linens appeared clean and soft but devoid of any personality. A single lounge chair that looked like it hasn't been moved in the past three decades sat in the corner near the window. The carpet is old but nice enough. Pretty sure the government lackey who furnished the place found great deals on the boring colors.

The refrigerator had been stocked with bottles of water, and I found a stack of ten MRE's tucked near the TV. The Meals Ready to Eat were in addition to the granola bars and two pre-wrapped pastries. Assuming they're consumed at a rate of three meals per day, that's a little over three days' worth of food. Part of me really hoped somebody would seek me out way before then, and part kind of hoped they forgot about me completely. The fewer dealings they have with me, the safer my family will be. That's probably a faulty conclusion based on a delusion, but I'm going to cling to it as long as possible.

With a little extra wall insulation and special locks, the hotel room made a perfect prison cell. My mind raced with the logistics of running a place like this. I hadn't seen many guards, but they could easily be explained as extra protection for the guests. Half the staff probably had no clue what really went on here. Admittedly, I'm right there with them on the ignorance scale.

I spent half an hour counting and recounting windows. I hadn't paid much attention to the room number getting here, but a check of the key card informed me that I'd been assigned room 1513. I wouldn't put it past government grunts to specifically design a system to confuse people, but it seemed to follow normal numbering logic. As far as I could tell, there was no distinguishable pattern to which windows had lights on, but that meant little because of the blackout shades and the relatively early hour. Real guests likely wouldn't be back for another two-to-three hours.

To satisfy the irrational part of me that needed to check again, I tried the door handle.

It didn't budge. I half-heartedly struggled with it for a few minutes, managing to make both arms sore. Thankfully, I stopped before the kicking phase could set in.

When I finally resigned myself to staying the night, I didn't bother pacing the room, but I decided to lay on the side of the bed away from the door. Despite the comfort of the shorts and T-shirt I'd donned after the shower, I got dressed in jeans and one of the long-sleeved T-shirts from the kidnappers' care package. It's probably tracked, but that's a problem for later. I'll probably even be darn glad to have that problem since it'll mean getting out of here.

There are still way more questions than answers. Why lure me to a fancy hotel in the heart of Las Vegas? If getting me to this room was all they wanted, they could have escorted me or shipped me here some other way. Why involve my family? Why the cloak and dagger bits? It's too elaborate. I'm not an evil government mastermind, but this seems like overkill to trap me. That means a lot more people are in deep trouble. Like a four-year-old, my mind keeps harping on who and why.

The Still Wide Awake One,
Danielle Matheson.

Chapter 14:
Can't Argue with Crazy

ITEM 251: Jillian's 121st post-kidnapping journal entry
Item Source: Jillian Blairington

Normally, if I wanna sleep naturally, I shut down my ability to enter dreams, but with the amount of stuff going on, I decided to leave the Gift partly on. That way, if something important came up, I could draw the event into one of my dreams. It's like taking a nap while holding tight to a fishing pole.

To my surprise, I caught something, though I guess it's more accurate to say something caught me.

About two hours into my normal sleep—as opposed to a working sleep—I got drawn into a video game world. I could tell right away that it hadn't been made by Varick, because it looked and felt different than one of his dreams. Varick spends a lot of time on world details. If ya looked into the water in any of his games, it would show you a perfect reflection of your avatar. This world felt like it was working with way less colors and details, like whoever made it was in an awfully big hurry to finish.

The room I arrived in reminded me of the dungeon Varick created for the first level of *The Immortal Warrior*. It held a wooden table and a metal folding chair. The four white walls lacked any kind of decoration or markings. I could only distinguish them in reference to the table and the chair's position. There wasn't even a door as far as I could tell, though the dreamer remembered to put on a ceiling with fluorescent lights. I regularly forget ceilings.

Reaching out with my Dream Shaper Gift, I tried to imagine a door into place. An outline appeared for a second before the wall in front of me rippled and smoothed out like somebody gave a sheet a good shake to get rid of a wrinkle. I tried again, putting more effort into the work. I formed a door that looked exactly like the one on our new house in the money sign state. We've been in the New Jersey house well over a year now, but it still seems new to me since I spent much of the time elsewhere. As soon as I stopped concentrating, the wall did that ripple thing again and fixed itself.

Frowning, I checked to see if I had the usual health, stamina, and mana bars I get in Varick's games. They showed up, but all three lines were gray like the game froze and would be making some hideous electronic death screech in the real world. The realization deepened my frown, but I wasn't worried yet. Wouldn't exactly qualify myself as a heavy gamer, but I'd played enough games to expect an annoying puzzle at some point.

Since the table and chair were present, I figured they must be important since the designer didn't waste details. Sitting on the chair, I stared at the table. A few game minutes disappeared while I studied every inch of that stupid table. The table itself seemed ordinary, but if I looked directly ahead, I could see waves in the air above the table. Wishing things made more sense changed the dream enough that the distortion grew more distinct. It now looked like a translucent square filled with smoke and small glowsticks. The glowsticks rotated but I couldn't move them. Their placement made me think letters.

Nadia likes puzzles, codes, and other cryptic head exercises. During some of our random training sessions, she tutored me in pattern recognition. I'm still terrible at it, but trial and error showed me that if I turned certain sticks so they met, they'd light up. It would have been worlds easier with Nadia present, but I finally discovered the hidden message.

It said: **Hello, Ashlynn.**

The glowsticks disappeared, and the square section turned opaque like a TV. Instinctively, I moved it back to the blank wall in front of me and stuck it to the wall because I didn't want to be that close to it.

Dustin appeared on the screen. He stared at me with a sly smile that told me it was my turn to speak. Several questions crowded my head. Since only his head and shoulders were visible on the screen, I couldn't tell much about his situation.

"Are you okay, Dusty?" I asked cautiously. "You had us worried when you left so suddenly."

"Sorry. I had some things to take care of." Dustin's voice sounded older and graver than I remembered. Something in his expression told me he wanted me to ask questions.

"It's late, and I'm tired. Tell me what you're gonna tell me," I said.

He laughed. It started harsh but changed to more of a giggle, making him sound younger than his ten-ish years.

"Mum's personality notes on you are spot-on," said Dustin, almost sounding like the cheerful boy I'd met when I first landed in Dr. Devya's old lab. "Among other things, she said you were 'Straightforward to a fault.'"

"So, make your point." I folded my hands and leaned forward to emphasize my eagerness to hear him out. "If ya did something, we can fix it, and if ya haven't done something, we can turn our heads to the real problems."

Every trace of playfulness vanished from his expression. I'd expected some reaction, but nothing quite so strong.

"I'm going to do what Nadia only dreamed of doing." Dustin's voice hardened even more with a crazy-high level of conviction. The effect made him sound a decade older even though the voice was mostly consistent with my memories of cheery Dustin. "I'm going to break every tie to our past and set us free for good." Dustin swept his gaze over me. His eyes flipped between asking for and demanding understanding. "I want your help. I'd like you to give it willingly, but I can force your hand if necessary. That's what this is about." He waved to indicate the room and whatever lay beyond the room. "Are you ready for a tour?"

A door appeared in the wall to my left.

Horror washed over me in two separate cold, wet waves as what he said sank in. I tried to remember what Nadia asked me to tell Dustin if I found him, but I drew a big blank.

Needing to move, I stood up. The movement bumped the chair back.

"Andrew. Mei Li. Agent Kanter." My inflection turned the names in to full-on accusations, but I fired the important question anyway. "Did you kill them?"

"Of course not," Dustin replied. "I was tucked up safe in the same compound you were until well after their fates were set. Besides, Agent Kanter's still alive."

"You know what I mean." My heart rate tripled with dread.

Dustin's mocking smile confirmed it.

"I may have given certain people some vital information." Dustin tilted his head back and tightened his jaw. The expression made him look less like my brother and more like Dr. Devya. "I needed certain parties to trust me, so I could get them to behave predictably. I'm happy to report that most predictions were accurate."

The time appeared on the lower right side of the screen.

"Now, if you want that tour, it'll have to be soon," said Dustin. "The night is ending."

"Let's skip to the part where I tell ya you're crazy and need to knock this nonsense off before somebody else gets hurt." I didn't need a tour to tell me I wouldn't like whatever he wanted to show me.

"As you wish." Dustin tipped his head forward in a slight bow. His face vanished from the screen.

Six pictures popped into place. They were too tiny to see much, but soon, the top left one consumed the whole screen. It showed Danielle exploring a hotel room. After a three second delay, that picture shrank and the middle one on the top row got big. This one featured Aiden and Maisha in a different hotel room. The tour of video camera views continued around in a clockwise fashion, showing me Momma and Michio, Agent Kanter, Nadia, and Dr. Devya. The image of Danielle vanished, replaced by a grainy view of Nadia's momma, Dr. Paladon, in a prison cell. Aiden and Maisha blinked out and a fancy looking office took its place, showing both Dr. Carnasis—that's my Second Momma—and Dustin's mum, Cora. Momma and Michio got replaced by the same picture of the Davidson's house that I'd seen earlier in the evening.

"There are more, but this should give you enough reasons to follow instructions," said Dustin, appearing on the screen again. "They're not even all meant for you, but you need to understand the stakes."

Nana always said ya can't argue with crazy, but I tried anyway.

"Speak with Nadia," I pleaded.

"She can't fix this!" Dustin snapped. "Only I can."

"It ain't a competition," I pointed out.

"Do you want to be a slave for the rest of your life?" Dustin's question held a sharp, bitter edge that made his British accent crisper.

"No," I admitted, "but I also don't wanna become the sorta evil we're fighting."

The thing Nadia told me to tell Dustin returned to me, but I had the sense not to mention her this time.

"You're not alone, Dusty. You never will be." I stared at my brother as I let those two statements sit in the air between us. "You can reach out to any of us any time. We're family."

"I have reached out to you," said Dustin, recovering his cool, mocking tone. "And Malia. And Nadia. If I'm right, I'll need the three of you to help me unlock the rest of my Gifts. Then, I can finish this."

"You ain't making sense," I informed him. "What are you trying to finish?"

He shot me a disgusted look that again reminded me of Dr. Devya.

"I told you. Purchasing our freedom," Dustin said scornfully. He heaved the sigh of those doomed to deal with idiots. "Nadia doesn't think I know what my Gifts are, but I do. I also know what they're worth. Freedom. Plain and simple. You'll help. You don't have a choice. You're going to meet Nadia and Malia here, help me with my Gifts, and we'll never have to worry about anybody trying to control us again. Not Father. Not the government. Nobody. Now, rest. I'll send instructions later today."

Dustin's face faded, replaced by Danielle lying on a large

bed in the same hotel room she'd been exploring before. She looked peaceful, but I could tell from her breathing pattern that she wasn't asleep yet. Gently, I reached out through the visual connection, found her, and helped her sleep. She could resist the impulse if she wanted to, but I'm guessing her brain wasn't letting normal rest come.

I still didn't understand the complicated web of who got threatened to control me and my other siblings or the full reason why my brother was playing several sides against each other, but Dustin sounded convinced of his plan. Though I sorta agreed with his goal, I had no intention of helping him unlock Gifts I didn't understand, but he was right about one thing. I didn't have much of a choice about playing along for now.

"How are ya gonna get me to come to you, Dusty? I don't even know where ya are." I muttered the question and observation aloud, even though my brother was long gone from the dream. The silence that answered me struck me as ominous. The big word reminded me of Nadia. She said it means creepy with a promise of bad things.

As I slipped out of the dream, I couldn't keep a small, terrifying question from running amok in my head.

Nadia, did you know?

Chapter 15:
Tour

ITEM 252: Danielle's 74th letter
Item Source: Danielle Matheson

Dear Dr. S.,

I'd say I have no idea how I eventually fell asleep, but it was probably Jillian. My wake-up call came at 7:00 AM. I didn't set an alarm. The phone rang four times, though once was enough to drive off sleep with a stick.

Mom. Dad. Katy! fired through my head. Don't tell Dylan. I thought of him, just not during that first, half-asleep moment. I dove for the cell phone, which I'd placed on the end table. Upon finding nothing, I flopped back to the prone position I started from. Varick popped into mind, releasing a different strain of worries. I know him—and Nadia and Jillian—too well to think they're not neck-deep in this. I've been in similar situations, but this feels way more personal.

The TV came on and flashed a series of instructions to get up and eat something. The lines between TVs and monitors have been blurring lately, so I can be excused for mistaking this one. My hands automatically clutched at the blankets, but I saw no reason to disobey the orders. I wondered about the absence of a *get dressed* order. Somehow, whoever had prepared the message knew I'd slept in day clothes.

Is there a camera in here?

I can't tell you how many times I've thought that question since my arrival in this strange hotel. I didn't include it in my previous letters because I didn't want to worry you, but this is not the time to be burying my feelings. That one's worth avoiding because the thought of anything less than a definitive "no" gives me the creeps. Nevertheless, the odds of there being a camera in here are very high. The other option for them having that kind of up-to-the-minute information involves Minders and is arguably even more disturbing.

Morning rituals, including eating, took maybe ten minutes. Once again, I ate without really tasting anything. Worry turned me off from the idea of food, but I forced myself to eat what I could. The prepackaged pastries were cheese and cherry, respectively. I ate the crusts off both and threw away the gooey centers, trying not to think about the fact that Katy and Dylan would fight over those scraps. The thought of never hearing their idiotic bickering again makes me sad.

As I sat on the bed and stared at that blasted phone, a gentle knock sounded at the door. Have I mentioned how much I despise gentle knocks? I instinctively looked toward the door and stood, tucking the phone away so my hands would be free. Despite a few dozen self-defense sessions with Varick, I had no delusions of being able to fight off whoever came to call, not with my family's fate still a giant question mark.

What should I do?

Varick would remind me that not fighting is a valid strategy, but he'd likely personally knock a few teeth loose from any captors dumb enough to politely knock at his door. The thought put a faint smile on my face.

It died as a second knock drew me close to the door.

"You know it's locked from the outside," I said, leaving enough room for the door to swing open. "But for what it's worth, you have my permission to enter." Not sure what to do with my hands, I let them form loose fists at my sides.

The door swung open, revealing three figures: Dustin and two male soldiers. They didn't wear uniforms, but their stiff stances and alert gazes gave them away. In other context, I might think Dustin was a prisoner, but his cool expression busted that notion.

"Are you surprised?" asked Dustin.

"Just confused," I admitted.

One of his shoulders rose in a partial shrug.

"It's not that complicated," said Dustin. "I need my sisters' help to unlock my Gifts so I can free us, and you're one of the best ways to control them and get Varick to stay out of it."

"Why involve my family?" I asked. "The more people you hurt and threaten, the harder it will be to keep the whole thing under wraps. Why risk the exposure?"

"Because your family is the best way to control you, and some important people think you're the ideal candidate for a new program." Dustin sounded like he was telling me the best condiment for a hotdog. "In addition to your role as my hostage, of course." He grinned cheerfully and stood taller. His voice still had the youthful chirp I'd come to associate with him.

"Do I need to sit down for this?" I asked. I planted my feet more firmly to keep from stepping back and inviting Dustin and his goons inside.

Dustin shook his head.

"We're going on a tour," he announced. "It was meant for Jillian, but she skipped the full version. Since she'll likely contact you soon, it will be good for you to have the knowledge to share with her." Dustin's head tipped left as he watched me closely.

I could tell calculations were happening in his head, but I couldn't begin guessing at what they could be about.

"I trust restraints won't be necessary," he commented at last. He sounded so much like Devya and Cora—his parents, my right fist tightened, itching to deliver the punch I owe Devya for creating this giant, unethical mess. I've made my peace with Cora, and anyway, I think getting kidnapped gave her a new perspective.

"Guess that depends on what you show me," I said. I tried for defiant but had to settle for barely keeping my voice steady. Weariness settled over my whole body. "Why are you doing this, Dustin?"

I didn't have a great mental hold on what exactly he was doing, but the current facts I had lined him up with the bad guys.

He stiffened, and his expression suddenly exuded anger.

He drew a few ragged breaths before his features reasserted their calm and cool setting. The switch happened as quickly as if Malia had flipped an emotional switch in him. I was almost grateful anger still smoldered in Dustin's eyes, so I could tell I didn't imagine the emotional spike.

"Nobody believes me," he muttered, "but I'll prove it." Straightening his posture, Dustin pivoted on his right heel and marched away from my doorway.

I hesitated, but one of the guards beckoned me out of the room and waved to indicate I should follow the kid. Neither guard had fluttered an eyelash at Dustin's Jekyll-Hyde moment. Since the guards weren't really asking my opinion, I followed the non-verbal order.

Dustin led the way to a steep stairwell and down three flights of stairs before entering a hallway identical to the one we'd just left. He stopped in front of a door midway down the hall.

"This one holds Maisha and Aiden," said Dustin. "I was going to let you see them, but they're probably still sleeping. They arrived late last night." He nodded to one of the guards flanking me.

A few seconds later, the man to my right shoved a phone at me. I instinctively accepted it and looked at the screen. It showed a surprisingly clear picture of Aiden and Maisha cuddled in the center of a king-sized bed.

That answers the camera question.

"Depending on how your meeting with Director Mulligan goes, you might have time to see them later," said Dustin.

It took some serious willpower to refrain from voicing the reflex questions.

What meeting? Director who?

But I refused to give Dustin the satisfaction.

As soon as I identified Aiden and Maisha, the guard snatched the phone back.

"Videos can be faked," I pointed out.

Dustin nodded agreeably.

"Check if you like," he offered, waving a hand in front of the lock. "Try not to disturb them. Aiden has some tests to complete later today."

A gentle push widened the gap enough to let me see the bed. Despite shaky legs, I stumbled forward a few steps and leaned heavily on the wall for support once I recognized the figures on the bed in the same pose as the video depicted. Curiosity satisfied, I swiftly retreated to the hallway.

The door clicked shut behind me.

"I have no reason to lie to you, Danielle," said Dustin. "I want your help. The Director's vision for our program could set us free. Don't you want Jillian to be free?"

"Help of any sort would be a heck of a lot easier to give if I understood what's going on and wasn't worried sick about my family." I fired the message a few additional times with my eyes before sucking in a frustrated breath, holding it for a three-count, and releasing it slowly. "If you need something, just ask your sisters. Threatening people will only make them less likely to want to help you."

"I'll let Dr. Mulligan explain, but we have a few more stops on our tour first," said Dustin. "My siblings might be willing to help me, but they're going to need some convincing to fully back the cause."

I puzzled over that last statement as Dustin and the guards guided me to an empty room a few doors down from Aiden and Maisha. It had the same basic layout as my current accommodations except for the back-left corner from the perspective of the door. In the space my room had a big chair and footrest, this one had several shelves of various building toys.

"This will house Michio and Mrs. Blairington sometime tonight," Dustin explained. "They are still traveling. I'd hoped they would be here by now, but sometimes, even the best plans suffer setbacks. It's inevitable when dealing with subcontractors."

I didn't comment on Dustin's ramblings, but his slightly exasperated tone annoyed me because at least part of me still understood he wasn't speaking about trivial things. Once again, the Devya-esque callous view of messing with many people's lives stirred my guts about.

After the empty room, we took an elevator down a few floors below the hotel's basement. The sight of the hidden panel of ten more floor options simultaneously intrigued and worried me. We went down to SL-5, which I'm guessing means the 5th sublevel below the basement.

The hallway here boasted the same harsh fluorescent lights as the rest of the hotel, but instead of rooms, it offered a wide variety of prison cells. Some were self-contained, opaque units. I couldn't tell if these were occupied or not, but most were either makeshift, temporary things or traditional cement and steel drab things. I found the sheer number of units disturbing. I counted at least twenty-eight, though I guess if they didn't care about personal space, they could double up the occupants. Few units had any privacy, but thankfully, most were empty. Still playing tour guide, Dustin led me to a more traditional prison cell tucked in the far-right corner from the elevator.

The occupant was sleeping on a mattress somebody had thrown against the back wall. She looked awfully familiar, but I couldn't readily identify her because she'd fallen asleep with her head tilted away from the door.

"I believe you've met before," said Dustin. "This is Dr. Paladon. She's—"

Varick's mother.

"I know who she is," I said, not letting him finish.

And Nadia's.

"She's going to be one of your instructors during the experiment."

Dustin's statement confused me.

"Why isn't she in a normal room?" I asked.

"We needed to conceal her presence from Nadia." Dustin pointed to four small boxes attached to the upper and lower corners of the cell bars.

I spotted more on the upper back corners and assumed there would be corresponding ones on the lower back corners.

"There's a suppression field that should distort her thought patterns enough to make her unrecognizable to Nadia, at least in the short term," said Dustin. "It won't hurt her."

I wanted him to elaborate on what Dustin's unseen masters wanted Dr. Paladon to teach me, but my heart hurt too much to do more than stare at the sleeping figure. She looked peaceful, but tell-tale marks on her wrists told me her kidnapping went about as smoothly as mine.

"Can I return to my room now?" I wasn't sure I'd even asked the question until Dustin shook his head.

"First, you have a meeting with the director," he reminded me.

Thrilling.

Guess I'm off to meet the head crazy guy. Maybe I'll get some answers. I'll keep you posted. It's going to be a long day.

The One Who Woke Up Weary,

Danielle Matheson.

Chapter 16:
I Ain't Surrendering

ITEM 253: Jillian's 122nd post-kidnapping journal entry
Item Source: Jillian Blairington

I couldn't sleep normally after that dream conversation with Dustin. The worry wired my brain to the *on* setting. Cheating by changing the oxygen levels in my brain woulda gotten me into some sort of sleep, but it certainly wasn't gonna be restful.

The clock on the end table read 3:32. I assumed AM since no light came in the windows.

I didn't have to go, but I figured since I was up, I might as well try. It'd give me a chance to rinse my face. The unsettled feeling from the dream intensified with each step I took toward the bathroom.

A creak on the stairs made me flinch.

Trying to tell myself the noise meant nothing didn't help, but the fear quickened my steps. I raced to the bathroom, shut the door, and leaned back against it. Relief filled me, like I'd reached a safe zone. Slowly, my heart rate dropped back to a non-painful pace, giving me a chance to take care of the necessaries and rinse my face. The tepid water felt good, but I resisted the temptation to take a drink. Nana says it ain't smart to drink water in strange places. I've learned to trust her on such matters. I felt bad for soaking the hand towel, but I wasn't eager to wear a wet sweatshirt either.

Once finished drying my face, I stared at the door for a

solid two seconds, afraid to open it.

A series of three hard knocks on the door sent my heart right back up into my throat.

As soon as I released the lock, the door whipped open, barely missing me as it swung inward.

Murphy stood in the threshold clutching a shotgun with his left hand.

"Come with me." His tone elevated the order to absolute command status. Without waiting for any response, he turned around, adjusted his grip on the shotgun, and started moving carefully toward the stairs. I say carefully 'cause he stepped like a man stalking a skittish deer.

My feet seemed rooted to the floor, but eventually, I stumbled after Murphy.

He led us down the stairs, then wove a swift path through the house to the kitchen. Before we could slip out the back door, every window lit up with harsh white light.

"Down!"

I didn't need to hear Murphy's hissed order.

Immediately, I dropped to my hands and knees 'cause being caught by those lights woulda made me a mighty fine target.

"Put the shotgun down and come out with the girl, Murphy." The man's voice sounded soulless 'cause it came through a bullhorn. "I'm on a tight schedule, so I'll be brief. You give me the girl, and Emma gets to live."

Murphy made a noise that balanced grunt and growl.

Leaning back against some of the cabinets, I put myself into a light sleep and reached out toward the man's voice. Nadia and I had spoken about me using some of her gifts, but the training hadn't gone far. Still, the people surrounding the house made tracking easy by being formed up in a regular semi-circle pattern.

The figures came in bunches of three or four. I guessed they'd brought three vehicles, but it coulda been a hundred if they had a second staging area. Reaching the first group caused enough strain to give me a mild headache.

I woke myself and reported the number of people to Murphy. Assuming the man spoke truth about Emma being one of 'em, we had twelve problems out there. My quick peek didn't reveal if they were armed or not, but their heads had the ultra-focused feeling of trained soldiers or agents.

"I can count 'em again, but I'm not sure I can deal with that many from here." Once upon a time, I'd dealt with more people in Dr. Devya's first lab, but that situation featured a closed room, Nadia and Malia for help and support, and a much closer distance to work with.

Murphy didn't reply. His expression held a lot of anger, resignation, and determination. I only recognized the emotions 'cause Malia had made me practice feeling those three.

"Get me closer to 'em. My Gift works better if I'm closer." I knew he could work that out for himself, but he had a lot on his mental plate.

"Is she there?" Murphy directed the question to me, of course, but the man with the bullhorn spoke up before I could confirm it.

"Emma is bleeding, but she'll be fine if she gets patched up soon."

Though the words were barbs cast at Murphy, they hit me too. It's one thing to hurt someone in a fight and another thing entirely to let them suffer to control somebody else.

I started to rise, but Murphy's strong hand landed hard on my left shoulder. He shook his head once. The bright light streaming through the windows let me see that the resignation now mingled with pain in his eyes.

"Murphy? Did you hear me?" called the man.

A few bullets crashed through each of the windows, showering both of us with glass.

"I heard you!" Murphy raised his voice so the man could hear. "Prove you have Emma."

"Gladly."

The man's answer worried me.

Gripping my left arm, Murphy leaned close and whispered, "Get to the basement. I can hold them off for a few hours. Help should arrive by then." The crisp delivery buried every emotion except determination.

A woman's muffled scream shredded more of my nerves, but I rallied enough to argue with Murphy.

"I gotta go to my siblings." The simple reminder I'd spoken a few seconds ago crystalized around my heart like confirmation of the right answer in one of Varick's video games. My Gifts work best in close quarters. If Dustin wanted me close, he'd get his way sooner or later by threatening Danielle, Momma, or Michio. My mind wandered for a few seconds, but when the thoughts snapped back into place, I had my path forward. "This is our mess to clean up."

Murphy eyed me like I wasn't making much sense. Dr. S. has given me the look enough to make it familiar.

"Your sister said to keep you safe. Handing you over to Agent Resnicki wouldn't exactly be following that directive."

"I ain't surrendering." I drew a big breath to gain a second to order my thoughts. Surrender had been my initial plan, but the way the agent talked about Emma told me that plan would likely get both of my protectors killed. "But I also can't do much good from here, so we're gonna have to make this look good."

"What do you mean?"

I spoke almost Nadia-level fast 'cause I knew the agent in charge out there wouldn't wait much longer before crashing in, even if it got some of his people killed.

"If we give up too easily, they'll know it's a trap, and if we wait too long—"

"They'll kill Emma," Murphy finished. "How are you going to make that call?"

I'd been working that question since the realization hit me, so by the time Murphy voiced it, I had an answer I didn't much like.

"Can't believe it's come to this," I muttered. That part didn't have a target, but I directed the next part to Murphy. "Stall them any way you can. I'll let you know when to move me." Another thought hit me. Nadia says that sometimes it's the smallest details that can sell a scene. Actually, she had a whole lot more to say on the matter, but that's the important part. "Do you have any rope or zip ties?"

Nodding, Murphy rose to a crouch, turned around, and trotted over to the sink. He stayed low so his head wouldn't reach the window height. After opening the cabinet housing the sink's guts, Murphy rummaged around until he came up with some zip ties. Since these were too small to make adequate wrist restraints, he started stringing them together to make a longer chain.

"Do you need more proof, Murphy?"

"Just wait!" Murphy's anger and irritation were a hundred percent genuine. He continued linking zip ties. "I'll need to subdue her." This part came out softer, but I guess they heard him well enough 'cause Emma protested.

"No—"

She got cut off almost instantly, but Murphy and I recognized her voice.

Dropping myself into another light dozing state, I used my knowledge of Varick's video games to sketch the scene outside. The figures for the men and Emma would never have won any artist awards, but they let me plot approximate positions and identify the head agent. I didn't need to keep the dream going long, an experimental program whipped up by Nadia showed me Agent Resnicki's patience wouldn't last much longer.

Letting the dream dissolve, I woke up and met Murphy's concerned gaze.

"We have to move now." I spoke softly, so the sound wouldn't carry out the windows. Next, I held out my wrists so Murphy could add the zip tie chains. "I'll go back to sleep and watch from a dream. Get me into the center of them as quickly as possible. Once they're unconscious, we can plan the next step."

Surprisingly, the plan unfolded without too many disasters. Murphy finished securing my hands, picked me up, shouted his intention to the guys outside, and cautiously exited the house. For a time, only the crunch of Murphy's boots and the buzzing of the spotlights could be heard. To keep the light from hurting my eyes, Murphy kept my head tucked in toward his chest. I ain't exactly a baby, but he made good progress.

The soldiers ordered him to stop while we were still a good distance away.

The guns aimed at us weren't normal ones. They were tranquilizers.

Murphy plodded on like he didn't hear the men.

They shouted louder for him to stop.

He paused, considering his options.

I almost panicked 'cause we were still out of range.

Turning around, Murphy let my legs drop to the ground, gripped my wrists, and sprinted backwards as fast as he could.

The soldiers let their tranquilizer darts fly.

Murphy ducked most of them, but three hit him anyway.

He stumbled and fell to his knees. Then, he keeled forward on top of me. Not entirely sure if he planned it that way or not, but the way Murphy fell shielded most of my body from the men firing tranquilizers at us. His weight made breathing more difficult, but it also forced the men to reposition and move closer, bringing 'em into a comfortable range for me to work.

Marking each position as swiftly as possible, I noted that the head agent and two soldiers stayed by the vehicles while the others moved in. Resigning myself to having a headache, I reached for every man at once and cut off the oxygen supplies to their heads. Typically, I try to be more subtle, but we were beyond out of time. Gripping their consciousnesses a different way wouldn't have worked. I knew that because I felt the buzzing sensation that means the person took something to artificially keep themselves awake. That's how Dr. Devya's head always feels.

Some of them managed to moan or curse, but most just dropped over like they'd gotten a good dose of whatever they shot at poor Murphy.

Agent Resnicki and the two men with him resisted the most.

Their guns—real ones, not tranquilizers—swung toward Emma.

I redoubled, then tripled, my efforts. I think I almost killed one of the men by cutting off the oxygen a little too long. That should probably disturb me, but the way they'd treated Emma didn't leave me with much sympathy for 'em.

Without all the shouting men, a strangely peaceful silence settled over us. After making sure the soldiers and agents survived my forced slumber, I checked on Emma. The dream state let me assess—that means something like get a feel for—her injuries more thoroughly than a normal visual scan 'cause I had access to knowledge from Nadia. I guess I always have the knowledge, but somehow, it's just easier to get to while asleep.

Anyway, I discovered that in addition to a lot of bruises, somebody had sliced Emma's left wrist. The knowledge made me simultaneously cold and hot with a mixture of anger, sorrow, and fear. The reaction knocked me up a few sleep levels. Riding the momentum, I made a few tweaks that would let me wake up.

Once conscious, Murphy's dead weight across my chest seemed more problematic, but I tapped into the adrenaline caused by fear for Emma to heave him off. Since Dr. S. wants an honest account, I guess I'll clarify that by *heaving him off* I mean I lifted Murphy just enough to wriggle free.

I'm no healer, but Michio left me with a semi-competent working knowledge of closing some wounds. Hopefully, it would be enough to save Emma.

My head hurt something awful by this point, but I tapped into Malia's Gift long enough to shock Murphy with cold. When that didn't work right away, I struggled to my feet and hurried over to try my healing skills on Emma's wounds.

Chapter 17:
Controls

ITEM 254: Danielle's 75th letter
Item Source: Danielle Matheson

Dear Dr. S.,

Despite being told I would be taken to meet Dr. Mulligan, my stomach fluttered when we piled into the elevator and went down two more levels to SL-7. I assumed the head honcho's office would be somewhere normal, like on the first floor next to the hotel manager's office.

Upon exiting the elevator, I noticed the soldiers straightening their shoulders. It didn't take me long to guess at why. This level featured uniformed soldiers at regular checkpoints and in front of several doors. Since the doors and white walls lacked windows, I didn't know what when on behind the many closed doors we passed, but several had convenient labels like SL 7-23 T or SL 7-28 H. The first part was the sublevel, and the second part was likely the room number. Before I could decrypt the letter part, we reached SL 7-45 O.

The door swung open as we approached. The soldiers flanking the door didn't react to the movement. Instead of entering the room, Dustin stopped and faced me.

"I'll be back when your interview ends." After dropping his announcement, Dustin walked swiftly back down the long corridor we'd just traveled.

"Come in, Ms. Matheson."

The businesslike tone to the man's summons simultaneously put me on edge and reassured me. My mind instinctively started sketching the speaker, basing him largely on a combination of Devya and Lanier. While I got the brown color part right, this man obviously put more effort into styling his wavy hair. He also had matching facial scruff that framed his entire face. He wore a white lab coat, but since it wasn't buttoned, I also saw his casual brown shirt and beige pants.

Dr. Mulligan's position behind a large, imposing desk brought back memories of Devya's office, but the similarities ended there. Whereas Devya's office had been tastefully decorated, almost everything about this office lacked a personal touch.

"Sit," said Dr. Mulligan, waving to the two chairs situated in front of his desk. His eyes tracked me until I did as bid. Then, he moved around the desk and perched against the corner near the empty chair and crossed his arms. "Do you know why you're here?"

"Dustin said you had a pitch for me," I said, keeping my tone neutral.

"I read your file. You have a lot of experience with the best results of Dr. Devya's work. Have you given any thought to having any of their Gifts?"

"No." I meant *no* in the sense that I wasn't interested, so I quickly added, "Yes. I've thought about it, but I don't want their Gifts."

It's complicated.

Jillian and her siblings possess miraculous Gifts. The idea that those abilities could be given to anybody is exciting and terrifying. Unleashing those Gifts upon the world irresponsibly is a big fat invitation to Armageddon. I really wish I was being melodramatic here. People get murderous over almost anything. Tech like this could break the world. For all its flaws, I'm not sure this is a step in the right direction. Through much effort, I did not elaborate on my thoughts for Dr. Mulligan, but if he had any skill in reading expressions, my face probably told him anyway.

"Really. That's interesting and disappointing. You're an

ideal candidate for the next phase of experiments."

"In what way?" The question put a bad taste in my mouth because I knew he wanted to hear it, but I didn't have the mental agility to put up much of a verbal battle.

"You're devoted to the current subjects. You've already experienced some of the Minder abilities by working with Nadia." Dr. Mulligan spoke with clinical dispassion that sucked any warmth from the words. "You're in good health. We'd have to check a few things, but I'm sure you'd pass with flying colors."

As the good doctor listed my attributes, I had a flashback to Cora doing much the same. Somehow her assessment was less disturbing. About then, I realized Dr. Mulligan was systematically trying to break down my will to resist the training through reverse psychology. The revelation made me wary, but dangerous curiosity stirred in me anyway.

"What are you trying to do?" Despite serious misgivings, I really wanted that question answered. I knew deep in my soul that continuing the conversation was a bad idea.

"Devya and his people have proven that humans can be bred with extraordinary Gifts. I want to take their findings to a new level." A gleam entered Dr. Mulligan's eyes as his passion for the work took over. "I want to know if those Gifts can be bestowed on anybody." He stared off into the space above my head for a moment before focusing on me again. "I'll need many subjects from various ages, races, and physical conditions. We have hundreds of desperate people signed up for last ditch therapies, but the medical possibilities are less interesting. The real power—and money—lies in unlocking the Minder Gifts. And for that, I believe a strong body and mind are better for the experiment."

"What are the risks?"

Dr. Mulligan lifted his left shoulder in a casual shrug.

"Every experiment carries some risk. If your body rejects the nanomachines or any of the chemicals they apply, you could experience anything and everything from discomfort to death." His features hardened slightly with annoyance. "Nothing has worked so far, but I think the problem lies with the subjects, not the science. Perhaps it's just the scientists."

He wasn't making much sense by this point, but I let him

ramble, hoping eventually something might click.

"I've requested that the original team be assembled, but the logistics are still being ironed out." A distant gaze announced that this part was Dr. Mulligan chatting with himself. "It's always a matter of leverage. I'd expected to use the controls one way, but perhaps it cuts both ways. I've seen it work before, but never with so many people. Who is the Dream Team lynchpin?"

"I'm confused."

Giant understatement.

Dr. Mulligan's head tilted ever-so-slightly.

"Perhaps it's you." He shook his shoulders like a dog waking up. "No. You're only connected to the original subjects." Dr. Mulligan tapped both index fingers rhythmically on his thighs. "It's got to be one of them. Devya. One of the women?" An expression of deep concentration came over him, but it soon gave way to a slow smile. "Cora."

"What about her?" An uncomfortable feeling socked me in the gut.

"She's my lynchpin." The man looked like a sated cat about to take a nap.

I knew he'd jumped clear off the edge of reason and was already plummeting, but the stubborn side of me needed to debate.

I wanted to say: *Leave Cora alone, you Devya wannabe*, but I settled for a rational argument.

"You can't get what you want through force."

The look Mulligan sent my way combined pity, compassion, and something sneaky and shrewd.

"I can and I will, but this will go much smoother if you help me. Let's make a deal."

"Let's not." It wasn't my smoothest comeback, but by then, I just wanted to return to my quaint prison to rest and forget this new flavor of idealistic nutter.

"In addition to truly getting a choice about volunteering for my next experiment, I'll let you choose whether the invitation even gets extended to your immediate family." Dr. Mulligan looked like a hard-pressed merchant offering a prospective buyer a one-time, amazing deal. "I'll even sign off on their exclusion from these proceedings."

It took my brain a few seconds to process the offer.

"You'll let them go?" My tone inserted a few tons of disbelief with a smidgen of blind hope. "Completely free and unharmed? No men. No guards. No bindings. Nothing."

"Completely free and unharmed," Dr. Mulligan echoed. He raised his right hand like someone swearing a formal oath. "Provided you come through on your end of this bargain."

Like a fish mesmerized by a shiny lure, I took the bait.

"What do you want?"

"Help obtaining Cora's cooperation." Mulligan folded his arms and resumed his perch on the desk corner. "She won't talk to me or most of my people, but she might speak with you. Right now, Cora and Dr. Evelyn Carnasis are well out of reach. That needs to change. I'll need both ladies to lend their expertise to my experiment, and I'd rather not cause an international incident in the process."

"They wouldn't risk their lives for me or my family." I didn't want to help Mulligan, even by pointing out the obvious. "They don't know us."

"You're not the control for them. You're the messenger."

"Who's the control?"

"Devya. He hasn't arrived yet, but he's contained. Nadia too, but I don't know how much influence she has upon them."

"Ask Nadia." Guilt slapped me right about then for making that suggestion, but I shoved it aside. "She can reach them anywhere."

"I have." Mulligan's admission surprised me. "She's not very cooperative at the moment. She may be more amenable once I clarify her mother's position, but the girl knows Dr. Paladon is worth far more than a simple hostage. The threat lacks substance."

The last statement made me feel like I should be offended, but for once, I knew what he meant. It even clarified some of the earlier mumbo jumbo.

The situation as I understand it this second is as follows. Please note that this is highly subject to change. Mulligan's trying to replicate the results of Devya's program in others, people already born. The Dream Team referenced is likely the original six stars: Devya, Sean Pauling, Evelyn Carnasis, Jessica Paladon,

Karita Robinson, and Cora. Mulligan hasn't mentioned Pauling, and I doubt he'd go after him since he's regularly in the public eye due to his political obligations.

Status check. Cora and Dr. C. are in England, presumably safe. Hence, Crazy Dude's blunt bid for my help. Dr. Paladon's already here with me in Hotel Hades. Sorry, cynical side flareup. Devya's *contained*, whatever that means. Pauling and Robinson are free. As previously mentioned, I think Pauling's career will keep him in the clear, but I'm pretty sure government thugs were after Dr. Robinson long before Mulligan's request. I only hope she can stay a few steps ahead of them.

My opinion, for what it's worth. I am not comfortable with anybody experimenting with people's genes, especially not somebody with Mulligan's attitude toward people. His callousness makes Devya seem warm and fuzzy.

"So, if I deliver a message to Cora and Dr. Carnasis, I get to choose my fate and my family goes free, right?" I needed the man to commit. The writhing mass of anxiety churning in my stomach said he could easily renege on any promise, but the part of me drowning in helplessness needed hope, even false hope.

"Once I have what I want, your family can walk away." Mulligan's summary did not sound favorable.

"That's not the same thing." The uncertainty settled and solidified. My conscience cleared even as my heart raced, then lurched like a faulty engine. "No deal."

Mulligan's disapproving frown seemed parental in nature.

"I'd hoped to avoid outright threats."

But I've given you no choice.

The thought contained a large bucketful of bitterness.

Standing, Mulligan turned enough to tap something on his desk.

"Dustin will be by shortly to return you to your room. We'll continue this conversation when your mother gets here. I'm not asking much of you. While I can't guarantee your success, you have nothing to lose by helping me."

The trip back to my cushy prison cell passed somehow. I don't think I noticed any of it. I've been lying on the bed for the past hour reviewing the entire exchange. The last sentence

Mulligan uttered haunts me because it sounds completely reasonable. I don't have much to lose by helping him, just idealistic notions of not being part of something every fiber of me screams is wrong. I have no doubt that if and when that vague threat against my mother gets more real, I will cave.

The Future Betrayer of My Own Morals,
Danielle Matheson.

Chapter 18:
We Ain't Them

ITEM 255: Jillian's 123rd post-kidnapping journal entry
Item Source: Jillian Blairington

Patching up Emma's left wrist took a whole heap of concentration. I made her sleep so she wouldn't be bothered by my clumsy efforts to help her. The blood loss had left her more than ready to pass out anyway, so that didn't take much out of me. The patching part did though 'cause it ain't my Gift.

For some reason, I have a harder time tapping into Michio's Gift than either Nadia's or Malia's, but that's probably 'cause they've got more experience and can explain things better than Michio. That's not his fault. He's a lot younger than us. When I was his age, I didn't even know I had a Dream Shaping Gift.

When I finally finished my work with Emma, I realized I still had five major problems. First, my wrists still sported the zip ties Murphy had applied to 'em. Second, both Emma and Murphy were unconscious and not likely to come around naturally for a long time. Third, the men I'd knocked out would be waking up in a matter of minutes. Fourth, I had no idea where to go to help anybody. Fifth, my head felt like somebody had taken a drill and driven it clear through the back of my skull. Spots of light danced behind my eyes every time I closed 'em.

My energy reserves had been burning backup fuel for the last ten minutes. If I fought hard, I had maybe one more move in me. Though I was next to Emma, I figured waking Murphy would be the smarter move. Aside from being thoroughly drugged, he didn't have any obvious wounds.

I had enough sense to know that cold was the wrong play here. Nadia's recent troubles and Dr. Lanier's insistence on drugging me had taught me a powerful lesson. The nanomachines that aided our Gifts could help get rid of the evil knock-out chemicals through natural body defenses, specifically sweat.

Since what I had to do involved Malia's Gifts, I let my body rest on the ground beside Emma. I hadn't had the foresight—that means good sense—to leave a mark with Murphy and I didn't have the energy to direct the nanomachines to move from me to him across the distance that separated us. So, I awkwardly checked Emma's pockets for something I could load with nanomachines and toss at Murphy.

She didn't have anything in her pockets, but Agent Resnicki had some pocket change. Taking two of the quarters, I loaded both with as many nanomachines as I could in a few seconds and tossed 'em both toward Murphy. One landed on his chest and the other landed a foot away from his left hand.

Closing my eyes, I activated a few programs Nadia had made me prepare recently. I don't know if she's really good at predicting odd situations and skills I'll need, or if she just assumes everything's gonna go wrong and plans for that.

The first series of instructions basically tricked Murphy's body into thinking it was super warm out. It's similar to the natural defense mechanisms that get a body to run a fever to fight off disease.

Next, I had the nanomachines make contact with each unconscious bad guy and monitor his level of sleep. It was a simple program that measured a certain level of brain activity. When their brains got too active, the nanomachines mimicked my Gift and cut off the oxygen supply to their heads until they returned to a deeper sleep. I didn't want to leave that system in place for too long for fear it'd malfunction and kill somebody, but I also didn't have the time or energy to play whack-a-mole with their level of alertness.

The third program kept me informed of the efforts to wake Murphy.

I monitored Murphy 'cause the microscopic machines

required constant attention. Nadia had warned me that it might happen that way 'cause she wasn't sure how much independence to give 'em. Guess she went with the cautious setting. I didn't mind. Once I knew what to do, the work helped me push past the pain still scrambling my brain.

Murphy's body did not want to wake up.

Not sure what would have happened if I'd gotten the same dose of knockout drugs he did. I mighta died.

Since directing the nanomachines from any distance wasn't going great, I repositioned my body and rolled toward Murphy. It didn't do nice things for my head, but at that point, I'm not sure the pain coulda gotten much worse. By the time I got in range to touch his head, I had to concentrate hard on not throwing up. Instead, I collapsed next to him.

After six rounds of purging as much of the chemicals as possible, I drove off enough to wake Murphy through Malia's cold shock method.

Murphy shivered, moaned, and started snoring.

Taking that as a good sign, I shocked him again.

Each breath hurt, but I forced myself to address him.

"Please, Murphy. Wake up. I need. Help." Feeling like one more thought would burst something in my head, I directed every nanomachine in Murphy to channel a sense of cold.

His body jumped like I'd touched him with a live wire.

Once conscious, he rolled away from me, then eyed me warily.

Couldn't blame him for that reaction. Besides, I was too relieved to be offended. For a while, I sat there and took some deep breaths. Tears of exhaustion fell. I musta looked miserable 'cause Murphy crawled over and hugged me.

He didn't say nothing, but the quiet comfort helped a lot. After releasing me from the hug, Murphy drew out a pocketknife, cut through the chain of zip ties, and helped me stand up.

"Can you walk?"

"Maybe." My answer was honest but not very helpful.

"We have to move." Murphy surveyed the prone forms around us. Something flipped in his expression. It turned hard even as he spoke softly to me. "If you can make it, get in that truck. This won't take long."

My time around Malia and Nadia let me follow the direction of Murphy's thoughts from his body language.

"Don't kill 'em."

"They'll come after you again," Murphy warned.

"There will always be more."

Murphy's skeptical look and scowl told me it was a terrible argument.

I sighed, frustrated that I couldn't explain my point well.

"We ain't them."

A sad smile replaced Murphy's scowl.

"Hard road, it is. How much time do I have?" He nodded at the nearest soldier to clarify his point.

"They're on a looped cycle, but I don't wanna leave 'em there too much longer," I explained.

Murphy nodded thoughtfully.

"Stay here and watch them. I'll check on Emma then take care of some details to strand them here as long as possible."

"She's asleep, but she should make it." I said this to Murphy 'cause it needed saying, not 'cause I thought it would change his need to check on her.

"There's enough food in the house to last the men a few days, but I'd rather they not end up with my gun collection."

I knew Murphy wasn't really talking to me by the time this statement came up, but my headache finally retreated enough for me to wanna attempt helping.

"How can I help?"

"Are you sure you're up for it? You should probably just rest."

I didn't need a mirror to tell I probably looked ready to keel over, but I mumbled something about resting on the way. It occurred to me that the head agent man probably had a lot of information that I needed. We should probably take him with us, wherever we decided to go. I told Murphy as much.

He nodded absently before giving me instructions.

"Gather their phones and destroy them. If you can let the air out of their tires, disable three of the four trucks. We'll take the last one. Then, grab some food for the road. I'll take care of my truck and Emma's motorcycle, if we can find it." Murphy didn't explain the rest of his chores. Instead, he rushed off to start 'em.

Dealing with the phones was easy and kinda fun. I put 'em in a pile and started a pyro program Aiden made. The phones melted together in one unsightly mass of metal and glass.

As I got to thinking I had no idea how to let air out of tires, the knowledge showed up in my head. It appeared like a fancy letter that dissolved as soon as I noticed it. When the scrap disappeared from my mind's eye, I had my answer to the question that had barely formed. Didn't take much head power to conclude Nadia had left it for me to find.

The thought packet led me to find the valve cap and remove it. Then, I needed something hard and thin to press down on the pin so air would escape. Nadia had suggested a screwdriver. Since I couldn't find one, I stole the keys from one of the unconscious guys. The loud hiss of escaping air scared me at first, but I soon got used to it. I'd gotten a good bit of air out of the first tire before Murphy saw and handed me a gun.

I didn't think that was a great idea 'cause it's been a long time since I held a gun, but as my hands closed around the weapon's handle, another thought packet activated. This one came with a short animation of a treasure chest opening.

"Be careful with that." Murphy looked like he had a whole heap more to say, but he merely shook his head and trudged back toward the house.

The Glock 17 was heavy, but I studied it from several angles while Nadia gave me the world's fastest crash course on safety and use. Finally, she let me approach the tire I'd already half-flattened. As I took aim, a weird instinct guided me back a few steps. That was certainly new, but I didn't argue with the feeling. When we get out of this big mess, I'm gonna have a long sit-down chat with Nadia about the extent of the programs she set loose in me.

While I dealt with the tires, Murphy bound every man except Agent Resnicki. He got bound too, but then, Murphy buckled him into the back seat behind Emma. She had been loaded into the front passenger seat. That left the seat behind the driver for me. Murphy insisted I get in and start searching the agent's dreams for information.

After collecting the nanomachines from the other soldiers and agents, I returned Resnicki's two quarters along with a fresh batch of tiny machines. It occurred to me that while I still had access to the other guys, I ought to work with them. Since I didn't have time to sort everything, I dove in and out of each man's dreams real quick-like and left a thought mining program and a mark. These wouldn't give us instant answers, but they might pay off later.

Nadia once called thought mining programs crab traps. While I hadn't been crabbing, I got her point.

Just before I entered a working sleep, I decided holding a loaded gun might not be the best idea, so I took out the half-full ammo magazine, cleared the round from the chamber, and held onto the two separate pieces of the gun.

A check of Emma showed me some disturbing dreams, so I replaced 'em with nicer ones before settling down to pull answers out of the head agent. I considered trying to use some of the healing protocols my brother left with me, but I couldn't afford to make any mistakes with my dream work. As far as I could tell, Emma had some nasty bruises, the long cut near her left wrist that I'd healed, and a shallow flesh wound inflicted with a gun. Murphy had patched her up with a First Aid kit, but the best healing aid I could offer was a few solid hours of rest.

I really hope the agent man knows where I need to go.

Agent Resnicki had orders to take me to a hotel in Las Vegas.

I guess I coulda gotten to the destination by letting 'em take me there, but that woulda left me with even bigger problems. At least this way, Murphy and Emma were free to help us and one team of government people would be temporarily out of the game.

Thoughts of the hotel brought Danielle to mind, but I also felt like I should focus on Varick, Malia, and my Second Momma. Nadia and I had talked about the possibility of projecting dreams to make them visible to others, but I'd never gotten to try it before. Danielle's mind buzzed with too much worry to submit gracefully to a deep sleep, so I connected to her head as well as I could and let the rest of my Gift carry me to some other dreams.

Chapter 19:
Depressing Company

ITEM 256: Danielle's 76th letter
Item Source: Danielle Matheson

Dear Dr. S.,

I've mentioned before that Jillian gets more tricks in her arsenal as the days go on.

I'm currently having one of the strangest experiences of my life. As with my last letter, I'm in bed, but this time, I think I'm legitimately asleep. Somehow, Jillian's sharing her Gift with me enough that I'm having incredibly vivid dreams of recent or currently unfolding events. At the same time, I'm aware enough to tap into Malia's thoughts-to-words program and give you live commentary. Lucky you.

The only reason you don't have eight more rambling exercises in nothingness is that I napped most of the day. I forgot how draining it can be to deal with crazy people. Mulligan's clinical, mad scientist approach almost makes me miss Lanier's brand of evil. At least with Lanier I expected that his influence had some reasonable limits. If Mulligan has the blessing of the US government's evil twin, things will likely spiral downward very quickly.

Don't know why there's a brief delay here, but as soon as the show starts, I'll shut up and just tell you what I'm seeing.

***

The first view makes me slightly dizzy. It's from the perspective of somebody walking through a long bare hallway lined with empty cells. The view then cycles through four different angles. It settles on a top-down perspective that shows me the top of Varick's head. The sight sends a deep ache through my chest.

The march continues, but I don't recognize either of the other two men. The last cell holds a sleeping Asian woman.

Before I can even think to wonder about her identity, I find myself watching Malia sleep in some sort of vehicle. Two arms wrap tightly around her. The close view prevents me from seeing more, but the perspective soon backs up as Jillian adjusts the dream. The ache that started in my chest quickly becomes a painful stabbing sensation as I recognize the owner of the arms as Malia's new mother, Mrs. Davidson.

The third shift doesn't surprise me, but hearing Dr. C's voice does.

"Have you heard from Nadia lately?"

"Yes, she said much is in motion and that someone would extend an invitation to us soon," Cora answered.

"Should we accept the invitation?"

***

I never got to hear Cora's answer to Dr. C's second question because the scene ended abruptly. In other news, I finally understand some of Jillian's frustration at the dreams made of *things she ain't supposed to see.*

I'm not sure whether to count that experiment as a success or a failure. Seeing Varick and Malia brought me some much-needed comfort, but they're not exactly getting to kick back and relax.

Now that I'm awake, the conflicting emotions get to have a proper row, as Varick would say. I know he's out there working hard and will eventually sweep in with a brilliant, probably doomed, rescue attempt. I love him for it, but I'm also tired of being a government plaything and watching my friends walk this fine line between strengthening their wonderful Gifts and being everybody's hostage.

This must end.

The fervor rises in me so quickly a burning heat flashes up

my neck. The passion gave me a reckless sense of bravery.

Figuring I ought to make Nadia a prophet before these whackos had a true hold on me, I hauled myself out of bed, put on a fresh set of clothes, and marched to the door. Not knowing the correct next step, I knocked on the door.

Nothing happened, so I retreated to the end table by the bed and tried the phone.

A polite young woman answered and asked how she could help.

I explained that I was ready to fulfill my end of Mulligan's deal. She didn't sound like she knew anything about it, but she transferred the call to another operator. This happened twice more before a young man finally obtained the clearance to patch my call through to England.

Mercifully, the runaround from that side of the pond didn't last long.

The epic phone journey finally ended when I reached Cora. She didn't bother with pleasantries.

"How bad is the situation?"

"Bad." The admission escaped before I could work out a nicer way to put it.

"Is my son involved?" The tone of Cora's question carried sadness and weariness.

"He is, but—"

"Tell Director Mulligan we'll be there as soon as possible." The statement came from Dr. C.

No! Stay back! Abort!

The random protests sailed through my head, but I could only manage to say, "That's a terrible idea. And how do you even know about Mulligan?"

"He's been sending messages for two weeks," said Dr. C.

Really? He gave me the impression nothing got through.

"I told him if he could get you to call me, I would consider his proposal." Cora's explanation stung.

"He was always going to pursue you." Dr. C.'s words didn't bring much comfort, but they did put some things in perspective. "This conflict has been a long time coming."

"What does he want from you?" I was too annoyed to care

if my question sounded desperate.

"Too many things to list," Cora said.

"We may not know every motive." Dr. C.'s statement came a split-second later. "If we have a chance to speak later today, we can discuss his motives."

"If Mulligan wants you two bad enough to break several dozen laws, shouldn't you be working to stay the heck away from this place?" I have never claimed to understand any of the women who worked for Devya, but Cora and Dr. C. always struck me as the most grounded and least likely to walk into blatant traps. On the other hand, I guess the saying that love makes people stupid holds some truth.

"We have been avoiding this for years," said Cora, "but the time for permanent resolution has come."

That sounded more like the scary version of Cora I met many moons ago.

A few more protests zipped through my head, but I kept them in.

"Guess I'll see you soon," I said. My tone added *even though that's a blatantly terrible idea*.

Since there wasn't much else to say, we each signed off.

I listened to the dial tone for a few seconds before hanging up the old school phone and sitting on the bed.

The next half-hour or so passed with my mind spinning on the hamster wheel of self-pity and worry. This time, I split the worry equally between my family members before adding Jillian and crew to the mix. As the worry threatened to make me completely useless, something shifted. It almost felt like Malia flipping an emotional switch in me or Nadia clearing cobwebs out of my head, but I guess it could easily have been my stubborn nature kicking in and driving off the victim mentality. We can hash that out if I ever make it to another therapy session.

Riding the wave of determination, I washed up. Next, I marched over to the pile of MREs and picked up the top one. It read chili with beans. I love chili but it doesn't always love me, so I set that one aside and scanned my other options. My stomach did not need more reasons to rebel. Meatballs in marinara sauce seemed the most innocuous of the bunch, so I dug into that one.

The meal wasn't exactly restaurant quality, but it did the job without making me sick. I count that as a win.

The food fortified me enough to get on that phone and make some visitation requests. I purposefully started with the names I didn't think they'd go for and worked my way down. The soldier fielding the request was kind enough to pretend to convey the messages, but for all I know, he could have just stuck me on hold and waited a painful amount of time before delivering the canned answer. My family, Dr. Paladon, Dr. Mulligan, Maisha and Aiden, and Dustin were *unavailable*. Not even news of my successful contact with Dr. C. and Cora earned me any favors.

I tried asking to go on a walk. Denied.

I asked about board games, a pack of cards, puzzles, or internet access and received four more no's. I expected it for the internet request, but the other requests were quite reasonable.

I asked if they needed any help. At that point, I would have settled for sorting MREs, helping in the kitchen, or even straightening up beds. My hospital corners are rusty, but I would have made it work. I think the man almost hung up on me.

"I'm bored! I need to do something!" Surprisingly, the cries of despair got some response.

After yet another painful wait, the man informed me that the director had some reading material he could have delivered.

I accepted without even thinking about what Mulligan would deem worthy of sending me. Shortly, I received my special delivery. The sound of the door opening made me leap off the bed, but the entire delivery process completed before I crossed into the small hallway leading to the door.

Upon realizing that the reading material consisted of three glossy pieces of propaganda, I groaned. Nevertheless, I snatched them up, grabbed a bottle of water from the refrigerator, and settled on the bed to be enlightened.

The first pamphlet made grand promises of curing diseases. The second read more like a comic book and harped on unlocking the secrets of the mind. The third and final was more of a recruiting tool than informational piece. It even had a tear-away section for obtaining more information. I read them twice, though to be fair, most of the second read consisted of me silently arguing with them.

I noticed that Mulligan's name was all over the three sheets. That irritated me because I knew each piece had its roots and probably whole trunk and most of its branches springing from Devya's work. Maybe you can help me square with that weirdness. I think I've sent you previous musings about the dual nature of Devya's work, but you get to hear it again because I get to spend the day stewing in my thoughts. Misery and company and so forth.

Devya's a genius, a madman, and a sociopath. The last description came from Cora, but I wholeheartedly agree. He's simultaneously the best and worst scientist I've ever heard of past or present, not that I know of many others. That seventh grade who's who among scientists projects is a blur. Devya didn't accomplish his feats alone, but he was certainly the driving force. The pamphlets make it seem like Mulligan's trying to hijack Devya's entire program. In the business world, that would be called a hostile takeover. I'm not sure what they'd call it here.

Most of Devya's crew has now adjusted their moral compasses to see Jillian and her siblings as people instead of objects. Nadia even claims they might grow a conscience in Devya one day. She's likely being a hopeless optimist on that score, but stranger things have happened.

Much as there is to hate about Devya, he deserves credit for his accomplishments. To have every two-bit, scruffy fanboy out there trying to steal his work is infuriating even without being the one directly wronged.

There must be some sort of nutter handbook because most of these jerks are running the same plays. When in doubt of being able to beat someone fairly or obtain their help by asking like a normal human, grab a hostage. In fact, grab hostages to control your hostage.

The only thing I can say in Mulligan's favor is that he doesn't do things by halves. Even Lanier only went after the children, me, and the main scientists. Mulligan's collecting the kids, the scientists, former employees, and innocent bystanders. It'll be an absolute miracle if nobody ends up dead. My gut tells me I know a small part of the whole picture and that the rest isn't pretty.

Half of me wants to just skip to the next big event, and the other half of me prays this terrifying time lasts forever. I want to see Varick and Jillian again, but if it would keep them safe, I'd suffer this aching sense of loss for a long time.

Guess it's a good thing we're not doing tea time.

The Depressing Company,

Danielle Matheson.

Chapter 20:
Freeing Captain McKenna

ITEM 257: Jillian's 124th post-kidnapping journal entry
Item Source: Jillian Blairington

When Murphy told me it could take us more than twelve hours to reach Las Vegas, I decided to get some real sleep. To accomplish that, I slipped into a light level sleep and used my Gifts to block most dreams. I kept just enough senses on to scan for thoughts initiated by Varick, Nadia, or Malia. Nadia can reach out to me on her own. Varick and Malia have marks that let 'em tell me when they want to be contacted, but if Nadia helps 'em, they can also reach out to me directly.

I think I got about twenty minutes of restful sleep before sensing Varick's signal that a new dream awaited me. Reaching out to him, I created a space within my mind for both of our avatars, but when mine arrived, I found only a glowing box. The bright light hurt my eyes, so I willed it to a dimmer setting. The move let me see the cover and title.

The figure in the picture had my face, and she held a shiny sword in one hand and a glowing blue-white ball of energy in the other hand. Big letters above the character read *The Immortal Warrior III: The Path to Truth*.

As I watched, the cover shifted to show me in a more relaxed pose wearing the same clothes I currently wore. This version of me held an unloaded gun in one hand and an ammunition clip in the other hand. The details impressed me until I remembered Nadia often added personal touches to Varick's games.

Varick hadn't spoken about a new game, but since the last Immortal Warrior game ended with a big reveal, it didn't surprise me. Bidding the box to open, I closed my avatar's eyes and entered the game.

I fully expected to be immediately fighting for my life, but for once, my avatar didn't enter to heart-pounding music. The theme music played softly in the background while a map showed me several cities around Terabane. A tab in the corner let me select a new era. It defaulted to medieval times, but I wanted to know what would happen if I set it to the farthest future date. Unfortunately, that was grayed out, telling me I had no access to that level.

I did have the ability to change my hair, facial features, clothes, and starting weapon. The knowledge made me uncomfortable, so I let the default settings stand. Varick had never given me so many choices. Usually, I just landed in the middle of a fight in a random game level. I know because I'd made Nadia tell me the entire story for *The Immortal Warrior* and *The Immortal Warrior II: Quest for the Lost Heirs*. I don't mind story spoilers, but I dislike having massive gaps. Momma and my New Daddy probably wouldn't like me playing the full version of these games anyway.

Sonia's melodious, unhurried voice addressed me. Hearing her made me think of Nadia 'cause it's her voice without the correct cadence. My sister always speaks like she's in a great hurry to get her point across.

"The time has come to right all wrongs. Chosen One, you must rescue your family and take back your throne or surrender to your uncle's will. Choose your path wisely, for many lives rest upon your decisions."

"What am I deciding?" My eyes automatically searched the clouds even though I knew Sonia wouldn't form an avatar. I know what she looks like from concept art, but she's always been a disembodied voice to me.

"Make haste to Torrin, former capital of Terabane, but do

not let your presence be known too soon, else your uncle vent his wrath upon those ye love."

The part about loved ones in danger hit me hard, but I forced myself to focus. Varick's games are nearly always training sessions. Even though it's all gussied up in fantasy wrapping, I'm guessing the game has something important to teach me about the situation I'm headed towards with Emma and Murphy.

My red health bar, yellow stamina bar, and blue mana bar looked normal, but I tested each to be sure. At certain times in past levels, one or the other would be useless for a time to make facing a particular boss harder. Picking up a small stick, I imagined it was a dagger. Part of my mana bar flashed and disappeared as my thought won. Touching the sharp blade to my left arm made the health bar brighten. I didn't cut myself since the health bar's reaction already let me know what I needed to know. Sprinting forward and leaping over a small stream convinced me the stamina bar worked fine.

Checking my inventory, I found two Transportation Stones. One was bound to my hidden cave in the Lost Souls' Forest. I left it alone because that would take me in the wrong direction. Using most of my remaining mana, I recited the spell to create a new Bind Point for the blank stone. I should probably bind it to a village near Torrin, but a nameless urgency bid me to hurry. Since I didn't know many safe places around Torrin, I chose one of the food cellars my character had played in as a child and made the Bind Point link to that.

I landed on a mountain of potatoes. Those aren't the nicest things to land on. They're only slightly nicer to one's backside than rocks and that's mostly 'cause they're packed in sacks that even out some of the lumpiness. I picked my way off the potatoes and wound through the other stacks of food.

The air smelled musty and slightly moldy. The damp feeling was familiar, but the paths had changed from those in my character's implanted memories. I used a mana restoration potion to help my bar recover. Then, I used some mana to activate a spell to learn the correct way out of the maze. Varick occasionally includes puzzles in his games, but I didn't have time to figure this one out the usual trial-and-error way.

As I neared the end of the maze, it struck me that I had no idea what I was supposed to do. Sonia's cryptic instructions had boiled down to get to Torrin and don't get caught. I'm not a big fan of sneaky missions. They're only slightly better than escort missions where you're trying to keep somebody alive.

Opening my character menu, I checked the mission log for current objectives.

- Save your family.
- Free Captain McKenna.
- Find the Lost Prince.
- Defeat your uncle and reclaim your throne.
- Uncover the True Enemy.
- Choose Terabane's future.

I got tired reading the list, but I knew from past experience that Varick's games often involved choices that made some objectives mutually exclusive, meaning you could only accomplish one of several objectives.

In a way, that's good for sales 'cause it means the games have good replay value. It also angers some fans who like writing ranty reviews. I read some while avoiding math homework. They're kinda entertaining.

I let these mundane thoughts ground me while I took my time sorting the objectives. Saving family seemed pretty darn important, but so did every other point. An uneasy gut feeling said family and a wider happy ending for the planet might be one of those either-or choices I dislike. I need to believe this is gonna have a happy ending.

The objective that said Free Captain McKenna changed from white font to red and faded back to white. The cycle repeated three times. That meant something significant was happening and the quest might not be available for much longer.

I snapped the menu closed 'cause the blinking objective was distracting.

Since my mana bar was only half-full, I used a little magic to turn myself into a mouse and created a tiny portal to take me to Captain Shamus McKenna. Learned that trick early. Some abilities, like turning myself into one of several small creatures, are linked to my core attributes, so I get a mana discount. Also, smaller portals have a lower magic cost.

I appeared in a dingy, gross prison cell.

A bearded man leaned against the wall. His wrists bore sores from the metal shackles.

A cutscene showed me a younger, beaming version of the man in fancy armor saluting me with a sword. That picture melted into a banquet hall with the same man kneeling before my father.

As suddenly as it started, the scene ended. The man's head slowly rose.

"It's good to see ye, princess." His soft, hoarse voice both warmed me and hurt to hear.

Returning to my human form, I laid both hands on the nearest of his broken wrists.

"No!" Captain McKenna clenched his fists. His words came out faster and stronger. "They will know. Ye must escape."

I must have hesitated too long because the game made me select the first suggested line.

"I can't leave you here." Sorrow put a painful ache deep in my chest. I didn't need to pass an intelligence check to see the former Captain of the Royal Guard would soon die.

His eyes lit with excitement.

I had a bad feeling about that look before he uttered a word of his barking mad plan, as Varick would put it.

"Take me Life Force. Add it to yer own."

I about shook a tooth loose turning that idea down.

"Please. I will perish either way, as a rat in this hole or doing my sworn duty. Let it be my choice, my gift."

The line reminded me of an uncomfortable conversation I had with Nadia, only this time I was on the receiving end of hard advice.

A check of the objectives paused the game. Under the Free Captain McKenna quest, I found a brief description of the offer.

In case I couldn't pick up on the giant clues the header before the description read: MORAL CHOICE!

Then, for added dramatic effect, Sonia spoke the description aloud.

"Captain Shamus McKenna is dying from wounds inflicted

by your uncle's interrogators. Adding his Life Force to yours will boost your maximum mana pool by 50% and increase the regeneration rate by 100% for the next three hours of gameplay."

"That will kill him." I muttered the statement aloud, but Sonia kept speaking since she was just reading the script to me.

"He will die a hero's death."

Since this was my dream, I shaped it to call to Sonia.

"Can I save him?"

"You are the Chosen One. You can do as you like, but all actions have a cost and a consequence. He may live. He may die. The future is unknown."

I'd been looking for a simple yes or no, and I suppose for Sonia that was straightforward. Releasing my hold on her, I speed read the rest of the description.

You can attempt to sustain his Life Force by donating some of yours. This will improve his odds of surviving. He can be a powerful ally as many soldiers are loyal to him. This choice will cost half of your remaining mana and slow your regeneration rate by 50% for the next three hours of gameplay.

When I let the game resume, I noticed Captain McKenna had passed out. In a way, that made my choice easier since I didn't have to argue with him about my decision. I chose the harder road. Aside from morbid curiosity, I figured I may as well train on the hardest setting.

Touching his right hand, I willed the game to do its thing. I'm sure it translated that into a fine spell, but I paid that part no mind. A faint white light drifted out of my fingertips and disappeared into Captain McKenna's hand. The wrist wounds still looked awful, but his breathing evened out. Using my Dream Shaping Gift on a character inside a dream was an odd experience, but I wanted to make sure he stayed out long enough for the Life Force transfer to do some good in his battered body.

A gate squeaked, giving me a good scare and reminding me to hurry up.

Freedom comes in many forms. Time will tell if you have chosen wisely or wasted an opportunity.

This time, Sonia's words sounded inside my mind.

A pleasant dinging noise told me I had earned a new

achievement. Curious, I dug into the character menu and checked the relevant tab. The new entry had a small orange exclamation point next to it.

The title read: LIFE GIVER.

Your selfless actions will be remembered for many generations.

The description gave me a queasy feeling 'cause it sounded like I'd already died.

Chapter 21:
I Believe You

ITEM 258: Danielle's 77th letter
Item Source: Danielle Matheson

Dear Dr. S.,

Things are about to get interesting. Guess it's just as well I have been staying in daytime clothes. These people aren't big on the whole knocking thing.

The phone woke me first, but when I answered, the guy on the other end only had two words for me.

"Get up."

I had about four seconds of processing time before three soldiers strode briskly into the room. I instinctively dropped the phone back into its cradle, grabbed some of the blankets, and held on tight like a kid warding off the boogeyman. I stopped just shy of burrowing in like a gopher.

The clean-cut goon in front held a bundle of clothes.

"Change." He gave the order mid-toss.

The bundle hit me in the chest and landed on my lap. The minty green color and soft fabric both said the clothes were scrubs.

I looked from the bundle to the intruders. My glance asked a question.

"Now." The speaker wouldn't have won a Mr. Congeniality award, but he was efficient. The curt answer shut the door on my question before I could voice it.

No worries. Having younger siblings is great training for such situations. Changing proceeded without incident, though I will say the scrubs felt weird. I kept fingering the fabric to remind myself I had clothes on. When I reached for my shoes, I received a set of three headshakes.

Before I could protest the odd decision, the talker retreated to the door and took point while the other two fell into step behind me.

My gut said they'd lead me down. It didn't warn me that they'd opt for the stairs. By the time we hit the third landing on our descent, I sorely missed my shoes and the bygone times of using the elevator. To my dismay, on the fifth-floor landing, the lead soldier quickened his pace. When I failed to increase my speed swiftly enough, the back left bundle of joy gave me a small shove forward. At least he had the decency to wait for the next landing, so I didn't take a set of stairs face-first. The next several staircases were embarked upon at a jogging pace. By the time we reached the correct floor, I had completely lost count. My lead escort charged through the door and ran down the hallway, then another, and another.

A few dozen complaints buzzed around in my head, but I held them back because I needed to conserve my breath and concentrate on not slipping. I'd worn socks to bed. That plus a lack of shoes meant treacherous footing.

By the time the trio brought me back to the large room divided into cells, my breaths came at a rate just shy of gasping.

Goon one saluted and stepped to the side. Thing two and three each gripped an arm and hustled me over to Dr. Paladon's cell.

The scene had obviously been carefully arranged. Somebody had already crammed a collapsed gurney into the cell. Dr. Paladon and Dr. C. sat on the cot beyond the gurney. Neither looked pleased, though I'd categorize Dr. Paladon as weary and Dr. C. as frustrated. Dr. C. clutched a syringe with a scary large needle. Her white-knuckled grip made my fingers ache with sympathy. Cora sat on the cot in the next cell to my right. Of the three, she looked the calmest, but my guess is she's got a better poker face than the other two.

Mulligan stood in the cell with her. My chatty escort entered the cell and stood slightly behind the aspiring Dr. Evil.

My heart pounded enough to let me feel it pulsing in my skull. The distraction of absorbing the scene let the silent muscle move me to the gurney and strap me in properly. One handled the foot restraints and a belt that would cross my thighs while the other buckled in my wrists and fastened another strap that fell across my stomach. Several protests collided. The best I could do was cough and keep from kicking the soldier restraining my feet.

Some adjustments raised the mattress up and tilted the whole bed, so I got a better view into the cell holding Cora.

So much for volunteering.

"Proceed." Mulligan directed the imperious instruction to Dr. C. and Dr. Paladon.

I'm not sure if he said more because a female voice spoke in my head. The British accent and voice pattern belonged to Nadia, but there was something distinctly different about the feel of these vivid thoughts.

Try not to react, Danielle. My name is Naidine. We've met briefly in the past, but you usually deal directly with Nadia. I apologize for the hasty explanation, but our collective efforts to reason with Dr. Mulligan have failed. We're arranging some backups to undo this experiment if you desire, but for now, I beg you to let it happen.

I'm not exactly in a fighting position.

Believe it or not, will is a key factor. If you let me help you, I can try to ease your body through the adjustment period, but it is possible for you to fight me on this. If we are at cross purposes, my help will be limited.

A crash and a cry caught my attention before I could give Naidine an adequate answer.

The soldier had shoved Cora against the metal bars separating the two cells. From her posture and expression, I guessed he also had one of her arms twisted up behind her back.

"What is happening?" I could guess, but I really wanted it spelled out because more time spent talking was less time spent experimenting on me.

"Dr. Mulligan is trying very hard to repeat past mistakes,"

answered Cora.

My gaze shot around the room like a pinball, trying to measure who would explain first.

"The nanomachines we developed do not give people special abilities. They enhance what is there and are programmable to a very small extent." Dr. C. spoke with the strained patience of one who has already explained something many times.

"I think you can do better than that; you simply lack the right motivation."

Mulligan's statement prompted a sigh from Dr. Paladon.

"That sounds familiar," she muttered. "Samson thought as you did, but coercion is a terrible substitute for real cooperation, which I guarantee you're not going to get."

Mulligan looked intrigued.

"You're not supposed to have those memories."

Dr. Paladon shrugged.

"Memory strippers don't always last forever."

What are they talking about? Who's Samson.

A mentor of Dr. Mulligan's. I will explain in full someday, but the conversation tells me there may be a way to keep Dr. Mulligan from running his experiment on you. Would you like me to try?

The curious side of me immediately asked for more details.

Naidine complied with a series of words and images so fast, I got dizzy taking them in.

The plan boiled down to offering up our connection as an interesting tidbit to distract Mulligan.

I wasn't convinced we should give him anything, but it sounded better than getting injected with random nanomachines.

"Does that mean I can count on you to help my teams with their Minder research?" asked Dr. Mulligan.

Do you trust me? If so, please allow me to speak through you.

I gave her the proper permissions.

"She does not have what you seek." Technically, the words came from me, but the syntax, word choice, and British accent was 100% Naidine. I even sounded like her. I have no idea how she managed to make my vocal cords work for her. Maybe it was just a mind trick. Much as I wanted to spend all day pondering the weird connection, I forced myself to focus on the odd experience of being a spectator in my own body.

I finally know what it means to have every eye fix on me. It was worse than one of those showing-up-to-class-naked dreams.

My close connection to Naidine enhanced my observation skills. Dr. Paladon winced and blinked back tears. Dr. C. looked intrigued but dubious. She shot me a warning look. Cora nodded thoughtfully. Mulligan's features cycled interest, excitement, caution, and doubt. Settling on interest, he gestured for the soldier to release Cora.

He did so but stayed in her personal space.

"You've been holding out on me," said Mulligan. "Tell me, do I have the pleasure of speaking with the famed Minder?"

"I am a part of Nadia. Danielle has been kind enough to endure my presence. I have a request to present. Will you hear it?"

We had collectively decided not to correct Mulligan on his assumption that he dealt with Nadia. Since I didn't really grasp the difference between them anyway, I concentrated on trying to be a good host while sharing my headspace with Naidine.

Mulligan adopted a semi-mocking, courteous tone.

"By all means, I'd love to hear your request … and what you plan to bargain with."

"Allow my father's work to continue unhindered. The more stipulations you place upon him, the harder you make his work. Ultimately, you will be disappointed by the results."

I'd personally been rooting for a list of hostages to release and got my wish a few seconds later.

"Furthermore, release Danielle's family, my mother, and Dr. Carnasis."

And Cora?

Cora is being held to control Dustin and my father. Should those reasons fail, Dr. Mulligan would seek to turn a profit through her family. He would never consider releasing her.

Which side is Dustin on?

His own.

Is he a prisoner or an accomplice?

A little of both.

"And what of Ms. Turner?" asked Mulligan. "I'm curious why you wouldn't include her in your bargain."

"You are not the first to attempt such tactics with us. Cora is perhaps the only hostage you need. Additional people are counterproductive."

"Stop talking." The plea came from Dr. C., but a similar request was written all over Dr. Paladon's face.

Naidine and Mulligan ignored the request.

"Despite her moral weaknesses and lack of vision, your mother is still one of the world's leading biochemists. Why should I let that much talent walk away? For that matter, Dr. Carnasis is possibly the only one with significant experience with the nanomachines. She could save my teams decades of work."

"*She* won't help your teams." The statement came from Dr. C.

Dr. Paladon placed a restraining hand on Dr. C.'s right shoulder. The move let me see the shiny handcuffs Dr. Paladon sported.

"I am in possession of some of my mother's memories, and I can access some of Dr. Carnasis's notes concerning her work with the nanomachines. Whatever I lack, I am certain Dustin has already promised you."

Naidine must have felt my alarm for she followed this up with silent reassurance.

I will not give him access to such powerful knowledge, I promise, but for now, he must believe I would consider it.

"I believe you." Of the terrifying responses we could have gotten from Mulligan, that was number one. He drew a small gun from somewhere.

Change of plan. Danielle, let Dr. Carnasis inject you with the nanomachines. They are blank slates, I can program them to save you if you get shot, but you must be swift. We need your permission.

Do it.

I didn't even want to think about the *if you get shot* part.

Oblivious to our conversation, Mulligan kept talking.

"So, here are my terms. You transfer every scrap of

information to me and maybe I'll let you save the girl."

What felt like the world's biggest needle rammed into my left bicep.

Mulligan fired.

I watched the bullet head for my stomach in slow motion.

Dr. C., who had already lunged forward to stick me with that blasted needle, reached out, caught the bullet, and redirected its flight. It thudded into the gurney's mattress an inch to my left. The soldier boys practically tackled Dr. C. Blood dripped from her hands and tears flowed down her face. Dr. Paladon tried to pull one soldier away from Dr. C. and caught an elbow with her face. I have no idea how I could even sense that since I was at an entirely wrong angle to see any of it.

Mulligan screamed an epic denial. His gun pointed at me again before swinging to Dr. C., Dr. Paladon, and around to Cora before he finally shoved it back into a holster. His beet-red cheeks clearly indicated frustration. That manifested in a series of sharp orders, one of which was that Dr. C. be brought to him.

The soldiers happily complied by dragging her around the gurney and hauling her into the cell with Mulligan.

He reached for her hands, turning them palm up to survey the damage.

Mission accomplished. Thank you for your help, and I apologize for the deception. It's probably best you pass out now.

Chapter 22: You're Family

ITEM 259: Jillian's 125th post-kidnapping journal entry
Item Source: Jillian Blairington

A few hours from Las Vegas, I helped Murphy take a nap while Emma and I kept watch. I needed a wakeful period anyway. Emma passed the time staring out the windows and thinking. I tried to order everything I knew about the new mess that faced both my families.

People connected to Dr. Devya's work were in a lot of danger. The most vexing part was not knowing how many enemies stood against us. Agent Resnicki's presence said the government was involved somehow, but that didn't explain if they were working with or against Dustin. The dream I'd met Dustin in had only told me he wanted my help along with Malia's and Nadia's. I still didn't know if that was a good idea, since I didn't know the full extent of his Gifts.

The thought of Malia made me drop myself into a light sleep to check on her. Despite the late hour, I couldn't find her dreams, so I assumed she was awake.

The part about Agent Kanter—AK—being held in a secret government lab didn't fit the rest of the puzzle forming in my head. I hadn't heard from Kay in a while, but he had left a mark with me to contact him since we hadn't gotten to talk after Nadia's council of war. We'd been about to chat when something came up, and Kay had made a hasty exit. He'd made the mark look like a gray box with a red button labeled *talk*. Figuring now was as good a time as any, I pictured the box and activated it.

Jillian?

You're not Kay.

Very astute. The thought made my brother sound an awful lot like Dr. Devya. ***Nadia wanted to keep you away from me by hiding you, but I outsmarted her.***

What do you want, Dusty?

I told you before. You're going to help me reach my Gifts. Go to these coordinates.

A series of numbers and random letters appeared in my head. As I prepared to tell Dustin they made no sense, an odd understanding moved through me. It felt like my brother was rearranging things in my head. I've had Nadia reveal stuff to me before. This was a completely different—and much more unpleasant—feeling.

Do I need to bring out my big threats?

A mental image of Isaac and my New Daddy appeared then faded. Another of Momma and Michio did the same thing. A third picture showed me Danielle. I couldn't tell if the threats had any teeth to 'em, but Dustin's confidence wasn't good.

What about Murphy and Emma?

A feeling of cold indifference filled me. The chill shot straight to my soul as I realized what that meant.

What about them? Bring them along or don't. I don't care.

Where's Malia?

She's safe with me. And before you ask, Nadia's set to arrive within the hour. You're the missing piece.

"I ain't comin'." I didn't realize I'd spoken aloud until Emma turned her head to give me a questioning glance.

Surprise then anger flashed inside me in a reflection of Dustin's mood.

You're really willing to sacrifice other lives to save your own? That's ... unexpected.

"Not what I said," I answered. "If Nadia and Malia help, I can reach ya well enough from almost anywhere, but I don't think it's a good idea to have us all in the same place."

Dustin stayed silent a few beats.

I agree to a point, but how do I know you'll help me?

"You're family. If this is about claiming your Gift, I'll help, even if I do think you're going about this all wrong."

I need to know who I am and what I can do.

Somehow, this thought was softer, almost pleading.

"Let me get somewhere safe. You know how to contact me. Let me know when Nadia arrives."

Dustin sent a feeling like a nod and a wave, then his presence left my mind.

I shook my head and grunted in frustration.

"I take it that was your brother, the other Minder." Emma directed her comment to me without turning around.

"I don't know what he is," I admitted. "That's mostly what this is about, I think."

"What did he ask for? And what do you need from us?" Emma's questions came out businesslike.

"Might as well tell us everything," said Murphy.

I spent a few minutes catching 'em up on my chat with Dustin.

"I've half a mind to turn around and drive across the country," Murphy declared, "but I don't think this is something we can avoid for long." He started the SUV and pulled back onto the road. "I don't have any contacts in this part of the country, but I'm sure we can find a cheap motel."

"I have a friend who could help."

My head was shaking no before Emma finished wording the offer.

"Too dangerous." As I hurried to make my point, Nadia's need to speak fast finally made some sense to me. "We should find two different places. Leave me at the first, then don't tell me wherever else ya go. Dustin knows how to track me, and I don't trust him not to send people after me, even though he agreed with me about not coming in."

"That would leave you defenseless," Murphy argued.

"It would leave me with two unseen guardians," I countered. "If I don't know where to find ya, they won't either. If ya take turns sleeping, I can let ya know how things work out.

There's a chance Nadia will be able to better direct ya anyway."

They exchanged a look I didn't quite catch, but Emma's thoughtful nod said they were at least considering my plan.

"What about Resnicki?" asked Emma.

"He comes with us." Murphy's answer was instant and had enough force to let us know he'd made up his mind on that.

"Ya could leave him with me," I said, sorta hoping they wouldn't take me up on that. "I can control him for a few more hours."

"If they capture you, they're likely to set him free." Murphy's clipped tone said he wasn't pleased by that notion. "Did you get the information you needed from him?"

"He didn't have much." I hesitated to admit that 'cause I knew the idea of getting a location from him was most of Murphy's reason for bringing him with us. "All I know is that his base is hidden in a hotel."

"Well, that narrows it down to a few thousand possibilities," said Emma.

"Can we get rid of him now?"

Murphy's question held only the barest hint of not being serious, but I answered as if he meant every word.

"Ya can't kill him. It'd haunt ya."

"You would regret it." Emma's statement and mine hit Murphy at the same time.

"I could take it," Murphy declared. "Who taught you kids how to argue anyway?"

"Nana says that part comes naturally," I answered.

"Mom. And she got it from you, so in a way, I learned it from you," said Emma.

The exchange lightened our mood a little. For a time, only Agent Resnicki's soft snores could be heard.

The closer we got to the city of Las Vegas, Nevada, the darker my mood got. I couldn't quite square my memory of Dustin as a cheerful kid and someone desperate enough to threaten dozens to get his way.

What happened to you, Dusty? Are your Gifts something the world's ready for?

Since I wasn't connected to a Minder, I didn't get an

answer, but I felt the questions burrowing into me.

***

ITEM 260: Jillian's 126th post-kidnapping journal entry
Item Source: Jillian Blairington

This place is creepy, but at least I'm not alone. Murphy, Emma, Agent Resnicki, and I are sprawled across a dingy motel room. Emma and I have the single, queen-sized bed. The agent is on the floor wearing a pair of handcuffs Emma found in the glovebox, and Murphy planted himself in the only chair so he could cover the door with his shotgun.

Despite letting me think I'd won the argument, Murphy and Emma refused to leave. Since Emma's side needed more care, I didn't feel right insisting.

We'd probably be better off seeking shelter in one of the tunnels under the city. I got that information from another of Nadia's packets. I'd ask how she knew we would be in Las Vegas, but knowing my sister, she might have prepared background information for every major city in the country.

Over an hour passed while we ate some food and took care of nightly rituals. The motel had a small store where we could buy toothbrushes, toothpaste, and soap. The guy manning the front desk didn't even look at us funny. Guess he gets to see lots of odd combinations of people coming and going.

Murphy patched Emma properly while I fed the agent. Resnicki glared a lot but didn't bother speaking much. He delivered a few more threats and dark promises, but we ignored him.

The place smelled weird, like desperation, sweat, and grosser things. Getting Emma's permission, I stripped the bed of the quilt, folded it a few times, and made a makeshift cushion for our reluctant guest. To be safe, I helped him into a deep sleep.

The sheets left on the bed had some odd stains, but they also reeked of powerful cleaners.

When I'd tried sharing a real-time dream with Danielle, the experiment got mighty messy. I had a lot of trouble keeping the connection, so I tried something else and dedicated part of my brainpower to recording the dream. As I finally started to relax, I remembered to check to see if it worked.

The dream with Malia and her New Momma didn't reveal much. They spent many hours in a car, then a few more in a small plane, and finally arrived in a hotel room.

The one with Cora and my Second Momma also didn't give me any new information. Mostly, they talked about arrangements to let Cora leave the business for a few days.

The short one featuring Varick surprised me the most because the recording didn't work. Curious, I dropped into a working sleep and searched for Varick. He wasn't asleep, so I set things in motion to draw his current situation into my dreams.

I couldn't find him. Given the tricky nature of hunting those sorts of dreams, that shouldn't have bothered me, but something nagged at me. My brain buzzed like I'd had a few energy drinks.

Kay!

The name popped into my head with full certainty.

What did ya do to me?

Nothing harmful. I'm just activating certain areas of your brain. I can't let you work right now.

Why not? I thought we was on the same side.

Unless your brother, Varick, or one of his contacts can free AK, I'm kind of stuck taking their orders.

Who's they?

I don't know! I'd tell you if I did. I don't like having to help them. I just want my siblings and AK back.

Kay sounded upset, but I couldn't tell if the frustration was real or very well faked.

Chapter 23: Smoke

ITEM 261: Danielle's 78th letter
Item Source: Danielle Matheson

Dear Dr. S.,

Once again, I apologize for not signing off on the last letter. I'd say I'm getting lousy at that part, but this time, it was entirely Naidine's fault. The letter is already out of my possession, or I would have simply edited it accordingly. Please allow me to set the record straight.

Everything about being hustled out of my room down into the dungeons beneath the hotel was true. Being strapped to a gurney and meeting Dr. C., Dr. Paladon, and Cora was also true.

However, Mulligan didn't have a gun. He—and everybody in that room—thought he had a gun because Naidine planted the idea in our heads. She did so to spin the tale that Dr. C. caught and redirected a bullet with her bare hands. The surprise overrode Mulligan's natural caution. When he examined Dr. C.'s hands directly, she transferred some nanomachines to him. This let Naidine negotiate with Mulligan directly. Like Father, he takes precautions against Minder influences.

The part about encouraging me to pass out spared me an interrogation and gave the others time to reason with Mulligan. You may wonder—as I did—how Naidine managed to bypass Mulligan's precautions to even give him the false story. She was entirely vague on details, but I think she used me like an amplifying rod. Picture Mulligan's precautions as the equivalent of putting on noise cancelling headphones. They're mostly effective, but if something's loud enough, you'll hear it anyway.

Although I've accepted Naidine's apology for the deception, we had a very long chat about trust and my absolute need to be kept in the loop from here on out. She agreed. I think. By that, I mean she will now consider my active wish to be involved in these harebrained schemes from the beginning, but if it's *necessary for my good* she will lie to me again.

While I had Naidine's attention, I asked about my family. She assured me they're as safe as they can be. My father and siblings are somewhere in South Carolina traveling with some of Mulligan's men. Ethan is still traveling with my mother. I am not sure which state they're in, but I assume they're coming here. I can't decide if the delay is a good thing or a bad thing.

It's honestly getting very messy with who works for whom. Naidine doesn't think Mulligan's the one fully in charge. Given that he works for the government, it's entirely possible he has both bosses and rivals. That would explain the disagreement I witnessed between Ethan and Agent Rydell.

I let Naidine see the memory of their argument. She didn't comment, and she didn't seem shocked. When we're connected this closely, I get occasional glimpses into her state of mind. She felt calm and in control. I took that as a good sign and am currently clinging to her promise to investigate.

I'm back in my plush prison. Having had a close look at the other accommodations they offer here, I'm grateful for what I've got, but I really wish they'd let me talk with Cora, Dr. C., and Dr. Paladon.

I can connect you to Cora if you wish, but you must hold the conversation in the lavatory for privacy. This room has at least three cameras. Dr. Paladon and Dr. Carnasis are currently sleeping. I can let you know when that changes. Would you like me to create the connection to Cora?

Will it bother her? Should I let her rest?

A short talk will do her good.

What ensued was just that, little more than pleasantries. I

got the impression Cora held information back, but I couldn't blame her. For all she knew, I was a Minder in disguise trying to breech her mental defenses.

When the awkward conversation ended and I safely returned to my own headspace, Naidine invited me into a training space she'd carved out within my mind. That should probably disturb me, but fascination overrode the creepy feelings.

Under Naidine's direction, I laid down on the bed and turned out the lights.

Pretend to sleep, but do not sleep. I have not quite mastered Jillian's abilities to reach dreamers. Where would you like to go?

Surprise me.

As I closed my eyes, I found myself at the beach. Thankfully, it wasn't the beach in Rodanthe, North Carolina. Before I could even wonder where we were, a location tag popped up in the bottom right corner of my vision. It read: St. George Island State Park, Florida. After a few seconds, the tag faded away, leaving a very realistic gorgeous beach scene in place.

I stood facing the ocean, listening to the rhythmic slap of waves reaching the shore. Salty air filled my avatar's lungs with each breath. A gentle breeze moved my hair. Tiny grains of sand pelted my pants. I wore those blasted scrubs until I frowned down at them. Then, they magically changed into my favorite pair of jeans and a TCNJ T-shirt.

An older version of Nadia appeared next to me at the perfect distance to inspect. Predictably, my avatar's head whipped in Naidine's direction. She wore a fitted black leather jacket and dark jeans. The somber colors in her outfit contrasted with her long, golden hair.

"I'm sorry we don't have time for a relaxed visit. I know you have a lot of questions, but I beg your patience. Much is in motion, and we will need your help soon. May I explain what has been done and what we're asking of you?"

Since words weren't really forming sentences for me, I nodded slowly.

She made a follow gesture and started walking along the shoreline, just out of reach of the waves.

"You were given a small batch of nanomachines. They were designed to give the bearer building Gifts like Michio and Aiden, but Dr. Carnasis wiped their programming before delivering them."

"How? Why?" The two questions crashed into each other on their way out of my mouth.

"Their programming was flawed in several fundamental ways. Unaltered, the nanomachines would have given you a lot of trouble. Dr. Carnasis and I used some of her nanomachines to reprogram the ones given to you. They no longer bear a specific Gift leaning, but they should accept instructions from you in time."

"What can I do with them? And how easy was it to reprogram them? Can they change their own programming or self-replicate?" I stopped walking. Visions of every technology-goes-rogue-and-destroys-the-world movie I've ever seen blundered around my head like the proverbial bull in a china shop.

Following those thoughts perfectly, Naidine smiled and waved the unhelpful things away.

"It's not like that." The smile faltered. "At least not with these. They can accept simple commands and little more. Self-repairing nanomachines are rare and self-replicating ones don't currently exist. Their uses never outweighed the dangers enough to justify their creation."

I gave Naidine a look that told her the last statement was terribly naïve.

"We monitor for such abuses of the technology, but to ease your mind, I shall increase our efforts in that regard." Naidine started walking again. "As to what you can do with them, you can train them in a specific task. If you do nothing, they will attempt to learn on their own. That will provide you with random enhancements but largely waste their potential. I have prepared sample scripts for you to test healing and telepathy. I can get other ones from Varick or Aiden if you'd prefer physical boosts or increased knowledge about engineering and design properties."

"Physical boosts?" My inflection made it a question. "Like, they can make me taller?"

Naidine chuckled.

"A simple growth serum could accomplish that, but I

wouldn't recommend it. The side effects are generally detrimental to mental health."

The last statement reminded me of Tyra and Ethan, Dr. Lanier's budding psychopaths.

"Noted and appreciated." Weariness caused my avatar's shoulders to slump.

"Last I checked they are getting the help they need."

"Good." Knowing Ethan was still a threat to my mother, I couldn't put much force behind the statement, but Naidine understood the mixed emotions. "What should I do?"

"Study the simulations and see which one appeals to you the most." Spreading her fingers, Naidine conjured five numbered and stoppered vials containing colorful smoke. They floated over to hover before me. "If you can come to a decision, release that program. The nanomachines should adjust accordingly. I must go but reach out if you need me."

Despite being tired enough to sleep for real, I spent the next two hours poring through the contents of each vial. Each contained a series of thoughts, instructions, and tiny memory capsules that delved deep into the given topic.

The green smoke went into more details on the physical enhancements the nanomachines could provide. Of the dozens of neat features, I'll mention the three that caught my attention. The machines could encourage bone marrow to form new red blood cells or attach to red blood cells and increase the capacity to hold oxygen. They could also form new blood vessels or repair existing blood vessels based on mathematical probabilities that would maximize efficiency. Muscles could be enhanced either through hardening them to make them more durable or softening them to make them more supple and flexible.

Gray smoke described a whole host of healing applications both internal and external. Naidine's notes said the nanomachines were close but not quite sophisticated enough to tackle something as complex as cancer on their own, but with training, I could probably accomplish what Jillian, Malia, and Michio did for Christy Roman's mother, Susan Kilpatrick.

Purple smoke covered the ins and outs of telepathy. This one didn't fascinate me as much as the others, but I think that's because my connection to Nadia and now Naidine has given me a little experience with the topic.

The red smoke showed how my brain could be altered to have better spatial sense. The tiny machines could also create more storage for memories, allowing for faster recall of details. I found it intriguing that they would also enhance any innate artistic abilities or forge some if none existed. At first, I questioned that, but I suppose such grand designing Gifts would be wasted if they couldn't be conveyed some way.

The last vial contained white smoke and provided deeper explanations and several thought packets that I should keep safe until later.

Cryptic.

Jillian always insisted that was a given with Nadia. I'm starting to believe her.

The Overwhelmed One,

Danielle Matheson.

Chapter 24: ATLAS

ITEM 262: Jillian's 127th post-kidnapping journal entry
Item Source: Jillian Blairington
Jillian! Get out now! They're coming!

Kay's thought pulled me out of the light dozing state I'd finally reached.

Who's comin'?

I don't have time to explain! These guys aren't us. They're the other team!

I didn't have much time to analyze Kay's frantic thoughts, but the quick filter Malia had given me said the emotions were genuine.

Next moment, it didn't much matter anyway.

The door crashed open.

Blind panic made me reach for the first guy through the door and knock him senseless. Pain shot through my head.

I fixed your Gift. You should be able to access it better now. Get free and get to the hotel. It should be safe.

Murphy shot the guy behind the one I knocked out. The man grunted as the bullets hit his bulletproof vest and made him stagger. That gave me time to reach him with my Gift too.

We braced for more attackers, but none came immediately. Murphy dragged the two unconscious guys away from the door and shut it as best he could. It didn't quite latch because the men had broken the handle with their brute force entry. Next, Murphy pushed the chair in front of the door to buy us a few seconds if there was a second wave. Emma searched the two men for weapons and identification.

Agent Resnicki muttered a curse.

"So that's how it is."

We looked at him, expecting a better explanation.

"If you have something useful to add, let's hear it," said Emma.

"Let's get somewhere safe first." The agent looked grim, but without Nadia or Malia helping, I couldn't tell the reason for the expression.

"This was supposed to be somewhere safe." Murphy sounded thoughtful. "Guess we could get in the SUV and drive around for a while."

The agent shook his head.

"Let me take you in. We can protect you."

The statements got a you've-lost-your-blessed-mind look from Murphy and an amused snort from Emma.

"You have a strange idea of protection." She lifted her left arm so we could see the white wraps covering the deep cut the agent had inflicted earlier.

"Things change." Despite the defensive words, Agent Resnicki's eyes dropped to the ground like a scolded pup. When he looked up again, he spread a determined look around to each of us. "We want to work within the system. They want to break it."

I looked to Murphy and Emma to get their opinions.

"It could be a trap," I said.

"It is," said Resnicki. "The next thing you'll receive is a nice invitation to surrender, but as soon as you do it, you're dead."

"I don't like any of this," Murphy declared. "I'd rather leave him here and take our chances on the road."

"Who do ya think's trying' to kill me?" I asked the agent.

A guarded look came over him.

"Whoever's in charge of ATLAS. It stands for the Automated Threat Level Analysis System. I only know about it because I was asked to transfer to a security detail over there. I turned it down because I thought it would be boring, and I didn't want to have to work my way up another chain."

"Speak to us like we've never heard of it before," Murphy instructed. His tone hardened as he fired follow-up questions. "What is it? Why is it dangerous? And how do you know it well enough to predict next moves?"

"I have some friends who accepted the transfer," said the agent. He shrugged. "Word gets around."

The phone rang before he could explain more.

"We're running out of time," said Agent Resnicki. "Make a decision. Shoot me or free me. I can help you, but if they catch us here, I'm dead anyway for telling you as much as I did."

"Who would know?" asked Emma.

The agent fixed her with a serious look that also managed to be sad and weary.

"Nothing is private anymore. If a Minder doesn't stalk your thoughts, something like ATLAS will track you some other way."

I'd heard the term before, but I couldn't immediately tell where. Wishing I had a few hours to work through the puzzle properly, I prepared for a different kind of battle.

"I'll go with ya, but I still don't trust ya." I delivered the first part of my decision to Agent Resnicki before turning to Murphy and Emma.

"Forget it," said Murphy.

"If you're headed for the lion's den, so are we," Emma added.

"Somebody's gotta stay free to plan a rescue." My attempt at a smile failed.

"You're going to be stubborn about this, aren't you?" asked Murphy.

"Only if I have to be," I answered. I didn't know if I had the courage to use my Gifts against allies, but if it came down to their comfort or their lives, I'd have to.

Something dark and metallic sailed into the room.

"Down!" The shout came from Murphy and Resnicki.

We'd been holding our little conference from the floor, so we didn't have far to go. Before I could lie down, Murphy's tackle flattened me. I clenched my eyes shut.

Bright light filled the entire room followed quickly by a

crack loud enough to shake the floor and rattle my bones. The noise rang through my head causing pain and dizziness.

Something crashed hard into the door which banged in to the chair.

I might have passed out, but if so, it was only for a few seconds.

Men with guns burst in. I could tell from the muffled footsteps. None of their shouts made it past the lingering ringing in my ears.

Tapping into some of Malia's Gifts let me clear my senses enough to focus.

Two men pulled Murphy off me and bound his hands with black zip ties. Another man drove the barrel of his rifle up under Emma's chin, pinning her to the ground. A fourth guy had a gun in my face, but it didn't bother me much because I couldn't understand a word he said. Finally understanding this, he quit shouting and secured my hands over my stomach with more zip ties.

I still dunno why everybody uses bindings. My Gifts ain't physical. Unless somebody like Kay is messing with my abilities, I should be able to access 'em whether my hands are free or not.

One guy pulled Murphy to his feet, and another did the same for Emma. Nobody moved to help Agent Resnicki.

"What about him?" That's the question I tried to ask, but from the puzzled look on the nearest soldier's face, I'm not sure that's what came out. I twitched my bound hands to indicate the agent.

"He'll be fine. My men will get him help as soon as we're away."

My hearing troubles forced me to read the answer on the soldier's lips, but at least he looked sincere. The way he took my arm to escort me out to an unmarked white van was downright gentle.

A soldier hopped up into the van, then turned and helped me climb in. Force of habit made me nod thanks. As the van door started to close, I caught it.

"My friends." The two words took a lot of effort to get out, but at least the soldier followed my thoughts.

"They'll be in a later shipment."

Darkness prevented me from reading his answer, but I heard it like a whisper.

The soldier with me in the van moved me to a bench secured to the far wall and strapped me in with the seat belt.

It's okay. This team won't kill you. They're not ours, but they're freelance, so they're in it for the money.

Good to know. Wait, what money?

There's a $10,000 bounty on your capture.

How do you know that?

I set it up. You can thank me later.

I'd been about to ask how they knew where to find us, but Kay's statement was answer enough.

Not feelin' too thankful right about now. Too busy trying not to throw up supper.

Sorry about that. I was very clear about non-lethal use of force only, but technically flash-bang grenades qualify.

Agent Resnicki had already convinced me to come in.

I didn't know that at the time.

Much as I wanted to stay mad at Kay, I needed answers more.

What'll happen to Murphy, Emma, and Resnicki?

Syler told you the truth. As far as I know, they'll be brought here. I don't know if I can get additional payment cleared to take them, but I doubt the mercenaries want to keep them.

Make it happen or see that they go free.

Dustin may want them kept in holding.

Since when does Dustin make such decisions?

Since he struck some kind of deal with Dr. Mulligan. You'll get to meet him soon. Just hang tight. The sooner this is over with, the sooner they'll release AK.

I didn't bother tellin' him he was being dumb for trusting the promises that AK would be released once they got what they wanted from Kay. They would have no reason to keep their word. Having a Minder willing to take orders would certainly be tempting. Kay could read my opinion well enough if he bothered searching my surface thoughts. I'm told they're quite loud.

They're not lying. We're not the real targets. My abilities aren't nearly as tempting as Nadia's. Once they control her, they won't need me or my siblings. We'll be free.

That's stupid logic and you know it.

I didn't have to be a Minder to hear the guilt filling most of Kay's thoughts.

We'd all get out of this mess sooner if you helped us.

Kay didn't answer with a thought, but his presence lingered. Nana says you can't force someone to do good. The best you can do is show 'em the right way and keep on loving 'em.

I chose to change tactics.

What am I walking into, Kay? Is everybody there?

Dr. Devya and Nadia came in a few hours ago. Your friend Danielle's here, so is your mother and Michio. Danielle's mother is still a few hours away. I'm not sure why her escort chose the long way. I wasn't involved in that plan. Most of the key scientists are also present. Dustin and Dr. Mulligan are eager to get started, but I argued that they may need everybody well-rested to get the best results. That's all I know.

Kay left before I could respond.

Guess Minders aren't much for goodbyes.

I tried not to think about seeing Momma and Michio, so that's all I could think about for the rest of the ride. I'd done my level best to keep my two families apart, but that wasn't an option now. I dreaded finding out whatever Dustin had in mind for us to do, but in a way, I also welcomed it. Too many questions had gone unanswered for too long.

All right, Dusty. Let's sort this mess. Not sure if you need a hug or a punch or both, but I'm prepared to deliver either.

Chapter 25: Motivation

ITEM 263: Danielle's 79th letter
Item Source: Danielle Matheson

Dear Dr. S.,

Looks like I get to reprise my role as a hostage. Jillian's here. She arrived late last night at some unholy hour. I think if it'd been up to Dustin the whole show would have commenced two seconds after Jillian's arrival. Thankfully, saner heads prevailed and postponed the meeting to a nicer hour.

Naidine let me feel a few seconds of Dustin's buzzing tension. I had asked about it because she mentioned it when she gave me the update at 4:03 AM. She also informed me my presence would likely be required at the reunion. I didn't think I'd sleep after an announcement like that, but Naidine promised to stay with me. I think she blocked my anxious thoughts or something. She wasn't using Jillian's Gift. I know what that feels like. Whatever she did worked swell though, and I got a solid four hours of sleep.

Since I wasn't in the mood for a full dinner at 8:30 in the morning, I cobbled together a light breakfast from sides stolen from random MREs. They pack a lot of food into each meal. The fruit puree squeeze was odd but fine. The corn bread had gone a tad stale since I had the rest of that MRE for yesterday's lunch. The nut and fruit mix provided a nice, crunchy finish. I stuck to bottled water without any of the protein powders because I can never predict how my stomach will receive those.

Why such gory details on what I ate this morning?

Because I'm waiting. Again. And the other option besides listing mundane life details is worrying about what Dustin could possibly want from his sisters that he'd need a dedicated hostage for each of them. An idle brain is a scary thing.

I'm only guessing here, but there aren't too many other reasons for gathering Jillian's mother, Malia's new mother, and Dr. Paladon. Dr. P. is the only one who would have been taken regardless of her status as Nadia's mother. Jillian once said that Devya claimed Nadia would be held hostage by any random street mutt. My second leap of logic this morning is that I'm the *random street mutt* in this scenario. Mulligan seems to want something from Dr. P. so I don't think he'd risk her life to threaten Nadia.

You are correct, but now that you are part of his experiment, Dr. Mulligan will protect you as well.

Who's in charge?

Naidine didn't answer, but I didn't blame her. She has a lot more important things to do than answer my random questions.

My thoughts churned the situation over a few times. I didn't think the government would be nuts enough to put a kid like Dustin in charge, but an awful lot of people have been taking orders from the little tyrant lately. I never liked that kid much. That's probably due to the unfortunate association with our first meeting and knowing little about his Gifts. He's got a strong mental link to Devya. That's the entirety of my knowledge on the subject. It's probably unfair to Dustin, but his behavior of late has also been appalling.

It may not be entirely his fault, but we don't know enough to render a judgement either way. If you can buy us some time to prepare, please do so, but do not further endanger yourself or the others.

My mind barely registered the marching orders. Instead, it numbly repeated *not entirely his fault*, then fired a dozen queries about what Naidine meant by that.

Once again, I didn't receive an immediate answer. This time, I did sort of hold that against her because she'd left me hanging. It's like running up to somebody and saying *boy, do I have a story to tell you, but I don't have time to tell it right now.*

Luckily, my escorts showed up about then and swept me off to meet Jillian. Our reunion was rushed, but I got to give her a long hug. That did my spirit good.

We're packed in the elevator and headed down. Despite being crammed in with four soldiers and Jillian, I'm happy to be doing something besides waiting and worrying. I might regret this optimistic feeling in a minute.

I'm going to switch over to Malia's thoughts-to-words program while leaving this other thing running. Hopefully, that will let you get this record of events even if I don't make it. You might call that pessimistic, but I'm not taking any chances with the kind of week I'm having.

The room we're taken to is small for the kind of conference halls these Vegas monstrosities can boast, but it's still about the size of half a football field. It's been set up like a small theater, complete with several rows of chairs for spectators.

Most of the gang is present with a few notable exceptions and one addition. Mulligan, Dustin, and Devya huddle on the stage's left side. I hadn't anticipated Devya himself would grace us with his presence, though I probably should have guessed that one.

A pair of scientists I didn't know stood near the threesome. Naidine kindly identified them as Dr. Kayla Burrel and Dr. Francis DeLuca.

Dr. Burrel and Dr. DeLuca are both consultants for the Central Intelligence Agency. Dr. Burrel's research centers on finding new, safer ways to deploy spies. She believes the job is perfectly suited for a Minder. Dr. DeLuca is more interested in future applications for the nanomachines.

Missing from the room are Dr. C., Dr. P., and Cora. They deserve to witness whatever this is, but they're probably safer in their makeshift prisons.

Present as prisoners are Mrs. B., Mrs. Davidson, and me. Any questions I had about my role get cleared up quickly when my personal soldiers move me to the front row seat between Jillian's mother and Malia's adoptive mother and apply some handcuffs.

What's with these people and wrist bindings? Having been desensitized to them by Devya and Lanier, I don't much mind cuffs at this point, but the matching expressions worn by Mrs. B. and Mrs. Davidson set a steady internal heat loose in me. I'm not the best at reading people and Naidine's busy with the current crisis, but I'm picking up simmering anger and colossal restraint at work. Whoever's in charge made a serious error in setting up this scenario. If these women are anything like my mother, they can endure a lot, but if you threaten their kid, you should make sure your affairs are in order because they will murder you, bury you, and plant pretty flowers on your grave.

Jillian's escorts pointed her toward the right side of the small stage where Malia and Nadia wait. Both appeared calm and collected, but that's not saying much because Malia's Gifts make her master of emotions and Nadia can borrow those Gifts under certain circumstances.

I started watching Jillian's ascent to the stage but got distracted by the setup at center stage. A gurney had been placed with the head facing Devya and crew and the foot facing Team Nadia. Normally, my vantage point would have been useless for seeing much, but tiny cameras had been mounted on poles coming down from the ceiling and rising from the four corners of the stage. The picture that showed up on a giant screen built into the wall behind the stage cycled through the various camera angles. The whole effect gave me a soap opera-y vibe.

Devya and Dustin conferred quietly. Mulligan's body language channeled impatience. Malia greeted Jillian with a brief hug. Nadia sent Jillian a nod and a distracted smile but didn't move from her spot which was about a half-foot closer to the empty gurney.

"This should not be done before witnesses." Nadia's voice rang out both soft and clear but still had her characteristic swiftness. "Our concern for their wellbeing will make the task much harder to accomplish."

"They stay," said Mulligan.

"You can handle it." Devya's answer was cool and dismissive.

Dustin didn't say anything. The kid looked ready to upchuck his breakfast. His normally fair skin looked like somebody had doused him in bleach.

"Ya having second thoughts, Dusty?" Jillian voiced the question, but if she hadn't said anything, I think it would have come from Nadia eventually.

He shook his head in swift denial, but his face did a fine job contradicting the sentiment.

"If this is what you want, lay down." Devya gently squeezed Dustin's right shoulder. "We should get started."

Nodding shortly, Dustin pulled free of Devya's light grasp and moved until he was even with the gurney before facing his sisters.

"Your job is to completely unlock my Gifts," said Dustin.

"You don't even know if we can do that." Malia looked from Dustin to her mother and frowned.

"You can."

Devya's confidence stirred up the queasy feeling already upsetting my gut.

"Once we get started, I might protest, but don't stop under any circumstances." Dustin cast a meaningful look our way.

His words made me think of the Narnia book, *The Silver Chair*. If I recall the story details correctly, listening to the ravings is exactly the right move. I tried not to react, but I don't know if I succeeded.

A surge of disgust sideswiped the protective instinct rising in me, leaving a bitter taste in my mouth.

"Say it," I challenged.

"I don't have to," Dustin replied. "They know the consequences if this doesn't work."

"But do you?" I pressed. "Do you understand the threat you're making?"

I didn't realize I'd popped to my feet until hands gripped my elbows. Looking right, I saw Mrs. B. shaking her head firmly. She tugged gently in a blatant plea for me to sit down and shut up.

Sorry, Mrs. B., I'm in stalling mode now.

To be fair, I was also genuinely fired up. I don't like bullies, and people who take hostages to control the behavior of others are the ultimate bullies.

"Can you back that up?" Real curiosity seasoned my tone as I realized I knew next to nothing about this kid.

"Of course. There are hundreds—"

"I'm not talking about the soldiers. I'm talking about *you.* Could you carry out the threats?"

"I can." Mulligan's dark declaration broke through the nice tension I'd been building. "And I will." He drew a handgun from a shoulder holster and held it up so everybody could see it. "This time, it's very real. Care to test me on this?"

Dustin pivoted to watch Mulligan.

Shaking my head, I let Mrs. B. and Mrs. Davidson pull me back onto my seat.

The cameras focused on Mulligan. His wild brown hair gave him a friendly guy air, but the glint in his eyes shouted fanatical madness.

"I'm a big believer in motivation, so allow me to provide some."

I'd be lying if I said I didn't expect a bullet to come flying my way.

I did not expect one to head elsewhere.

Wheeling on Devya, Mulligan shot him in the side from point blank range.

Aside from sharply drawn breath, I'm not sure anybody made a sound as Devya pitched forward onto his left side. I don't know about the others, but the gunshot must have echoed in my head a hundred times.

Soldiers snapped into action. They must have had preassigned targets because two each approached Nadia, Malia, Jillian, and Dustin. Malia's guards backed down quickly. Another soldier pulled Mrs. Davidson up and pushed her to the edge of the stage. He stepped to the side so Malia could see the gun he pointed at her mother. So many people shouted, nobody could be heard.

Stop!

The command blasted through everybody's head courtesy of Nadia.

We will do what we can, but the ultimate decision lies with Dustin. Nothing you say or do can change that fact.

I tried to make heads or tails of Nadia's cryptic words for the three seconds I believed they were directed at me, but Mulligan's cheerful next words clarified the situation.

"I think they're suitably motivated. Somebody get a pressure bandage for Devya. I don't want him bleeding out before they're done."

The soldier returned a dazed Mrs. Davidson to the chair next to me. I offered her my hands to hold. She latched on with both of her hands and squeezed hard.

The soldiers with Dustin strapped him to the gurney. The camera fixed above the gurney got a clear shot of his wide eyes and trembling jaw, but otherwise, he hid his fears well.

The Shaken Random Street Mutt,

Danielle Matheson.

Chapter 26:
Jailbreak

ITEM 264: Jillian's 128th post-kidnapping journal entry
Item Source: Jillian Blairington
Jillian, make Father sleep deeply and put Dustin into a dozing state. Then, pull us into a dream. We must work quickly, or Father will die.

Sitting down hard, I yanked my sisters down with me so they wouldn't hurt themselves when I made 'em sleep. The touch gave me more control than I usually have. Working swiftly, I set up a small, bare room for us to chat in and fashioned avatars for each of us. I even remembered to add chairs and a roof. Plopping onto the nearest chair, I waited for Nadia to speak. Even in the dream, I could tell she was busting to say something.

"Malia and I have been establishing people's true loyalties for a few days. Our lists are far from complete or perfect, but they should suffice. I have mapped the hotel and color-coded friend, foe, neutral party, and innocent party as blue, red, gray, and white. Leave blue and white figures alone but take down red and neutral ones."

The promised map appeared in my head. There musta been over a hundred people marked for takedown. I shot my sister a look that told her what I thought of the plan. An image of the previous night's struggle to subdue Agent Resnicki's men flared to life. Since we were in my dream, Malia and Nadia got to share the memory.

Malia gripped my left hand and shored up my courage.

"You can do this … because we're with you." She sounded out of breath.

"What's wrong?" Concern for Malia made my return grip pretty tight.

"She is holding the most dangerous parties at bay until you complete your task," Nadia explained.

I growled at them like TJ does when he's miffed. Then, starting with the closest ones, I reached for small groups of targets Nadia painted and dropped 'em into a medium level sleep. Deep sleep woulda taken more effort and light sleep woulda risked letting 'em wake up early. Every time my Gift felt strained or I got a headache, Malia would set me to rights. Every time I wasn't sure what to do next, Nadia highlighted a new section to concentrate on.

Working together, we knocked out 197 people. It's a good thing I didn't know the real number we'd be tackling at the time or I mighta quit before starting.

"What now?" I demanded, looking between Nadia and Malia. I tried not sounding grumpy but was too tired to put much effort into it.

"Now, we cause a small jailbreak," said Nadia.

My sister's got a knack for understating things. By *small jailbreak*, she really meant everybody held here against their will. This facility wasn't meant to be a prison, but that still meant Nadia's momma, my Second Momma, Cora, Aiden, Michio, Maisha, Murphy, Emma, and Kay's brother, Que. Nadia summoned portraits of each person to be rescued and set 'em to file past me.

"Find each target and help them. If they have not yet escaped their personal prisons, lend aid. Malia can help you with the locks or you can find the codes from people's dreams. Direct the freed captives here. I will help with instructing them, if necessary, but you must accomplish most of the work on your own. We must begin the work with Dustin."

Quicker than blinking, I was alone with the nine portraits. When I wished for some order, the pictures formed up in three lines of three with my Second Momma, Dr. Paladon, and Cora in the top row. Next came Murphy, Emma, and Que. The bottom row showed me Aiden, Michio, and Maisha. That surprised me 'cause Aiden and Michio have healing Gifts. Those seemed important given what happened to Dr. Devya.

They will never reach their destination without help. Murphy and Emma can protect them. Que can deal with any locks they run into.

Figuring I ought to get to work, I lowered myself a few sleep levels and checked on the top priorities first. I didn't know where to find 'em, but Nadia's map was thorough. I pictured the building like a 3D blueprint with the objectives as yellow dots and moved my consciousness there. Once in the right place, I arranged to draw the scene into my dreams. I'm getting better at that, but it takes some patience. Being rushed makes patience hard to come by. Finally, I had to ask for Malia's help. She channeled enough peace into me to make the wait bearable.

"I believe your daughter has arrived, Evie." Cora waved to indicate the guard slumped against the metal door of her prison cell.

"They must all be here if Jillian is using her Gifts to this extent," said my Second Momma. She and Nadia's momma were in the cell next to Cora's.

Several rows of prison boxes had been set up side-by-side. They looked identical, but the one holding my Second Momma and Dr. Paladon gave off a strange buzzing energy that caused my teeth to tingle.

"Something must have happened." Dr. Paladon leaned heavily against the cell bars. She sounded mighty sleepy. "They wouldn't make a move like this without cause."

"They don't do anything by halves either. We should get ready to move." My Second Momma climbed off the cot and sent a concerned look Dr. Paladon's way. "Can you stand?"

"Leave me." Dr. Paladon smiled faintly. "Come back when all the dragons are slain."

"Best get that out of your head now," said Cora. "I feel like I'm telling you yanks that a lot these days."

"I will drag you out of here if I have to, but can we try

walking first?" My Second Momma sat down next to Dr. Paladon and tucked her left arm under the other woman's shoulders.

By this time, I had enough control over the dream to create an avatar. I wasn't really there, of course, but my connection to Nadia and Malia let me reach into each of their minds and form an image of myself right outside Cora's cell door.

"Jillian. Brilliant. I see you've adopted the ghost look from Nadia." Cora stood in the center of her cell and nodded a greeting to me. "Do you have a plan?"

My mother will need significant help getting to us, and they should probably all eat before moving. Private Peter Chadwick and Sergeant Mario D'Aleric can help. They are headed your way and will arrive shortly.

What's wrong with her? I could see she was listless, but that didn't answer how she'd gotten that way.

Dr. Mulligan ordered the soldiers to withhold food. He thought that a weakened body and mind would prevent her from reaching out to me.

Anger sprang up in me, but I tried to control it. Letting it run wild woulda made my job harder.

"Help's coming." The anger made my words crisp and sharp. "What can I do?"

"You've done your part," said Cora. Kneeling by the cell door, she reached through the bars and rummaged through the man's pockets. The right one was in range, so she started there. "Once I release us, you can show us the way." Finding nothing, she muttered, "Of course, the bloke is left-handed. Probably the only one in this entire building." She tugged the man's right shoulder to get him to flip onto his other side.

"I can do that." My Gifts didn't extend to moving objects with my mind, but I could reach sleepers. I'd done something similar when I tricked Mr. Clark into helping Cora when Dr. Lanier had put her in danger.

The soldier wasn't at a good level for taking suggestions, so I first raised him to the proper level. Next, I searched for his name 'cause people are way more likely to take suggestions if ya know their name. Steven James Forchester hid his name better than most people, but I found it in a memory of his momma yelling about playing soccer in the family room with his little brother. They broke a lamp and put a big hole in the wall before their momma halted the game.

Steven shifted as I pulled the bad memory to the surface. His agitation level spiked, which almost woke him, so I buried the memory deep enough to let him relax. He wasn't dreaming of much. Pulling up the image of his momma, I replaced it with his sergeant and painted the picture that he'd just been caught sleeping on the job. In the real world, his body twitched.

Scrolling through Private Forchester's memories let me cobble together a simple command in Sergeant Kouten's voice.

"Get up and unlock that cell!"

The voice scared me and the soldier.

Still sleeping, he launched to his feet, dug the key out of his pocket and jammed it into the lock to Cora's cell.

Fearing he would wake up and be beyond my control, I dropped him into a much deeper level of sleep. The soldier collapsed against the metal bars and landed close to where he'd started, only this time he faced the door. The movement almost pulled the key from the lock, but Cora caught it in time to hold it in place and twist it open. She had to shove the door hard a few times to move Forchester enough so she could slip out, but soon, she was free. The same key also worked on the lock holding my Second Momma and Dr. Paladon.

Private Chadwick and Sergeant D'Aleric arrived as Cora and my Second Momma got Dr. Paladon to a standing position. Chadwick had a bag with some power bars and protein shakes.

Having accomplished my first goal, I left while they were still doing introductions.

As soon as I needed it, Nadia's map popped back into my head and led me to Murphy and Emma. Freeing 'em took some time 'cause I first had to find a sleeping soldier who knew the code to their door and sort enough dreams to find a memory of the soldier entering that door code. Once I had the code, I put Murphy into a light sleep long enough to give him the information and Nadia's instructions to free Que before coming for me.

The code to Que's door was different, but now that I had a system, the code retrieval went faster. This time, I gave the code to Emma so she could plug it in. As the door swung open, Que charged. I knocked him out in time to prevent him from seriously hurting Emma, but she still grunted from the impact of suddenly catching the teenager.

Diving into Que's head, I formed a dream for him. It consisted of him bound to a chair in an empty room and me standing before him.

He screamed and thrashed against the ropes.

"Calm down. We're trying to help!" I didn't bother telling Que he about clobbered the help I'd sent.

My Gift struggled to shift the boy's panic to a level where I could deal with it. When I got smart, I asked Malia for help. She had him calm in short order, but he still looked plenty angry.

"I ain't here to trick ya, Que." I spoke almost Nadia-level fast. "We're setting ya free 'cause we promised your brother, Kay, we would."

My sisters and I would have enough problems without having to deal with interference from Kay. If setting Que loose got some cooperation, we'd do it.

"What about AK?" Que's question snapped out like an accusation.

Varick is working on that.

I passed the message on even though I think he heard Nadia's thought too.

"How do I know this isn't a trick?" asked Que.

"Ya could ask Kay, but I dunno if he'll answer," I said with a shrug. "I got other things to do. Murphy and Emma are coming to help me. If ya travel with 'em, I'm sure they'll protect ya. Otherwise, good luck. Opening yer cage was my job and I've done it. Whether ya walk on through is your business, but we'd welcome your help."

Ending the dream, I let Que wake up. The curious sense I got from him said he had a lot more questions, but he'd just have to get answers from Murphy and Emma.

My next task took me to Aiden and Maisha. I beat the lock on their door same as I'd done for the one holding Murphy and Emma. I musta had some luck left cause the first soldier I checked knew that code.

If I'd been smarter about the whole thing, I woulda checked with the soldiers who work at the front desk since they've probably seen every room code. They mighta been able to change the codes to suit me if I'd asked.

Anyway, the hard way worked fine. Maisha accepted the code, gave my avatar a huge hug, and woke up on her own. I didn't know people could do that, but I guess it's possible since I wasn't actively keeping her asleep.

Michio woulda been my last captive to free, but Nadia had already gotten two blue soldiers to fetch him. One of the helpful soldiers had been assigned to watch our little brother when they took Momma up to the conference room.

I checked in again with my Second Momma and the others in her group. They'd finished eating and started the journey to get to us. Maisha and Aiden found the soldier with Michio and another two who'd come along for protection. Murphy and Emma were still chatting with Que. I asked Nadia to send 'em a reminder to hurry.

Do not worry about them. I will set them up in a security room. They should be able to help contain some of our foes if they awaken before the events set to transpire here have completed their courses.

I got the feeling she wasn't telling me everything, but I couldn't devote much head power to it right then. Only sorta satisfied with her answer, I drew my attention back to the conference room to see if I could help Malia and Nadia with their work on Dustin or Dr. Devya.

Chapter 27:
Glorified Gopher

ITEM 265: Danielle's 80th letter
Item Source: Danielle Matheson

Dear Dr. S.,

The scene on that stage looked like a Shakespearean tragedy. Bodies everywhere.

Jillian, Nadia, and Malia had fallen together like a collapsing house of cards with Jillian sandwiched between her sisters. Mulligan, Dr. Burrel, Dr. DeLuca, and all the soldiers except one had dropped as awkwardly as if they'd been done in by bullets. Devya—the one with an actual bullet in him—was ironically one of the few conscious people. The only peaceful looking one was Dustin since he'd been strapped to the gurney before Jillian's blitz attack.

Back in Devya's first lab, I'd seen a similar scenario unfold, but this one was much better documented. The camera view cycled so we got a look at each portion of the stage in turn. Since nobody rushed the stage, I assumed the guards stationed at the various exits had also been knocked out.

A small part of me feared I'd be in for another boring wait. The idea died a second later.

Dropping my hand, Mrs. Davidson leapt to her feet. On my other side, Mrs. B. was maybe a half-second behind her. I scrambled to catch up, now afraid I'd be left out of the action.

I didn't see the source of their panic until the camera angle showed me a closeup of the only soldier left standing on the stage. He'd drawn a syringe out from his right pocket and taken off the safety cap. His eyes moved from the syringe to Jillian. No grand leaps of logic were needed to guess what would happen next. Several bodies lay in his path, but a few careful steps would successfully answer for them. My brain did rapid calculations of the man's distance from Jillian and my distance from the stage and the man. My heart sank as I realized I'd be too late.

An animalistic cry exploded out of Mrs. B. The noise unstuck my feet, letting me stumble to the stage's edge. It had the opposite effect on the soldier. He froze.

Bounding forward like a mythical predator, Mrs. B. planted her bound hands on the stage edge and vaulted up as gracefully as a professional gymnast. Next instant, she regained her feet and headed for the soldier with the purpose of a rampaging bull seeing red. Tucking her head down and leading with her right shoulder, Mrs. B. rammed into the guy. He'd picked up on the peril with enough time to begin twisting. The move resulted in him rolling left as Mrs. B. clipped his right side.

The syringe went flying toward Mrs. Davidson but landed a foot short. It barely missed skewering another soldier's hand. Snatching up the syringe, Mrs. Davidson stabbed it into the stage carpet and depressed the plunger.

Muttering, the soldier drew a dagger from his left boot and moved to rise.

Lunging, Mrs. Davidson latched onto his blade-wielding hand and held on tight.

Instinctively, I clambered onto the stage and pounced on the guy's right hand.

Bellowing a noise filled with rage, adrenaline, and frustration, the man sat up and yanked his arms forward, pulling me along for the ride.

Mrs. Davidson yelped and lost her grip on his hand, but before the man could plant the dagger in me, Mrs. B. ended the struggle by hammering the lower half of his jaw with a fantastic right hook. I'm not even sure how she managed that much momentum with her hands bound together. Guess the cuffs had enough give to allow the move.

The man slumped to the ground.

I sagged with relief but also prepared to intervene. I didn't want Mrs. B. to end up with a murder rap. The look she leveled at that guy chilled me head to foot. The way she cradled her right hand told me she probably hurt herself.

Sitting up slowly, I scanned for more threats.

Mrs. Davidson broke the silence.

"Let me see it." She gently placed a hand on Mrs. B.'s good arm. "I may not be a doctor, but my three grown children showed me a wide variety of injuries over the years."

Danielle, free your hands. Then, please see to my father. There is a First Aid Kit down the hall to your left. It should have something to slow the bleeding. We need it fast.

I tossed a worried glance at the older women.

I will see that they get free soon.

Nadia highlighted one of the unconscious soldiers. When I searched his pockets, I found a handcuff key. After using the key, I tossed it to Mrs. B.

Nadia's next trick showed me where to find the first aid supplies. She made it like a video game. The wall went transparent and a yellow outline with a big red cross in the middle flashed a few times. Then, the wall returned to normal, and a path created by large yellow dashes paved the way to the door that would let me reach the item in question. My first steps were halting at best, but once my body and head coordinated, I ramped up to a full sprint.

The case was surprisingly heavy, but I grabbed the whole thing anyway because I didn't know what else we would need from it. In my haste, I almost dropped the thing on Devya. Instead, it thudded to the ground next to his head.

He opened his eyes but didn't comment. After confirming my identity, he closed his eyes again.

I didn't know where to start. Devya had landed on his left side then flopped onto his stomach. His left hand clutched his right side. Blood had pooled under him, but I couldn't tell how much without moving him. I didn't want to do that if it would make the bleeding worse.

After a period of numbing panic, clarity swept through my head along with detailed instructions on what to do. Mrs. Davidson came over and helped while Mrs. B. stayed on guard duty, watching for more trouble like the syringe wielding soldier.

First, we pulled off half of Devya's suit jacket and cut through large sections of his dress shirt and once-white T-shirt. With the clothing gone I got a good look at the wounds. The bullet had entered the lower right side of his back and exited through the center of his gut.

Michio and Aiden will be here soon. Meanwhile, use the rapid release sponges to staunch the blood flow.

Heedless of the blood on my hands, I snatched up one of the tubes of sponges and drew out the plunger on the needleless syringe. Holding my breath and scraps of courage, I stuck the nozzle into the bullet's entry wound and drove out the dozens of tiny sponges.

Mrs. Davidson helped me roll Devya onto his side so the exit wound could get a similar treatment. We packed every nonstick gauze pad that medkit had to offer into the two wounds, then rigged up pressure bandages to hold them in place. For good measure, we also wound an ace bandage around the whole mess. Devya didn't look very comfortable on his side, but I didn't want to roll him back onto the puddle of blood after cleaning him up. Didn't think he'd appreciate being rolled the other way onto the side bearing bullet holes either, so he stayed on his side in a CPR rescue position.

A soldier I hadn't seen enter the room brought us some water and paper towels to clean up. It helped, but I couldn't get the last bits of blood off my hands and arms. Nadia directed me to the restroom before I could go all Lady Macbeth on my hands.

Mrs. Davidson followed.

I treated my hands and arms to lavish soap treatment, rinsed off, and repeated the process again. Next, I threw cold water onto my face and dried off. When I finished, Mrs. Davidson pulled me down into a hug. Embarrassed by needing the comfort, I tried to pull away, but she only tightened her grip.

"It's not over, but you're doing fine. Have a quick cry, then we can see what else needs doing."

The words and tone struck down my idiotic resolve to be strong, but I still struggled not to sob.

Pulling back, Mrs. Davidson cupped my face with her hands. Tear streaks already lined her face. Her voice was hoarse, but her words struck home.

"Tears are not a weakness. They'll wash away what was and clear the way for what lies ahead."

I wanted so badly to follow the advice, but shock prevented the emotions from surfacing.

Mrs. Davidson closed her eyes and let her head dip downward. I couldn't tell if she was praying or just waiting, but seeing her concern finally moved me enough to surrender to the sobs.

The hysterical phase didn't last long but it did me a world of good. After washing up for a fourth time, I was ready to face the crises still bubbling under the surface calm.

By the time we returned, several soldiers had arrived with Dr. P., Dr. C., and Cora. One soldier busied himself by pulling the unconscious guys off the stage, dragging them to the wall, and fitting them with zip ties.

Cora checked on Dustin, then settled next to Devya.

Dr. Paladon sat with Nadia's head in her lap. The leaning tower of girls had been dismantled, but the three still lay next to each other.

Dr. C. checked vital signs on the CIA reps.

Mrs. B. hovered near Jillian's head.

Mrs. Davidson, of course, made a beeline for Malia.

I stayed off the stage feeling redundant.

We still need you. If you are willing, please go get some food from the kitchens. I have asked Chef Suledad to prepare something light but filling. My mother and the others have not eaten a real meal for some time.

Well trained by this point, I waited for the yellow dashes to show me the way. The path took me down some service stairs to a fancy set of kitchens. A self-conscious feeling settled over me until Nadia assured me she'd provide a proper illusion if necessary. The caper reminded me of the time Christy Roman and I snuck through a crowded club with Varick. That made me miss him. A longing to have him by my side and somewhere safe contradicted each other.

The thoughts distracted me enough that I found myself in the kitchens with no knowledge of the last few minutes. A clock set high on the wall declared the time to be 9:48 AM. I stared at it for a while quite sure it was telling me a bold-faced lie. The recent events felt like they should fill a few days at least.

The kitchen was massive and bustled with activity. I spent most of a minute dodging wait staff darting everywhere. Finally, a large, bearded man with dark skin darted out of the chaos and directed me to a large cart already loaded with four trays of food. He explained the offerings at a clip that would make Nadia proud. I missed most of the words due to the din around us, but Nadia repeated them as I pushed the cart through an empty back hallway and onto a service elevator.

He has prepared caprese pasta salad with grilled chicken for my mother, vegetable paella for Dr. Carnasis, and fish tacos for Cora. The fourth tray is for you to share with Mrs. Blairington and Mrs. Davidson. The three of you did not eat well this morning. It has a platter of eggs, a plate of sausage links, some toast, and a small selection of fruit.

Since I had nothing else to do in the elevator, I questioned Nadia.

Who said they shouldn't be fed? And what brought that about anyway?

It seemed unnecessarily cruel. Dr. Lanier had considered pulling a stunt like that when he held us, but he didn't exactly have an army to control us. That wasn't the case here.

Dr. Mulligan initially gave the order because he didn't want my mother to reach out to me, but his preparations backfired. The absence of thought due to the suppression field drew my attention to her prison. Such fields have a very distinct, cold feeling. I may not have been able to see into the prison, but the minds of the soldiers who drew guard duty were quite clear.

Instead of dwelling on Mulligan's cruelty, I complimented Nadia on her low-tech victory over the high-tech challenge.

She accepted the praise with good grace and guided me back to the correct conference room.

I distributed the food to those who needed it most before forcing myself to eat some of the orange slices and a few sausage links. The last food item made me think of Jillian, so I checked on her. The regular rise and fall of her chest and rapid eye movements told me she was likely still working, but I had to satisfy my curiosity anyway.

Mrs. Davidson and Mrs. B. thanked me but barely glanced at the food. They only had eyes for their slumbering daughters. Seizing the challenge that presented, I prepared small plates and hand delivered them. It took some serious nagging, but I got them to clear the plates.

We're back to waiting, but at least we're fed and watered at this point.

The Glorified Gopher,
Danielle Matheson.

Chapter 28: Edward

ITEM 266: Jillian's 129th post-kidnapping journal entry
Item Source: Jillian Blairington

Danielle and Malia's new momma helped Dr. Devya until Michio and Aiden arrived. Nadia, Malia, and I waited for that situation to settle before fully diving into the work with Dustin. During the wait time, they did some setup work while I made sure the sleepers around the building stayed unconscious. A handful had risen quite a few sleep levels on their own, so I dropped 'em down to a much deeper level.

It is time to help Dustin.

Nadia's announcement drew me back to the conference room where my body rested. Our close connection let me feel her frustration at not being able to know what would happen with Dr. Devya. She would probably send Naidine, Queen Elena, or another personality to monitor, but we couldn't afford to split our attention when it came to Dustin.

Since I can only touch dreamers and Nadia has some skill using my Gifts, we decided to work within a dream. Malia can't fully use either of our Gifts, but she can make her ability to influence emotions available to us regardless of sleeping status.

I drew the room into my dream to check on the situation. Somebody had moved me, but I didn't mind. The new position looked a lot more comfortable than the random way I'd left us. I mostly wanted to know Dustin's exact position since knowing that would help me reach him. It would be best if I could touch him. Realizing it was a good idea, I let Nadia know, and she informed Danielle and some of the good soldiers.

Drawing a new map of the room, Nadia added tiny figures and let me move them around to see where everybody should go. We tried a few arrangements and finally chose the one where they collapsed the gurney holding Dustin and laid me along his left side. My Second Momma and Danielle carried me to the assigned position. Mrs. Davidson and a soldier set Malia to my left, and Nadia's Momma and a different soldier placed her next to Malia.

I thought about having Nadia on Dustin's other side so she could reach him, but she's got a whole heap more practice influencing people from any distance. It was better to let Malia have access to us 'cause her Gifts work better through direct contact.

Before we did anything, I figured we oughta find out what Dustin wanted from us. If it was a simple matter of something locked in his head, Nadia alone shoulda been able to help him. For him to summon the three of us, he musta been expecting a real tough fight to get at his Gifts. That fact got me curious 'cause most of our Gifts are straightforward. Nadia deals with head matters, Malia controls heart matters, Aiden and Michio build stuff and heal, Varick fights well, and I touch dreams.

After getting into Dustin's dreams, I cleared out a space, built another bare room, and created avatars for us. For convenience, I'd outfitted the figures with clothes identical to those we currently wore. I didn't bother adding chairs this time 'cause I didn't expect us to be there long.

The figure of Dustin changed. It surprised me even though I know my brother is one of the only people who's aware he still has some control over his dreams. He became older and more serious looking than the boy I'd met in Dr. Devya's first lab. Facial hair covered most of his cheeks and a good portion of his jaw except for a few scrappy patches of smooth skin. He even had a neat mustache. I ain't overly fond of 'em, but somehow, it looked good on him. The cut of his sandy brown hair had changed but remained neat and short. The most striking change was his eyes.

For as long as I've known him, Dustin has had green eyes, but this version had pale blue eyes. Varick can change his eye color if he wants or strong emotions can change the color for him, but I had no idea Dustin had that ability.

In addition to the self-changes, Dustin modified the room around us. Instead of the bare, windowless room, we stood in a cozy living room that look liked it'd been plucked from a lake house magazine. Four sets of large windows gave us a fine view of pine trees and water. Between the windows lay a stone fireplace, complete with crackling flames. The mantle had some pine cones and some fat candles. A candle-bearing chandelier hung in the center of the room above a low, rustic coffee table. A sprawling, oddly cut carpet lay beneath the coffee table, and two beige couches faced each other, left and right of the coffee table. A tall table behind the left couch held a lamp. Blocks of wood flanked the couches, serving as end tables for more candles.

And I thought Aiden was the pyro.

Nadia also changed, taking the form of Naidine. Her blond hair appeared more golden in this version, though there were still strands that appeared white too. She wore her traditional dark pants and black leather jacket. She's always been pretty, but now, she looked like she walked straight off a movie set.

I considered aging the avatars for Malia and me so we'd fit in, but I chose not to bother.

"Hello, Edward." Naidine's greeting was cool but not unfriendly, and she spoke positively slow for Nadia standards. "It's been a while. What brings you to the surface today?"

The man's expression, which had been neutral, immediately darkened.

"I came to stop this." Like Dustin, he spoke with a British accent, but his voice was a lot more serious than I'm used to. Deeper too, seeing as he's probably what my brother will be in his mid-to-late twenties.

Thick shades covered the windows, making the room seem smaller.

"Stop what?" I wondered. "Wait. Back up. Who are you?"

Naidine handled the introduction.

"Jillian, this is our brother, Edward. As you can guess, he's a part of Dustin."

"*He* won't exist if you do this." The young man's eyes flashed with conviction and more than a hint of anger.

"Better start explaining." Stepping over to the right couch, I sat down and waited on the edge for somebody to get to the explaining part.

Malia sat next to me and picked up my right hand.

"Dustin's full name is Dustin Edward Ayers. Dustin can mean 'stone' or 'brave fighter.' Edward means 'rich guard,' and Ayers means 'heir to a fortune.'" Malia's fingers compressed mine. "I think we're about to find out what that truly means, but Edward doesn't want us to carry out the task."

"You can't!" cried Edward. "It would destroy me."

I gave Edward my best Evil Eye. It ain't got nothing on Nana's or Momma's, but hopefully, it got my point across.

"Ya keep saying stuff like that, but I'm still good and lost. Start at the beginning and make it snappy. Your other half was pretty sure we oughta ignore ya, but I wanna hear whatcha have to say first."

Naidine crossed to the other couch and sat down on the far end, leaving room for Edward if he wanted to sit.

Edward ran his hands through his hair and gripped the sides of his head while he gathered his thoughts. Everything about him still read agitated. Finally, he sighed, let his hands drop to his sides, and stared at the floor.

"His Gift—my Gift—is knowledge." Edward raised his eyes and connected with each of us briefly before sending Naidine a longer look. His words flowed faster. "If you unleash it, they will come for him, for me. Once they have what they want, they'll kill me before moving on to the rest of you." Tears made his pretty blue eyes shiny. "Don't you understand? They won't need us or our parents once they have the records, recordings, and notes. What I know is locked up tight, but you three can reach it. She wants you to reach it. That's why we were drawn here."

I only caught about half of what he said but understanding swept over Naidine.

"The data repository does exist." Catching my make-some-sense glare, she continued, "There was always a rumor that every part of the successful experiments was well-documented and stored someplace. Now we know it's true. It's in Dustin."

Knowing the words should have an impact on me, I waited, but I felt nothing. At the risk of sounding dumb, I broke down and asked the obvious question.

"Why's this a big deal?"

"Many of the dangers we've faced recently are due to people trying to control us," Malia explained. Releasing my right hand, she turned her hands palms up and studied them. "But the information on how to make people with our Gifts would be infinitely more valuable."

I nodded to let her know the explanation was sinking in but stopped when I realized she'd left out a huge point.

"Who's *they* and who's *she* that has him in a twist?"

Naidine fielded that query.

"They are those who work for ATLAS. It's an acronym and a series of computer protocols the US government uses to analyze threats. Uncontrolled scientific knowledge of this nature would be a threat as would anybody who wields such information."

"I'm still confused," I admitted. My gaze landed squarely on Edward. "Why bring us here if you're afraid of us getting to this information?"

"He didn't," said Malia.

"Dustin did," Naidine finished.

I squinted at Naidine.

"You saying Dustin acted without Edward's knowledge?"

"Precisely. For a time, Dustin did not know what the Gift would be because Edward hid it from him. Even once he guessed what the Gift might be, he had no way to know for sure." Naidine finally spoke at proper Nadia speed. Her eyes flitted over to Edward. "I suspect ATLAS may have prompted his actions some way."

"She did." A single nod added to Edward's confirmation. "She's been against us for a while. Remember Katharos? That was ATLAS stirring up fanatics to do some of her dirty work. She changed tactics when she realized how inefficient zealots can be."

"What does she want?" I asked the question 'cause

Edward's answer kinda took us down a bunny trail.

"Dustin." His tone added that it ought to be obvious. "I discovered the true nature of the Gift a few years ago and kept it from him because he's not ready to bear the burden that comes with it."

"Ready or not, we gotta fix this now." My head threw a couple of pictures of the people in danger into the air above the coffee table.

"You are correct, Jillian," said Naidine, "but the ultimate decision still belongs to Dustin. He must be a part of this." She pushed my pictures up and away so they wouldn't distract us.

I let them disappear.

Edward clenched his jaw but reluctantly agreed with Naidine.

I didn't.

"How do ya figure that?" I demanded, referring to the part about involving Dustin. We were gonna have a hard time reaching a decision with just the four of us, let alone bringing in a fifth person.

Malia summarized our options.

"There are only four things we can do with Dustin's Gift: destroy the knowledge, give it to ATLAS, scatter it, or bury it."

"It is currently buried, but now that the location is known, it is compromised," said Naidine. "If we don't retrieve it, somebody else will likely take it by force."

"Is that possible?" I wondered.

Naidine sent me one of those sad smiles I've come to associate with my sister.

"Anything is possible with enough will, the right equipment, or the right threats."

Given that nearly everybody we knew was under some kind of threat, I couldn't argue with her.

"If ATLAS pries the information out of Dustin, we're all dead," said Edward. "So, how do we keep the information safe?"

With Edward's grim summary hanging over us, we settled into our own heads.

My mind batted the options Malia mentioned about like a cat with a yarn ball. None of the options sounded great. Destroying what they wanted sounded like a fast way to get everybody killed. Same for giving up the information. Scattering the information might buy us some time, but it wouldn't solve the problems. The Gift was already buried, so that last option boiled down to do nothing. That didn't sit right either.

"We gotta do it all." I wasn't sure I'd spoken until the others fixed their attention on me.

Thoughts zipped through my head faster than I could track dousing me with doubts.

Malia placed her left hand on my shoulder and subtly shifted things until confidence surged and fears faded.

"Should Dustin be present?" Naidine asked.

"Lemme explain my plan first. Everybody's gotta agree or this will go nowhere."

Chapter 29:
A Theory to Test

ITEM 267: Danielle's 81st letter
Item Source: Danielle Matheson

Dear Dr. S.,

Jillian's about to do something stupid. She hasn't told me exactly what yet, but I was asked to distract Mrs. B., Mrs. Davidson, and as many of the soldiers as possible. One does not get such requests if the asker is planning on behaving in a predictable, safe manner.

As I futilely searched my brain for possible distractions, Michio and Aiden finished their work with Devya and provided the perfect distraction. I proposed that we take the boys to the restroom to get cleaned up.

There wasn't a drop of blood on either tyke, but mere moments ago they'd been covered up to their little elbows in Devya's blood. I think my help suspected something, but they didn't deny that the boys needed a good washing on principle.

I'd taken the easy way out and watched Jillian, Nadia, Malia, and Dustin instead of seeing how Michio and Aiden fared, but Maisha was with them the whole time. I think Mrs. B. had tunnel vision focused on Jillian, so she didn't even realize Michio was there. He might have recognized her, but the healing kept him busy.

"Momma!" Michio's loud announcement made most of us

flinch, but the heart-melting reunion that took place was beautiful to behold.

Mrs. B. cried.

To keep from joining her, I spent the reunion time checking out Devya. A miniature mountain of small white sponges sat next to him as fresh as if they were still inside their syringe. Devya lay on his back sleeping. The tattered clothes made him look like a shipwreck victim. His exposed side looked raw but healthy. The speed at which Michio and Aiden worked astonished me. Jillian and Nadia had used Michio's knowledge to stitch up Dr. C.'s side from a nasty knife encounter a few weeks ago, but that healing had taken them hours. I hadn't kept close track, but this closing of ginormous bullet holes had happened in mere minutes at most.

The soldier who'd been in charge of Michio stood nearby but waited respectfully. I invited him along in case of an impromptu potty time. I'd never asked about Aiden's potty-training status, but I knew Michio to be fully trained. It's probably thanks to genetic engineering and being raised around Nadia and Malia. In any case, the young gentlemen were small enough to warrant supervision when using adult facilities.

The soldier paused at the threshold to the women's room, but we assured him he wouldn't spontaneously combust if he entered upon our invitation. He helped Aiden do the necessaries in the roomy handicap stall while Mrs. B. crammed herself into a normal stall with Michio. I don't think she had to do anything besides listen to the little guy yammer, but afterward, she helped him wash up and dry off properly.

Michio's a pro at getting wet while washing off, but his idea of drying involves madly waving his arms about trying to see how many surfaces he can soak in the process. Even though my cover story for getting Mrs. B. and Mrs. Davidson out of the main conference room had been a stretch, it took our collective efforts to complete the washing up business without destroying the restroom.

With the task done, we headed back to the conference room. The soldier, Kirk Keller, had introduced himself sometime between lathering Aiden's arms with soap and holding him still for the rinse. Kirk ended up in the lead, but he stopped a step inside.

That was my first clue something had gone horribly wrong.

The second clue, a gun appearing near the right side of my head, was even clearer.

Kirk sidestepped in front of me, caught the tail end of the other man's rifle with his chin, and dropped with barely a sound.

A noise that mashed groan, moan, and yelp together slipped out of me, and I tightened my hold on Aiden. He sat up in my arms, stuffed a thumb in his mouth, and tucked his head near my neck.

"Go to the stage." The gruff order got followed by a shove in that direction.

For a scary second, I forgot how to walk. I could only stare down at Aiden in horror.

Mrs. Davidson came up behind me and gently steered me toward the correct destination.

When I got to the stage edge, I stopped and perched Aiden on the edge because the other option was drop him.

The scene hadn't changed much but the small differences told a completely different tale. Before people had been huddled near either Jillian or Devya. The groupings had changed. Maisha, Dr. P., Dr. C., and Cora sat in a line by Devya. He was conscious but still flat on his back. The camera showed us that Cora had a restraining hand on his left shoulder. Jillian, Nadia, and Malia knelt in a line behind the gurney holding Dustin.

The tides turned decidedly against us. Around the room, soldiers who helped us were knocked out, bound, or both. The fatalistic side of me wondered why they didn't just shoot us. Soldiers Jillian had knocked out woke up and were set free by their friends. A futile wish for things to be clearer resulted in a helpful color-coding system courtesy of Nadia.

Mulligan and the CIA flunkies stood between Devya's party and Jillian's party arguing with a well-dressed newcomer. I must really have been out of it to not notice her before now. She wore tight black pants and a long gray blazer that looked simultaneously powerful and stylish. A large, heavy necklace chain with flat white stones hung around her neck. Without the stones it would have looked like a studded dog collar. She had long, slender fingers and short nails with a French manicure.

"I just want the boy and his mother. It won't even be for long, maybe an hour or two. You can keep the rest, including the Minder." The woman's brown eyes shone with amusement. "For now. I'll be in touch if I need to question her or the others."

"You have no authority here, senator." Mulligan's shoulders rose defensively. "I—"

"Should be grateful I'm not taking them all." The woman made a show of looking around. Her low voice with its cultured Southern accent had the quality of somebody who's had lessons in public speaking. "The security in this facility could use an overhaul. I'll see to it when I take over next month."

Veronica Santelli, US senator from New Mexico.

That tidbit came through without further explanation, but I shot silent thanks at Nadia anyway.

"That hasn't been decided yet." Mulligan's tone hardened considerably.

A scuffle broke out as Dr. P. stood and stepped toward Jillian's group. A soldier stepped into her path, assumed a shooter's stance, and centered his gun on her chest. Another man held her in place by her left shoulder.

I'd been so caught up in the drama with Mulligan and the unknown senator that I'd not paid any attention to Jillian, Malia, and Nadia. The first two held their kneeling postures, looking resigned to their fate. That surprised me because I've never known Jillian to go down without a fight. Then again, the armed soldiers surrounding her and her siblings would be powerful motivation to not try anything daring.

Nadia stood between two soldiers. Only her stiff stance spoke of her unease.

A young woman wearing a lab coat and blue nitrile gloves prepared an injection.

"Don't hurt her!" Dr. Paladon's plea tugged at my heartstrings. "Please. Knockout drugs frighten her."

Is there anybody they don't frighten?

Moving closer to Dr. P. the senator spoke kindly.

"I'm not here to hurt children, but I have a job to do. I can't risk having any interference. Once it's done, you can stay with her if ya like. That should be of some comfort."

Not looking comforted, Dr. P. stared longingly at Nadia.

For her part, Nadia forced a small smile and shook her head. Tilting her head toward her sisters, she said, "Jillian, Malia, can you help her?"

They nodded and closed their eyes.

Slowly, the tension left Dr. Paladon's shoulders. Shaking off the soldier's hold, she returned to her spot by Devya, sat down, leaned on Dr. C., and appeared to fall asleep.

The senator looked impressed, but she merely waved for the soldiers and scientist to carry on.

"Nadia sleep?" asked Aiden.

My hand flew to his mouth to cut off more words. We did not need to draw attention to ourselves. Holding him felt like clutching a warm blanket fresh out of the dryer. That might have worried me if Jillian hadn't mentioned Aiden's body temperature tends to run high.

"That's right, dear," answered Senator Santelli. "Just a short nap for each of them."

First Nadia, then Jillian, and finally, Malia received injections of some unknown sedative. Someone had laid out a blanket near the gurney. Mrs. Davidson wept when it was Malia's turn. After each shot, the soldiers carefully moved the unconscious girl to the blanket. The cameras cycled various faces, revealing Devya's blank expression, Maisha's worry, and the murderous glare Dr. C. fired at the senator.

Something warm and wet touched my palm.

Aiden giggled.

I glared at the little imp, but it did my heart good to see his brilliant smile. After wiping my hand on his shirt, I adjusted my grip and silently vowed to sock the first guy stupid enough to try and take him from me.

Bizarre ceremony over, the senator motioned for her people to collect the gurney holding Dustin and faced Mulligan again.

"Dr. Mulligan, tell me, which of these ladies should I be taking with me? I need the boy's mother, Cora. The files I received contained names but no pictures, a curious oversight I intend to correct someday."

Dr. C. looked up expectantly before checking on Dr. P.

Cora shook slightly but kept her eyes cast down toward Devya. Her right hand curled around the pendant hanging from a delicate gold chain.

Thankfully, nobody was paying any attention to me, or they might have read my puzzled frown.

Dr. C. pushed Dr. P. up and leaned her against Cora before standing.

"Is this the one?" An arched, well-maintained eyebrow repeated the question aimed at Mulligan.

He didn't respond, but to be fair, I'm not certain he registered the question since he wore a nine-mile stare.

"Are you Cora?" asked the senator.

"They are all our children," said Dr. C., dodging the question. "The notes should have been clear on that."

"Not an answer." The senator affected a thoughtful pose by resting her chin on a closed fist. "I suppose we could take the three of you, but it'll be an uncomfortable ride in the van." Letting her hand drop, she sighed. "I'm not sure why there's any reluctance to telling me the truth. Cora will be fine and returned in a few hours as long as the boy is compliant."

"You only need one of us."

"Agreed, but I'd rather have the right one." A triumphant grin formed. "I do have a theory to test." Snapping her fingers at me, Senator Santelli said, "You. Girl. Let the boy go."

A gun muzzle reappeared in my peripheral vision, clearing up any doubts I had about being addressed.

"Down?" Aiden tilted his head and wriggled.

Setting him on his feet, I turned Aiden to face the woman and gripped the kid's bony shoulders.

"Go to your mother, darling." The woman's tone managed to split the line between kind and commanding.

Turning his head, Aiden glanced back at me.

My fingers slipped from his shoulders. I had no advice for him because I didn't know the consequences either way, and I needed every scrap of willpower to keep from doing something suicidal.

Feeling the attention, Aiden straightened and sprinted to

Dr. C. Leaping clear over Devya's legs, the boy landed in her arms.

Looking defeated, Dr. C. shut her eyes and hugged Aiden close. Her shoulders shook, but I couldn't tell if she was crying until Aiden spoke.

"Why sad?" He sounded worried. "I bad?"

Pulling away so he could see her, Dr. C. shook her head and forced a smile.

"Not your fault." Leaning forward, she kissed his forehead before tucking him close again. Her right hand cupped the back of his head in a protective gesture.

The drama drained everyone, even the evil lady.

"Take that one," she said, nodding to Cora. "No drugs. I want her alert."

That's it. The woman *suggested* to Mulligan that everybody with questionable loyalties be taken to the holding cells. Then, she and her people swept out, carrying Dustin and Cora in their wake.

The Hollow One,

Danielle Matheson.

Chapter 30: Everything to do with Love

ITEM 268: Jillian's first letter to Danielle
Item Source: Jillian Blairington

Dear Danielle,

Stay with Momma if ya can. Try to keep her calm, but don't tell her what I'm up to unless ya gotta. I'm sending her a letter too, but it's gonna contain a lot less details 'cause she'd probably stop me if she could. That ain't a criticism. Her momma's heart wasn't made to stand by while I do something dangerous.

I ain't a fan of that part either. If we had another option, I'd take it, but this is about the only projected plan that might keep us alive a little longer.

You once helped me get to Nadia 'cause it was important to me. That kind of loyalty don't come easy or cheap, and I know it cost you plenty. Don't know if I ever put a thank you in writing. I really gotta find a better reason to write people than walking into something I might not be able to get out of. Anyway, thank you for everything. You've become one of my best friends, and I love ya for that. Hopefully, I can tell ya this in person someday.

I'm switching places with Dustin. I'll tell ya the whole story someday, but for now, the short version's gonna have to do. Somewhere deep in his head, he's got the project notes for each of us. That might not sound exciting, but it's the cause of most of this mess. Nadia, Malia, and I are working to get at it so we can protect it better or bargain with it if we must.

Right now, it's a really dangerous shell game. We gotta keep Dustin out of Senator Veronica Santelli's hands. She's working for ATLAS. Dunno if anybody's mentioned that to you before, but it's a program powered by computers and ruthless people. I think it was meant to analyze threats to the country as a whole and come up with solutions. Unfortunately, we are a threat to ATLAS, and gaining the knowledge to create more of us that could be better controlled is a goal worth pursuing by any means necessary.

The charade will collapse soon enough. We're trying to buy time. We gotta find the information buried in Dustin and answer for it before Senator Santelli or ATLAS realize what we've done. The fear is that if they get a hold of the original files, they won't need us. We're the originals. We have free will and stubborn natures. Those flaws cannot be abided in government tools. Least, that's how Nadia put it.

Maybe we're being overly pessimistic, and ATLAS will decide to keep some of us if we stop fighting. That's the more likely scenario. Our brothers would likely be enslaved for one reason or another. Their Gifts are generally more physical, so they give the illusion of being easier to control. As a Minder, Nadia's the biggest threat, but Malia and I are probably close seconds because our Gifts connect well to hers. If she truly believed the loss of one life could right things for the rest, Nadia would be first in line to pay the price.

She said, "We cannot cast our fate upon heartless machines and people who lost sight of mercy long ago."

Thus, our bid for time.

Hug Aiden and Michio for me. They're brave little guys, but they're still very young. Our mommas will try to protect 'em, but they're in danger too. Currently, they're being held 'cause of their connection to us, but it won't take ATLAS long to discover the deeper threat they represent. We can't let that happen.

I refuse to sacrifice one side of my family to save the other. We will come through this together or perish together. I'm not saying that to scare ya, but I do want to prepare ya in case things I do don't make sense immediately.

Do whatcha gotta to save your family. I mean that. Even if ya gotta turn against me, I understand and won't love ya less for it.

Forever your friend,
Jillian

***

ITEM 269: Jillian's second letter to her mother
Item Source: Allison Blairington

Dear Momma,

I know this is strange and new for ya. It ain't natural to receive letters in one's head. My sister, Nadia, is making this possible. I'm sorry I can't explain everything right now, and I'm sorry you're in this mess.

If ya need to see the letter again, think *repeat Jillian's explanation* and it'll replay from the beginning. There's a written copy on the pink mental sticky note. If you close your eyes, it should appear. Imagine touching it, and it'll expand for ya.

I gotta do something that's dangerous. If it works, we'll be in a better place. I don't mean that in the *we're dead* sorta way, I mean we'll be free of the dangers that have been haunting us the past few months. If it doesn't work, the situation will stand much as it is, and bad things are gonna continue happening to everybody connected to Dr. Devya's programs.

There's a chance this only sorta works. In that case, most of the innocents like you, Mr. Blairington, Isaac, Mrs. Davidson, and Danielle's family will be all right, but me and my other family will have to disappear for a long while.

Last Nadia checked, Mr. Blairington and Isaac were fine. They're in hiding with somebody Varick knows. For their safety, Nadia wouldn't tell me more, but I trust her with my life.

Before I face this thing, I gotta clear my conscience, but I honestly don't know if you're gonna wanna hear this. Nadia helped me prepare it in such a way that it'll be your choice. That's the red mental sticky note. It has to do with your past and has the chance of bringing you both pain and joy. I'm sorry that's about as clear as mud.

You're probably gonna get an odd feeling something ain't right. Please don't pursue it. Everything will get sorted one way or another sometime today.

Follow Danielle's lead and instructions. I told her some of the plan. Telling her while keeping it from ya has nothing to do with trust and everything to do with love.

I love ya both something fierce, but Danielle has a part to play in seeing this through.

Malia may also seek to direct ya if you are willing to help. She'll show ya which emotions will best sell the story we're weaving.

Lots of love,
Jillian

***

ITEM 270: Allison's eighth letter to Dr. Sokolowski
Item Source: Allison Blairington

Dear Dr. S.,

I have another son. Jillian just told me about him. Guess the ultrasound didn't lie to us. I don't even know his name. Jason and I were gonna name our baby boy Kyle Robert Antel, but Fate—and Nadia—gave us Jillian instead.

That's not a complaint. I love that girl with all my heart, mind, and soul. She's challenged me in ways I never would have imagined.

Jillian was right about one thing. The news I have a son comes with heavy loads of pain and joy, but she forgot to add uncertainty. I wanna know my son, but I can't help thinking it's probably best for him if I stay away. That's a faulty assumption that implies I bear some guilt for the things that have happened to us, which I know is accepting false responsibility, but I can't help it. My boy has a different momma and a life that's got nothing to do with me.

Do I risk upending that life just for the chance to know him?

My brain kicks up dozens of other questions I have no answers for. Is my boy safe? Is he happy? What does he look like? Is he as handsome as his daddy? What does he like to do? Is he kind? Loud? Athletic?

Jason wasn't much for responsibility, but he's always been easy on the eyes and excellent at woodworking. Can our son build things with his hands?

I'm sorta surprised I have the mental capacity to worry about this boy. Between Jillian, Isaac, and Michio there's plenty to occupy my thoughts. Jillian and Michio are here but out of reach. I miss Isaac's comforting weight in my arms. I miss Jeffrey too.

I don't know how this ends, and I already feel like I ain't gonna like the outcome.

I thought I'd prepared my heart for steering clear of Jillian until it was safe, but the last few days have shown me that such a time may not exist.

Can I let her go?

She's my daughter. I raised her from infancy. Nobody can take that away from me. She's still got a ways to go 'til she's a woman, but her Gifts give her concerns no kid should ever have to face. She still needs me, but I can't say in what capacity. Michio and Isaac still need me too, and there at least I feel somewhat qualified to help.

In some ways, it feels like I've already lost Jillian.

As terrifying as this whole experience has been, I am grateful for the insight into the things she faces.

I trust God, but I do not trust people.

I am not throwing away my life, but if there is a way to free my children from these dangerous people, I will see it done, whatever the cost. I see that same determination on the faces of the women around me.

If ya think of it, pray for us.

Sincerely,

Allison Blairington

Chapter 31:
The Vault

ITEM 271: Jillian's 130th post-kidnapping journal entry
Item Source: Jillian Blairington

My audience of three looked at me expectantly. The growing distance between us stretched my Gift, but I'd conserved strength while being directly connected to Nadia, Malia, and Dustin.

Drawing a breath only bought me a second more to order my thoughts, which wasn't nearly enough time, but I started speaking anyway.

"We're thinking of Dustin's Gift as one thing, but if it's information, it's probably in a lot of smaller pieces."

In tune with my thoughts, Naidine nodded slowly.

"It could work."

Edward and Malia still looked lost.

"What are you proposing?" Edward straightened like a man bracing for bad news.

"As I said, we do it all," I answered. "We break in and get the information Dustin holds. Then, we destroy part, hand over part, hold back part, and spread the rest around to trusted people."

"Won't that put them in danger?" Malia wondered.

"Only if the bad guys know who got the information." I added a look that said we oughta keep that part to ourselves.

"Why take the risk?" Malia folded her hands on her lap, projecting a calm I envied. "Destroying the information would answer for the threat it represents."

"We would lose any bargaining power we have." Edward's shrug acknowledged that such power was highly limited anyway.

"The knowledge itself is not the problem," Naidine explained. "Properly applied, the notes could save decades of work in many scientific fields. That is worth preserving."

"You want to bargain with ATLAS?" Edward's tone called us all kinds of crazy. "This program has tried to kill us for months."

"Programs can be rewritten," Malia noted. "It's the people we'll need to reach."

"I have a list prepared. These are the people we must convince we are not a threat." Naidine conjured a copy for each of us, but I didn't bother looking at it. "Jillian, please summon Dustin. We have much to do in very little time."

They hadn't heard my whole plan, but I didn't mind since it wasn't completely formed in my head anyway.

"Shouldn't we decide what to do first?" I kept my tone tentative 'cause I didn't wanna argue with Naidine.

"Everything hinges on Dustin's permission." Naidine spoke gently but firmly. "We can present our case, but we cannot force him to part with the Gift unwillingly."

"Why not?" I demanded.

"It would be wrong," Malia said.

They were ticking me off. My avatar's cheeks flushed and the urge to laugh and cry hit me at the same time. I blinked to keep from crying.

"We are hundreds of miles and many states away from home. A lot of people we love are counting on us, and you wanna sit here talking about right and wrong." I didn't bother hiding the bitterness.

Malia closed her eyes, but she didn't touch me.

Peace didn't immediately sweep over me, but I calmed down enough to at least start thinking again.

"Edward agrees with us. Don't he get a say?"

Edward looked uncomfortable to be caught in the middle of this philosophical debate.

"I want to live, but that will not happen if Dustin gives up. You must have his cooperation."

I poured my frustration into a groan but did as bid since it was now three-to-one against me and common sense.

"Why haven't you started yet?" Dustin's demand hit us almost before his avatar finished forming. His gaze made the rounds starting with Naidine 'cause I'd put him in the empty spot on the couch next to her. When he reached Edward, a puzzled look formed. "What are you doing here?"

"Listen up, Dusty. We gotta talk about your Gift." I wasn't speaking quite Nadia-level fast, but the words were quicker than my usual pace.

"What's to talk about? Did you get it yet?" The questions had a bouncy quality that reminded me of the Old Dustin, the one who didn't betray his siblings to government crazy people. "What has he been telling you?"

"He didn't need to tell us much," said Naidine, "but he did confirm the nature of your Gift. You hold the sum of what fashioned us from ideas to powerful realities."

Dustin flushed as his close connection to Edward brought him up to speed. His neutral expression turned to a grumpy one.

"You had no right to keep this from me." Dustin directed the words to his older self.

Edward accepted the scolding with a short nod and ran his right hand through his hair.

"Can't change that now but listen to them. We're in deeper trouble than you can handle."

"I made a deal."

I about said one of the bad words as a memory of the last time Dustin made a deal stabbed me with needles of panic. Malia's hand landed on my right leg, giving me enough calm to stay seated, but my face channeled my worry. I dunno what kinda deal Dustin struck this time, but in the past, he has been painfully naïve. He'd promised to work for Dr. Lanier in exchange for Cora's safety, but Dr. Lanier had already broken his side of that bargain.

"Explain." I kept the command short 'cause anything else woulda involved a lecture we couldn't afford right now.

"We'll be free once I transfer the information to ATLAS." Dustin's posture dared us to contradict him.

The defiant look he shot Naidine struck me as significant,

but I couldn't tell why right then.

"Death is a form of freedom," Malia said.

My brain had to chew on that a few seconds before I got her meaning and how it fit with the rest of the conversation.

"They wouldn't betray us." Dustin's defensive tone told us he shared our fear of that fate.

I snorted, and Naidine beat me to the obvious statement.

"They most certainly would."

Sensing the moment was right, I conjured the pictures of our loved ones facing danger and had them file past Dustin. The last two were Cora and Dr. Devya 'cause those are the two he cares about the most.

"Help us, Dusty." I paused to let him get a good look at the pictures. "We can win our freedom, but only with your help 'cause it involves your Gift."

Dustin fell silent for a long time. His expression turned sad, then despairing, and finally, scared.

I only know 'cause Malia's presence enhanced my ability to recognize the very subtle differences.

He settled on a mixture of sad and scared.

"If you take my Gift, what will happen to me?"

"The Gift will always be yours," Naidine promised. "We ask only that you allow us to access it to truly purchase the freedom you sought and do some good where it is safe to do so."

"Won't that put him in danger?" I did not want to solve this problem only to have it kick us in the teeth in another few weeks.

"Naidine and I should be able to select pieces that won't be dangerous." Edward sounded more confident than he looked.

I couldn't tell if he was downplaying to help us or genuinely innocent enough to believe the danger wouldn't pop up again.

A dull throb in my head caused the room to shake. Several candles tumbled to the floor, but before they could set anything on fire, Edward and I caught 'em and put 'em back in place.

"The Gifts were always meant to work together. Let's find yours fast before keeping this connection proves too difficult. We can argue its fate after we have it."

We ended up doing both. Upon Naidine's suggestion, I

created a copy of the entire room, including the avatars. The copies continued discussing the ins and outs of various plans to deal with any information we got from Dustin while the originals broke the lock surrounding the data vault.

Holding two conversations at once was a very strange experience.

If the stakes weren't so high, I mighta enjoyed the exercise. Dustin had protected the vault with a few puzzles and code systems that required our combined knowledge to beat.

The first bit was much like the lock Nadia had put up to protect her throne room when she fell into a coma. Two hundred colored bricks lined up in twenty rows of ten. I imagined they had numbers. Nadia made the suggestions on which to press next, and Malia recorded our success or failure with each of the twelve different codes. Every time we got a wrong block, we had to start over. Working alone, it mighta taken close to forever to get the correct combinations.

The next puzzle had trivia questions from Dustin's life. Nadia had some of the answers and Edward supplied the rest.

The third challenge resembled the old game Frogger or the newer game Chicken Chase where ya gotta maneuver across dangerous terrain before something comes outta nowhere and flattens your character. It tested my reflexes and patience, but after about a thousand tries, I memorized the moves to get us across.

The last obstacle consisted of a simulated corn maze. I wanted to wish us right to the end but figured I should humor Dustin. I got lost after three turns, but Nadia and Malia kept better track of our progress and guided us through.

At last, we stood before the Vault. The way Dustin presented it made me think of it as a proper place. It surprised me to not find a lock on the door.

A queasy feeling kicked me right before Edward swung the huge door open. Inside, we found a warehouse stretching as far as my avatar could see. Each row had many shelves lined with little wooden cubes. The room appeared to be moving 'cause each cube had moving shapes and colors crisscrossing it. The effect reminded me of Nadia's teardrop crystals, but these didn't show a coherent picture as far as I could tell.

I stole a look at Naidine in time to see her puzzled frown melt with understanding.

"They're encrypted."

"Is that gonna be a problem?" Wasn't sure I wanted the answer, but the question needed asking.

"Perhaps." A distant look crossed Naidine's face. "But I think it more likely we can turn this to our advantage." Her expression cleared. "We must find the key."

Chapter 32:
Fever

ITEM 272: Danielle's 82nd letter
Item Source: Danielle Matheson

Dear Dr. S.,

I wanted the day to end but feared what Mulligan would pull next. If he hasn't lost his mind, he's doing a stellar impression of it. Guess that was apparent when he shot Devya.

Never thought I'd see the day when I pitied that man but getting shot in the back must hurt in multiple ways.

Does Mulligan have a plan or is he running on insane instinct?

Does Devya have a role here, or is he a prisoner too?

I am tempted to say Nadia has cracked as well, but I half-suspect, half-hope this is a brilliant scheme I don't understand yet. That is probably unfair to her. I tend to expect Old Testament style miracles from the girl. There's no question she has extraordinary Gifts, but she also has limitations and an impressive list of enemies.

Allow me to lay things out as far as I can gather from Jillian's letter and a few lightning-quick instructions from Naidine. Whatever they're up to must be a massive undertaking because I have never seen Naidine this distracted.

Because I'm nosy, I took careful stock of who ended up where in this makeshift prison. I have copious amounts of downtime on my hands, so I shall now recount for you the situation as it stands.

Most of us are back in the cells that originally held the lady scientists from Devya's old crew. I'm in a jail-like cell with Mrs. Davidson. If memory's playing straight with me today, this box was formally occupied by Cora. Dr. C. and Aiden are to my right in the cell she'd shared with Dr. P. That's where I was strapped to a gurney and injected with blank nanomachines. To my left, you'll find Michio and Mrs. B. sharing the last cell in our quaint row of three. They're both napping. Across from my cell is Doc P. Somehow, she ended up with no cellmate. The remaining cells are crammed with soldiers who had helped us.

Jillian's not here. She and Cora were kidnapped by the well-dressed senator who thought she was getting Dustin but really took Jillian. I'm going to have to grill Jillian on how they pulled off that switcharoo. For the record, it's very disconcerting to see Dustin wearing Jillian's features and clothes. I can't tell if it's solely an illusion set up by Nadia or if there are nanomachines involved. I don't even know how she's still working if she's unconscious. I guess the whole drugging ceremony could have been an elaborate illusion.

Great. I'll never trust my eyes again.

The location of Devya, Malia, Dustin, and Nadia is unknown. Since they were not moved with us, it's possible they're still up on the stage. It's just as possible Mulligan moved them to a completely different building or packed them up to ship out to a new state. I really hope that's not the case though because having them close is psychologically comforting.

I began this round of waiting with a nap, but that didn't last long because I was too keyed up. When I woke up, I watched Dr. C. play with Aiden. The soldiers had refused to bring the boys any toys, so Dr. C. lent Aiden her necklace. She helped him use his nanomachines to move the necklace around in a circle.

It wasn't exactly fast-paced entertainment, but I didn't mind. I was tired, annoyed, and I felt lousy. Watching a necklace do circles on its own was about my speed. My head hurt too.

"Danielle, come here, please. I want to check something." Dr. C. tried for a casual tone, but I heard notes of quiet concern too. Getting no response besides a curious glance from me, she appealed to Mrs. Davidson. "Does she have a fever?"

A cool hand landed on my forehead. It felt fabulous. I wanted to hold it in place, but my hands ignored the order from my brain.

My eyes drifted shut.

"Yes, she feels warm," said Mrs. Davidson.

"I'm fine," I mumbled. I wasn't, but I also didn't want to be fussed over.

"You're not fine, but you will be in a few hours," Dr. C. promised. "Get her to lay down."

My addled brain tried to make sense of the instruction and got nowhere.

Someone pulled me forward and laid me on my side, then straightened my legs and tipped me onto my back.

"Where … you sit?" I wondered. The fatigue set in so strongly, I had to concentrate to keep my eyes open.

"Right here," replied Mrs. Davidson. She'd changed positions to be perched on the edge of the cell's single cot. She rested her right hand on my left arm to reinforce her presence.

"It's a side effect of the nanomachines." Dr. Carnasis spoke slowly and clearly. "Your body doesn't recognize them and isn't receiving any instructions about them, so it's attacking. They should be able to adapt soon and do a better job of blending in with normal cells, but until then, you'll run a fever."

"You might be achy too," added Dr. P. "It's rare, but it happens."

"How do you know?"

I silently blessed Mrs. Davidson for her innate curiosity because it saved me the colossal effort of voicing the question.

"It happened to me," said Dr. P. "That's why I didn't stick with that experiment even though they were short of test subjects."

"You knew this could happen." Mrs. Davidson's statement had the bite of accusation in it.

"I honestly forgot about that part," said Dr. C. "It's been so long since my first dose." She paused a few beats. "It really does get better, and you might be able to speed up the rough parts by choosing a path."

Since I didn't have much strength, I stared my confusion

up at Mrs. Davidson and she relayed it to the others.

"What do you mean? What are her choices?"

"She's talking about a specialty," said Dr. P, "but I'm not sure we should be talking about this aloud. The less Mulligan knows, the better."

"Keep talking." The instruction came in a gruff male voice I hardly recognized as Mulligan's. "I want to hear this."

Where the heck did he come from?

Nobody spoke for a while.

"Do I need to insist?" asked Mulligan.

My current position—flat on my back—prevented me from seeing much beyond Mrs. Davidson, some cell bars, and part of the ceiling, but it didn't take much imagination to picture him threatening somebody.

"No. She should have the information anyway." Dr. C. sounded weary. "Danielle, the nanotechnology experiment is newer than our work on the children you know. You don't have a high enough machine count to mimic Jillian or Nadia. Their Gifts are highly complex, but you might be able to begin touching upon empathic Gifts like Malia's. I suggest you try something even simpler like physical enhancements, increased blood flow or muscle enhancement. That will probably make you feel better the quickest."

"She's going to be a Healer." That declaration came from Mulligan. "I'll just have to pick the right poison or wound to inflict. Should we do both?" The last part was a conversation he had with himself.

Well, strike Healer from my wish list.

If Mulligan favored it, I wanted nothing to do with that Gift, no offense to Aiden and Michio.

"You're going to introduce too many variables," Dr. C. warned. "Healing physical wounds and clearing up a poison involve very different skill sets. Ideally, the nanomachines can handle both, but Danielle doesn't have that many in her. To see any results, the ones she has are going to have to be united in a purpose."

"Why does that matter?" asked Mulligan. "If she can close a wound, we'll know the machines work. The confirmation should be enough to warrant a small production run. How long do they take to make? Could we begin trials within three months?"

"It matters because everybody is different." Irritation hardened Dr. C.'s tone. "If you've been listening as long as I think you have, you might recall Jessie mentioning her poor reaction to the nanomachines. That's why we always start with very small batches."

"You can program them to create more, can't you?" Mulligan sounded petulant.

"Yes, but it's dangerous." Dr. C. sounded like she wanted the conversation over ten minutes ago. "Every copy risks an error. Too many errors will harm the host."

The word *host* struck me weird. It brought up images of aliens, viruses, and cheap horror flicks.

"Let's stick with wound then. Should the injury be inflicted on her or somebody else?"

I imagine Mulligan was garnering some glares from Dr. C., Dr. P., Mrs. B., and Mrs. Davidson.

That's about the point I questioned if the entire exchange might be a bizarre fever dream.

"Answer me!"

Big surprise, nobody answered him.

He growled.

"You. Bring me the boy."

I didn't know which boy he meant until Dr. C. spoke. If somebody took the temperature of her voice, I'm pretty sure they'd end up with icicles.

"Hurting Aiden won't work. He's a Healer. You won't be able to tell which work belongs to him or Danielle."

A huff confirmed that Mulligan hadn't thought of that.

I internally cheered and awarded Dr. C. an arbitrary point in the verbal contest.

"What about you?" Mulligan's voice bled innocent curiosity. "Your machines aren't geared toward healing."

"True, but their presence is another variable." Dr. C. sounded too calm to be discussing the idea of wounding her to see if I could develop a healing Gift. "There's no way to predict how the machines in me will react to the sudden need to heal. They may be able to develop such an enhancement on their own."

Mrs. Davidson stiffened slightly, and her fingers squeezed my arm gently.

I imagined Mulligan's predatory gaze landing on her.

"I'm your best option," said Dr. P. "My body has rejected nanomachines in the past. I'm as close to a control as you'll get."

"Do you agree?"

I couldn't tell whom Mulligan was addressing, but eventually, Dr. C. answered.

"No. Everybody has some healing capacity in their bodies. If you truly want to know if the machines will take orders from Danielle, you have to start small and with her."

"How would you approach it?" asked Mulligan. "Hypothetically, of course."

The hypothetical part fooled nobody.

"I wouldn't," answered Dr. C.

"You will," Mulligan said cheerfully. His voice immediately darkened with his next words. "Because if you continue to annoy me, I will shoot one of the boys. They're both Healers. They'll be fine, but it will cause them some distress."

The disturbing nature of his threat gave me a little strength.

"It's okay. Tell him." That's what I wanted to say. Not entirely sure what I really said, but they got the gist.

After a long silence, Dr. C. sighed and explained her plan.

"Open a shallow cut on the underside of her left arm. Place it near the median cubital vein, but don't cut the vein. That should let the nanomachines be delivered near the site without being forced out by blood. Time how long it takes for the wound to close itself. If it's within a few hours, you can assume the machines are receiving adequate instructions on how to heal."

Mulligan made a random noise that indicated he was thinking.

"I want to move to more extensive human trials in the next few weeks, but I'll accept your bid for a slow start. See that it's done."

The next minute contained a lot of confusing movement and door opening and closing noises.

"Momma!" A high-pitched, child screech split the air.

Sounds of a scuffle followed.

A man screamed.

Then, heavy silence fell.

A child's sniffles disrupted the stillness.

"What did he do?" Mulligan sounded giddy. "How bad is the burn?"

"Hold still," instructed Dr. C. "He can heal that if you let him."

"Wait, let the girl try. This could be the perfect test for her."

"She's still struggling with the initial influx of machines," called Dr. P. "Until that sorts itself, she won't be up for much of anything, including healing."

Mulligan dismissed Dr. P.'s claim. He even had the poor burned guy hauled into my cell and shoved Mrs. Davidson aside to bring the soldier close to me.

I probably could have rallied enough to lift my head, but I faked an even worst state of listlessness than I was feeling. Eventually, Mulligan let Aiden heal the burns inflicted on the soldier. My curious side really wants to know exactly what went down. The cowardly side is grateful the chaos delayed my date with a knife.

The Listless One,

Danielle Matheson.

Chapter 33:
Negotiations

ITEM 273: Jillian's 131st post-kidnapping journal entry
Item Source: Jillian Blairington

The van door slid open, letting in a blast of cold air. I shivered but kept myself at the lightest level of sleep I can work in so I could monitor the situation.

I didn't know if Nadia's illusion would last, and I suspected it wouldn't be long. I think she alters people's perceptions directly, so anybody new wouldn't have been influenced. I had a few nanomachines altering some of my features but that was just to reinforce Nadia's work. We didn't change anything about my clothes. That wasn't a dead giveaway since people don't often pay attention to that sorta thing, and I had been wearing sweatpants and a sweatshirt.

My guess got confirmed a few seconds later when the guy who opened the door gave the woman an odd look.

"Wake him." The lady spoke without even looking at the scientist guy. "He needs to be conscious for the hard wire connection. I want the information in his head on the analysts' screens within the hour."

"Are you sure you got the right kid?" The man spoke with the cautious tone of someone who had bad news but didn't want to be yelled at.

"Of course, I—" The lady cut herself off and whipped her

head toward me.

Cora unbuckled herself and stood near the gurney holding me.

"Who do I have?" The lady's tone was dark and dangerous, like a storm about to get real loud.

Before waking myself, I pulled Cora into a dozing state and transferred a thought capsule Nadia had prepared for me to give her. She hadn't told me what was in it, but that's typical Nadia behavior. Sensing my cover wouldn't last long anyway, I dropped my side of Nadia's illusion.

"This is Jillian." Cora placed a hand on my right shoulder as she made the introduction. "She's the Dream Shaper."

Frustration and disgust played across the lady's features.

"Why do I have her instead of your son?"

"To protect him." Cora reached beneath my head and smoothed out the hair that had gotten bunched there. "And I suspect the children have a proposal for you."

We had tucked a lot of my hair under my head to make the illusion easier to create, but now that I was awake, it was lumpy and bothersome.

The lady glared at us, then sighed and ordered us taken inside to Containment Cell Three.

I tensed but didn't put up a fuss 'cause there was nothing to gain right then. Somehow, I got elected to present our case to ATLAS. I figured I might as well get it over with.

Since we had arrived underground, I couldn't tell much about our surroundings. Such an investigation would require me to be asleep, but I paid attention to where we were in the building in case we needed the information to escape.

Containment Cell Three consisted of a bare room with two cots, two chairs, and a small table. Three sides had off-white walls. Thick metal bars formed the fourth wall.

Cora guided me to the left cot before sitting in one of the chairs.

Since I'd just had a long, working nap, I got comfortable and leaned back against the wall. I needed the time to think about how to get the computer program to listen to me. I didn't even know what I could bargain with 'cause Nadia hadn't reported they got the information yet.

Two soldiers stood guard outside the door.

Curiosity shone in Cora's eyes, but she didn't ask me any questions with the soldiers present. Since the cell also had a few video cameras, I guessed anything we said would be witnessed by ATLAS.

After a while, a man brought a tray with two plates of food. The beef stew looked kinda questionable and the bread was stale. I dunno about Cora, but I wasn't hungry. I forced myself to eat anyway 'cause it gave me something to do, and Maisha would yell if she knew I intended to enter important negotiations without eating.

I tried not to think about the importance of the upcoming meeting, but I couldn't shake the idea that a hundred things could go wrong and get somebody killed. Nadia and the others could fail to figure out how to decrypt the information. ATLAS could keep thinking of us as a threat. Dr. Mulligan could do something desperate before the deal was complete. Dr. Mulligan could do something desperate even if we got a deal in place.

"You'll do fine." Cora's statement cut off the stream of horrible scenarios marching through my head.

"How do ya know?" The question wasn't a fair one, but it slipped out on a wave of self-doubt.

Cora didn't answer right away, but her body language said she would eventually.

"I know because I have watched you grow in your Gift, and I trust your siblings and my former colleagues. Dean is many things, but fool is not one of them. Nadia has her mental Gifts plus a good dose of Jessie's stubbornness. If there is a favorable solution to our situation, it will be found."

The senator returned before I could respond to Cora's observations. She dismissed the guards and tossed something small into our cell.

My heart skipped a beat 'cause my first thought was *grenade* thanks to my last experience with something that size entering a room unexpectedly.

Instead of exploding, the metal thing sprouted three delicate legs and moved to the center of the cell. A flat area formed on top of the legs and the rest of the blob took the shape of a woman. The entire figure woulda fit in my palm.

"Hello. I am ATLAS. I apologize for the limitations of this representative. My communication suites are being upgraded, but this model is convenient." The female voice coming from the figure sounded like a normal lady, but the way she spoke and her word choices didn't seem natural. "Why are you here?"

"Why is she here?" I waved at the senator lady in case the machine missed my meaning. I hadn't expected to be making my case from a jail cell, so I said the first thing to pop into my mind to buy a second to adjust.

"Senator Santelli has been tasked with helping me achieve my goals," replied the voice from the figure. The effect made me think an action figure had come to life.

I glanced at the senator. She didn't take out anything to write with, but if her expression could be trusted, our conversation had her complete attention and she'd be taking very thorough mental notes.

After my brief delay to get my bearings, I figured this was as good a location as any to bargain for our lives.

"We don't have whatcha want yet, but my siblings are working on it." I almost panicked 'cause that was not how I imagined starting. Since I couldn't take back the words, I blundered on. "I came to buy time." I frowned 'cause I hadn't meant to admit that. Usually, I'm better at keeping important stuff secret.

"It's all right, Jillian. The meal must have had a truth serum in it." Cora's expression hardened as her attention shifted from me to the figure of ATLAS. "I could have told them that was unnecessary, but they didn't ask. It won't hurt you."

"Continue," said the machine, still addressing me.

"We have the same main goal," I said.

"How do you know my main goal?" asked ATLAS.

"You told us by everything you did to gather us." I didn't know which parts the program could claim credit for, but it was safe to assume a lot of the problems had their roots in her. "You want the information stored with my brother, and you won't get it without our permission."

"Not complete, but not completely wrong either," said ATLAS.

The rhythm of that statement did seem natural to me.

"Why would that be your goal as well?" asked Senator Santelli.

"Our goal is to live in peace, but to get there we gotta do what we were made to do," I answered.

"And that is?" The prompt came from the senator.

I glanced at Cora to see if she wanted to answer the question.

"The original contract had a lot of subpoints about national defense, thus that objective was integrated into each project."

"If our Gifts can protect lives, then that's what we're gonna do," I explained. By this time, thoughts ordered themselves in my head. I didn't know if that was 'cause of the truth serum, but I didn't question it. "The same holds true for the information Dustin has in his head. The key difference is that even without knowing the sum of what he holds, I can tell ya that a lot of it is dangerous. We ain't gonna hand over a weapon that powerful for any reason."

"Do you place no value on the lives I hold?" asked ATLAS.

"You hold my life, and you hold Cora's. Those are the only sure things." I made sure to address both ATLAS and Senator Santelli. "I value our lives enough to fight for 'em, if that's what ya wanna know, but what I'm saying is that this doesn't have to be a fight. We can work together to protect the country and advance science without compromising every moral law ever invented."

"Why should I agree to this?" The figure representing ATLAS tilted its head in a sign of universal curiosity.

"Because it is in your best interest, Senator Foster," said Cora.

Senator Santelli and I gave her looks that said she'd taken leave of her senses.

The figure of a woman changed to that of a man and a male chuckle rose from whatever it used as speakers.

"Do I have the Minder to thank for that revelation?"

"Dad?" Senator Santelli's face flipped through a few emotions. Confusion and anger won out in equal measures at first before anger pulled slightly ahead.

"You do." Cora nodded even though the figures still faced me. "She sends her regards and suggests you take Jillian's words to heart."

The figure twisted around to see Cora and spoke in the same older male voice.

"What is the cost and the offer?"

"They can improve ATLAS exponentially. Malia and Que will work on that as soon as Nicole Kanter is released, assuming she's still in your custody."

"She is not, but I can return Tae."

The senator mentioned the switch far too casually for my tastes, but I kept quiet 'cause I knew Cora had taken over the negotiations.

"You'll return all of them if you want this deal," said Cora. "The complete release of everyone threatened to control these children is not negotiable, nor is their personal freedom. That is part of the cost."

"How will I ensure compliance?"

"You don't need to." Impatience hardened Cora's tone. "As Jillian explained, the goals are compatible."

"The world is becoming more dangerous," said Senator Foster. "These Gifts may be our salvation. I want the ability to create more people like them."

"I doubt they're going to give you that ability." Cora spoke carefully like she expected the words might make him angry. "However, Nadia has promised their aid with the nanomachine project if you agree to her terms. That should be an adequate compromise."

The tiny figure shook its head.

"Not good enough."

"Why not?" To my surprise, the question came from Senator Santelli. "The program has the potential to outperform the children anyway."

"The materials to make such machines will always be limited," explained Senator Foster. "Creating people with the innate ability to do what those machines can do would be far superior."

"It's also not an option," said Cora softly. "That part of the research is gone."

Nadia spoke directly to me.

It is not quite gone yet, but we have put the plan into motion. The samples related to our project have been destroyed, and the notes will soon follow. Jillian, please be prepared to intervene should either senator react poorly to that revelation.

Chapter 34: Conspiracy

ITEM 274: Danielle's 83rd letter
Item Source: Danielle Matheson

Dear Dr. S.,

I missed lunch because I still felt really crummy. Not sure the others—besides the boys—ate much of the sandwich offerings either. Guess the whole captivity thing is rough on one's appetite unless you have the innocence of youth on your side. If I can judge by the chatter, Michio might have eaten one and a half sandwiches.

Dr. P. and Dr. C. insisted I keep hydrated, so I let Mrs. Davidson pour water down my throat at regular intervals. I worried what would happen when that water ran through me, but the intense fever I ran prevented the need.

By mid-afternoon, I started feeling human again. The first sign of improvement manifested as the ability to keep my eyes open for more than thirty seconds without feeling nauseous or getting a headache. Next, Mrs. Davidson's worried expression lessened in intensity. She still checked my forehead every two minutes for the next half-hour, but eventually, the timing lengthened to five minutes, then ten minutes. Finally, she only checked occasionally.

I'm glad your fever has broken. Are you well enough to help us?

A portrait-style image of Naidine formed in my head.

Do I have a choice?

You—

Don't mind me. I get grumpy when I don't feel great. Of course, I'll help. What do you need? And does it require standing? That might be a dealbreaker if you want this done now.

I need you to gather the necklaces from my mother and Dr. Carnasis and give them to Aiden or Michio. Either one will know what to do with them.

She left before I could ask any clarifying questions. I didn't have any, but the option to ask them would have been nice.

I almost despaired until I remembered Dr. C. had already given Aiden her necklace. I didn't know if he still had it, but the precedent had been set. Come to think of it, that may have been the primary reason for the exercise, but I had no way to verify the hunch.

Deciding to start right away, I asked Mrs. Davidson to help me sit up. She protested a little, but I finally convinced her without spilling the beans on my new mission. The actual getting up piece was easy. Staying upright proved to be the tougher battle.

"Would you like some water?" asked Mrs. Davidson.

"No thanks, but I am sort of hungry." As soon as the words left my mouth, my stomach concurred.

The win was two-fold. It earned a small smile from Mrs. Davidson and gave her a mission to concentrate on. I only half-listened to the conversation she had with the soldier standing outside our cell, but he wasn't too keen on the idea. She reminded him that Mulligan wanted me in tip-top shape as soon as possible and implied he would look good if he could get me to that point. I mentally checked out of the conversation around then, but I think it took a few rounds of convincing various people that taking good care of me was in everybody's interest.

My mental energies went into planning out my mission. If Mulligan wanted me to practice controlling the nanomachines, perhaps he'd agree to let me train with Dr. C. I also needed him to allow Dr. P. out to play, but by her own admission, she had nothing to do with nanomachines. She did sort of volunteer her services as a control, but the idea of holding her to that made me feel like a coward and a lousy human being.

My food came before I could choose a gameplan, so I took a mental break and let Mrs. Davidson spoon some chicken soup into me. At first, I felt silly, but since the act of sitting upright took some effort, I submitted to the pampering. The soup tasted deliciously salty, but I could only eat about half before my body decided more would be rejected violently.

Reading me perfectly, Mrs. D. quickly set the soup aside and helped me back to a prone position. From here on, you'll notice there's a switch in how I think about Mrs. D. Tending to sick people—and being tended to—is quite the bonding experience.

I needed a short nap to recover from the feeding exercise, but before taking my nap, I extracted a promise from Mrs. D. to wake me in an hour.

The nap lasted only about twenty minutes, but I stayed flat because nobody disturbed me and it gave me some quality thinking time. I started with the same lines of thoughts as before and ran into the same main problem. I needed an excuse to see Dr. P. up close and personal if I was to have a hope of getting her necklace. My brain chased the problem around in circles until I finally had a breakthrough. Ultimately, both necklaces needed to get to one of the boys, but that didn't mean I had to be directly involved. The control freak in me cringed at that point. I also realized trying to do everything myself was dumb.

Grand plan step one became enlist more help.

Despite feeling somewhat better, I weakly waved Mrs. D. over and whispered my mission to her. She made a show of helping me sit up and propping a pillow behind me to cover for some of the whispering. I didn't have time to explain why I needed to get the necklace to Aiden or Michio, but she didn't press for an explanation. I think her time with Malia has trained her to accept oddball requests without question.

Mrs. D.'s first cause had been getting me food. Her next objective became entertainment for the boys. Our guard wasn't moved much by the initial plea, but Dr. P., Dr. C., and the boys soon adopted the battle cry as well. I think we wore the poor fellow out. He eventually agreed to talk to his superiors. Given the inefficiencies of the army when it comes to taking responsibility for a decision, that took a while, but word eventually trickled down that we'd be granted a short walk for exercise.

I nearly groaned aloud.

Mrs. D. must have read the frustration in my expression.

"It would be better for everybody to be able to socialize. Isn't there a room where we can watch the boys play together?"

The counterproposal took its sweet time about trickling through the system. I think Mulligan suspected an ulterior motive because he accepted the plan but decided to oversee the social session and brought twenty buddies along for the experience.

I had to prove I could stand without aid to earn my spot on the excursion. I thought that might be a problem, but the long delays gave my body time to adjust to the idea of functioning again. Unfortunately for me, the symptoms didn't vanish as quickly as they came on, but slowly, the aches dulled, the fever died down, and moving became less of a chore.

Mrs. D. hovered in case she needed to catch me, but I held my own on the walk to the elevator and then down a few hallways to the gym they'd cleared out for us.

The boys squealed with delight and sprinted to the giant exercise balls. Michio took a flying leap at the nearest one and belly flopped onto the top. I thought he'd break his skinny neck, but instead, he ended up surfing across three of the exercise balls before tumbling off. It looked like fun, but I didn't think my body would greet the experience with as much enthusiasm.

Aiden tackled a different body-sized ball and rolled head-over-heels with it a few times before smacking into a wall and falling off. Only his bouts of uncontrollable laughter kept me from rushing over to check the kid for injuries.

Mrs. B. and Mrs. D. wandered over to keep an eye on the boys while I went to Dr. C. and Dr. P. Since we were well-within earshot of Mulligan, I took some time to plan my approach. I couldn't outright ask for their necklaces without looking crazy-shady.

Dr. C. solved the problem.

"Let's take a walk. We might not get the chance to do so later."

Mulligan ordered a soldier to walk with us, but after a few

annoyed glances from Dr. P., the man dropped back a pace. Not satisfied with the space, Dr. P. fell a step behind us. The move forced the soldier to split his attention. Still not satisfied, Dr. P. struck up a conversation with the man. Her masterful handling of the soldier gave Dr. C. and I the chance to chat in relative peace.

Dr. C. didn't waste any time diving into the heart of the matter.

"Do you have a plan?"

"Nadia wants me to get your necklace and Dr. Paladon's to Aiden or Michio. She didn't tell me why." I left the statement hanging, hoping Dr. C. would take that as an invitation to fill in the gaps.

She didn't take the bait right away. We finished our current circuit of the room and started around again. I tried not to rush my companion, but my impatience made me keep stealing glances at her. Dr. C.'s expression changed from neutral to thoughtful to sad and finally, accepting.

"Why would Nadia say that?" I asked, ditching subtlety.

"To destroy the pendants."

I strained my ears trying to hear Dr. C's response. My expression must have fired a follow up why because she quietly elaborated.

"It's not about the necklaces. This is an information war. When we formed Votive, Cora commissioned six pendants, one for each of us. Nadia can explain the design symbolism later, but long story short, they contain a microchip that can decrypt some of the information stored within Dustin. Destroying them will make it impossible to access some of the data."

"How does that help us out of this rather large mess?" I consciously delivered the question slowly because that was the only way to control the volume.

"Guess that depends on which information she wants to render useless. Knowing Nadia, it's probably the notes related to the most controversial projects, like Minders. It's the most sought-after data because it's the most dangerous."

"If you think it's dangerous, why haven't you destroyed it before now?" I wondered, trying to distract myself from delving deeper into what exactly makes Minders dangerous. I love Nadia, but the thought of a world filled with people like her hurt my head. They could topple entire governments, sow chaos and mistrust, and mess with the global stock markets without breaking a sweat.

"Because I learned about the plan a few seconds before I told you." The hint of a sympathetic grin formed, and Dr. C. added, "Time with Nadia makes such surprises a regular occurrence."

Even as I agreed with her on that last point, my logical brain choked on the scenario being presented.

"Didn't the pendant presentation pre-date Nadia's existence?"

"It did." Dr. C. didn't seem disturbed by the timeline issue. "I suspect when Cora gave them to us, there was only sentimental and symbolic meaning in them. Dean has a habit of giving Nadia tasks like increasing security on something. My guess is the encryption plan came about later, once Dean realized what kinds of people wanted his research and why they wanted it."

"Wouldn't Nadia remember something like that?" The question came out low and fast as incredulity battled caution. "It seems like a pretty big point to forget."

"She wouldn't remember if one of the subsequent nanomachine injections suppressed the memory," answered Dr. C.

"They can do that?" I didn't bother masking the horror that socked me in the gut.

"In Nadia, yes. That's probably how some of her Gifts work in terms of storing and accessing information, but since I didn't work on that design, I'm only guessing." Dr. C.'s words flowed faster as she mentally connected the dots. "I do know she received regular injections of nanomachines in the guise of controlling a genetic disorder she never had. Jillian helped her uncover the deception when she was trying to break Nadia out of the coma."

I didn't respond right away because I needed a moment to absorb the idea that Nadia could be tricked on such a massive level. It also struck me as sad. These children—all of them—should be behaving as carefree as Aiden and Michio, not concerned about keeping world-changing secrets. The boys are currently darting around the room screaming at random. I futilely imagined Jillian and Varick doing the same. Try as I might, I couldn't picture Nadia ever acting with reckless abandon. That made me sadder.

"Will it help save them?" The heaviness of despair weighed the question down.

"I'm not sure this is about saving them," Dr. C. said softly. "It might just be about saving the world from a future where Gifts like theirs are used and abused. Whatever the motive, we need to tell Jessie."

The plan smacked of something Nadia would set in motion. Determination crystalized in my chest. I'd help her carry out the mad scheme, but then, somehow, I would free them. They deserved that much.

Doc C. and I took a few more laps in relative silence before I drew even with Dr. P. and our guard escort. We chatted about the boys' antics for a few minutes. Then, Dr. P. sped up enough to draw even with Dr. C. I busied myself distracting the guard, so I didn't catch their conversation. I assumed Dr. C. was recounting some of our discussion.

That's where things stand now. We're on the precipice of doing something drastic, but the boys still need to be brought into the folds of our conspiracy.

You might think I'm delusional for believing I can help people with superpowers, but I see myself as a guardian for Jillian and her siblings.

The Fired-Up One,
Danielle Matheson.

Chapter 35:
Magic Bullet Things

ITEM 275: Jillian's 132nd post-kidnapping journal entry
Item Source: Jillian Blairington
You also need to destroy the pendant on Cora's necklace.

I wanted to question Nadia about her two strange orders, but I could tell she'd already left. There ain't much I can do to prepare my Gift, so I watched Senator Santelli carefully and thought about ways to destroy a necklace. I wanted to ask Cora for ideas and permission, but that sounded like a conversation best had in private. My sister would probably warn her, but we weren't exactly in a great place to melt something made of metal.

Maybe a microwave would work. Momma and Nana always said to never put metal in a microwave 'cause it could be dangerous. My Old Daddy and I did it once anyway. We microwaved a ball of aluminum foil. That was the end of that microwave and the beginning of a very long lecture from Momma, but it was rather exciting. On the other hand, I accidentally microwaved a fork once and nothing happened. I dunno what metals went into making the pendant. It looked gold, but that didn't mean it was only gold.

My next thought was to crush it, but the cell we were in didn't have anything that capable of crushing something. Stepping on the necklace would do a whole lot of nothing.

"It's not gone."

Senator Foster's declaration pulled me out of my thoughts

on destroying Cora's pendant.

"I have almost every scientist involved from the very beginning, and I can get the remaining two if necessary." The torrent of words sounded odd 'cause they came from the tiny figure of ATLAS. "If samples are the issue, we'll gather more. If will is the issue, we'll find the weakness and exploit it. Starting from scratch won't be a problem with the wonder kids' knowledge accelerating the work."

"You're not listening," said Cora. "Dustin may try to appease you, but Nadia will not."

Senator Santelli shifted uncomfortably.

"We should cut our losses and work with them."

"I'm not having my program exist on scraps handed out on whims!" If he'd been standing before us, spit woulda sprayed us. "They'll give us the information, or we'll take it."

The aimless threat didn't hit either Cora or me.

Senator Foster musta sensed our lack of concern. The machine shifted around to address Senator Santelli.

"V, keep them in isolation. The girl is dangerous. Give her something to keep her awake. That should block her ability to work. Hurt the woman if you must but not permanently."

The lady senator looked uncertain about that order, but reluctantly, she nodded.

That's about as far as I let her get.

Before she could reach for something to call soldiers for help, I put myself in a working sleep and knocked her out. I pulled the scene into my head in time to see her legs fold underneath her. She kind of sat down before falling onto her left side.

An alarm started blaring and four men rushed in.

I knocked 'em out too, along with another three about to enter.

The move hurt my head, but I pushed the pain back and prepared to continue defending us.

Cora rushed over to my cot, sat down, and picked up one of my hands.

"Jillian, stop. You'll hurt yourself."

Her plea distracted me enough to miss two more soldiers entering the room. They had to hop over the ones I'd already dealt with. One reached the door to our cell and stuck a key in the lock. I dropped him into a deep sleep before he could finish his task. The man with him caught him and eased him down. He was luckier than most 'cause he didn't have far to fall when I made him sleep.

Even with the preparation Nadia, Malia, and I had done, I could tell I neared some kind of limit.

Eight more soldiers entered and waded through their companions to get to us. I handled four before the pain woke me.

Tears moved freely down Cora's face. Seeing that I was awake, she pulled me into a hug.

The four soldiers I'd failed to knock out fanned out in front of my cot. At first, they pointed guns at us, but they soon realized that was dumb 'cause they weren't supposed to kill us. Tucking their weapons away, they pulled us apart.

Cora didn't fight as two soldiers forced her to kneel and handcuffed her wrists behind her back.

I wanted to scream or fight, but the head pain made me concentrate on my breathing. Tears blurred my vision until I used my Gift to ease into a light sleep. I watched horrified as the people I'd dropped all over the room stirred.

Senator Santelli groaned and sat up. Her expression read furious. A long dart with a hot pink end struck her in the upper part of her right arm. She stayed conscious long enough to glare at the newcomers, then slumped to the ground again.

By the time I paid attention to the other people in the room, they each had hot pink tranquilizer darts sticking out from somewhere on their bodies. Following the trail of wreckage led to my brother, Varick, my Old Daddy, and a smiling young man I didn't know. The trio wielded strange rifles that had long, blocky cartridges sticking out of sides, making the guns look a little like unbalanced crossbows.

Varick handed the young man his bulky rifle, drew a handgun, and shot each of the cameras watching over the cell. Then, he turned the gun on the figure of ATLAS.

"Pardon the interruption, but I'll be taking my sister back now. Cora too." He then shot the small black object. Instead of a bullet, this time, the gun spat a glob of something I couldn't identify.

The stuff landed on the machine portraying ATLAS and coated the entire top of the figure. A keening electronic noise started then cut off abruptly. The top section turned an ashy gray color and crumbled to dust.

Varick beat the lock with a simple touch. He did the same for my handcuffs.

My Old Daddy almost knocked Varick over at that point. After removing the cuffs, my Old Daddy tossed 'em to the cot's far corner. Then, he sat next to me, pulled me close, kissed my hair, and held me.

"You'll be all right, baby, but we've got more to do. Come on back to us."

I wanted to wake myself, but I ain't Malia and didn't have her with me. Waking people without her ability to shock 'em with cold made it tough. Usually, I can wake myself just fine, but I'd also exhausted my Gift to a dangerous point.

"What's wrong with her?" My Old Daddy looked to Varick for an answer.

"She's knackered." Varick finished removing Cora's cuffs and helped her sit on the other cot. "Did you see all the blokes she knocked out before we got here? That's a lot of work."

"Speaking of the numerous blokes lying about, we should be on our way before they regain the ability to walk, talk, and shoot." The guy I didn't know had stayed near Senator Santelli. He kept his tone light, but even I could read his concern. "Should we take V with us?"

"Won't that wind her up?" asked Varick.

"Pretty sure shooting her accomplished that already." The young man shrugged. "I think I'm off her Christmas card list this year, but it's okay because she always gets ugly cards anyway."

"Is there a chance she'd take our side over your father's?"

"Not much of one," said Cora, fielding Varick's question. "She has tied her career very closely to Senator Foster's success. That will be difficult for her to break away from."

"If we leave her, she'll be free to plot evils in a few hours. If we take her, she'll be a thorn in my side in a few hours." The young man gave an exaggerated shrug. "I don't see a win here."

Varick had spent the exchange watching the lady senator.

"Let's take her with us. Some time with my sisters might help change her loyalties." His grin had a slightly wicked quality. "At the very least, they'll probably drive her bloody mad."

With the matter settled, the group prepared to move out but decided to wake me first. My Old Daddy coulda carried me, Cora could walk on her own, and the new guy could carry the lady senator, but an arrangement like that would leave all the guard duty to Varick. Rubbing my wrists just made 'em raw. Gently slapping my cheeks and pinching my arms both failed too. Finally, Varick made my Old Daddy lay me out on the cot and step back.

When Varick drew his gun, I thought he was gonna shoot me.

Instead, he took out the magazine holding the bullets and ejected 'em one by one, letting most fall to the floor. It reminded me of the time Nadia scolded him for littering the lab floor with bullets. I almost missed the part where Varick popped the clip back into place and aimed the gun at the cot holding me.

Cora looked stunned but not worried. That encouraged me.

Varick fired.

The bullet was another globby thing that landed on the mattress somewhere near my right side.

An intense feeling of cold shot through me. It felt like lying on a giant ice cube. Two seconds later, the cot shuddered and collapsed beneath my weight. I landed on the floor with a thud that jarred me awake. The cloud of dust that raised made me choke and covered me in a chalky substance.

I scowled at Varick and got a cheeky grin in return. Nadia supplied that word when I let her review the scene later.

"Rise and shine, sleepyhead." Varick held a hand out to help me up.

If we didn't have more important things like get back to the others, I mighta let him struggle to get me upright. Given the short time, I gave him one of my finest Evil Eyes and accepted his help.

Once I was up, Varick batted at my pants to dislodge some of the dust. Catching my half-curious, half-annoyed look, he explained.

"It's a modified chemical based on liquid nitrogen. When it hits certain substances, it turns them cold and brittle. Sorry about the mess. You're a right heavy sleeper."

I grunted to let him know I'd heard him before systematically considering my physical condition. Aside from general soreness and a dull headache, my body seemed functional. Near the end of my inventory, I stiffened.

"Do you have any more of those magic bullet things?"

"One. Why?"

I held my hand out in a gimme gesture.

Varick hesitated but handed over the gun.

"What would you like destroyed?"

"Cora's necklace." I drew a breath for a long-winded explanation, but Cora readily handed over the necklace. I explained Nadia's instruction anyway to satisfy their unspoken curiosity.

I thought there'd be a big to-do, but I placed the necklace on the ground near the former ATLAS thing, lined up the shot, took it, and hit my target. The blob settled over the pendant, turning it from gold to ashy gray. Varick nudged it with his right boot, and the pendant broke into dozens of frozen little shards.

I dunno about the others, but I was emotionally rung out by the whole affair.

Chapter 36:
Done

ITEM 276: Danielle's 84th letter
Item Source: Danielle Matheson

Dear Dr. S.,

Once reasonably certain Dr. P., Dr. C., and I were on the same page concerning the necklaces, the next goal became getting the boys to do their part. If we could count on Nadia to bring them up to speed, the task would have been extremely easy, but unfortunately, at the time, we had no clue about the status of Nadia, Malia, or Dustin.

There was also no safe way to update Mrs. B. and Mrs. D. I felt bad about that because both women looked extremely worried. Even knowing a plan was in the works might have brought them some comfort.

"We need to hurry."

Dr. C.'s whispered statement made me pay more attention to our surroundings.

A soldier had rushed in clutching a phone. He scanned the room for Mulligan and headed directly for him.

Panic stabbed me in the chest.

"Go for Aiden." Dr. P. tossed the order at Dr. C. and me and sprinted for Michio.

I couldn't tell if she meant to include me in the instruction or not, but my body reacted to the urgency in her voice. The soldier with us overheard and reached for Dr. C.'s arm. I sidestepped directly into his arm to throw off his aim, then dashed forward to stay out of reach.

The move gave Dr. C. an extra second to get to Aiden. For the last few minutes, he'd been ramming his body into another of the exercise balls. Dr. C. caught Aiden as his body flew back from another headlong flight. He screeched and wriggled to be set free, but Dr. C. had enough sense to immobilize his legs. Dropping low, she leaned close and whispered to the boy.

A soldier approached them, but I stepped in his way.

Intent on passing, the man pivoted around me and shoved hard, sending me toward some of his colleagues.

I managed to halt myself before I fell straight into their arms, but the state of unbalance also effectively left me flatfooted.

One guy latched onto my right arm, used it to spin me around, and wrenched the poor arm up behind my back. In another context, it might have been an exciting dance move. Instead, I got shooting pain in my shoulder. A hand clamped down hard on my left shoulder close to my neck. The influx of pain weakened my knees, making it child's play for the guy to force me to kneel.

I tried to stand, but the soldier put a stop to that by tugging the arm up and back.

I'd like to say I stoically bore the pain, but I didn't. I yelped.

The pain spiked then disappeared as the man let go. My arm flopped to my side, still tingling. Pitching forward, I caught myself with both hands. The abused shoulder complained but held. As my head cleared, I remembered the others and wrenched my head up to check on them.

Before I could get my bearings, Mrs. B. and Mrs. D. landed to my left and right, respectively. Danger sense flooded me with mind-numbing fear. I couldn't see behind me, but I could practically feel the guns pointed in our direction.

It felt like the universe had ground to a halt, but nothing could be further from the truth.

Because I was facing them, I spotted Dr. C. and Aiden first. Their position as the focal point of four guns wielded by soldiers clarified the situation behind me. The sight burned into my brain.

If somebody had photographed it, they'd likely win a Pulitzer for capturing the perfect balance of despair, determination, and pure love.

Aiden lay on the ground. Dr. C. knelt by his right side with her left hand cradling his head and her right hand positioned on the other side of his body, down by his stomach. The position of her head and shoulders placed most of her body between the boy and the guns. It also brought the pendant of her necklace directly above Aiden's chest, within easy reach. When my mind took its snapshot of the scene, the boy's fingers barely brushed the pendant.

My breath hitched and held as if even the slightest release would break the spell holding the bullets at bay.

Eventually, ingrained need forced me to breathe again.

My attention darted to the last standoff.

Dr. P. had one soldier hovering nearby. His gun was inches from her head. Like the rest of us, she was on her knees, but Michio's position differed. He stood behind Dr. P. with his left arm encircling her neck, like someone preparing for a piggyback ride. His other hand gripped her necklace.

Mulligan's glare moved from scene to scene. His wild eyes shouted his suspicions.

"Grab the boys."

Dr. C.'s pendant started glowing red like someone had thrown it into a furnace.

I looked to Dr. P. to see if hers would also glow. As I watched, the chain disintegrated. One second, Michio clutched the delicate necklace, and the next instant, it was gone. I couldn't see the pendant from my current angle, but I was almost certain there wouldn't be one to find. Michio stepped back and clapped. Gold dust puffed out from between his hands and fluttered to the ground.

A soldier swooped in and picked Michio up.

Dr. P. started to rise, but the guy with her swung his gun like a club. She turned her head swiftly but still caught some of the weapon's tail end across her forehead. The blow knocked her down but didn't kill her spirit. That much was apparent by the way she sat up and immediately looked for Michio, even while pressing a hand over the head wound.

For his part, Michio fought like a grease-covered octopus.

His flailing arms and legs made it seem like he had double the amount of appendages. One lucky swing clouted his captor on the chin. The guy grunted and tightened his grip. Michio unleashed an impressive screech that made the soldier cringe.

"It's all right. Put him down," said Mulligan.

The soldier all but chucked Michio in Dr. P.'s direction.

Landing on his feet, the boy scrambled to Dr. P. and plopped down beside her. Crossing her legs, Dr. P. drew Michio onto her lap, and embraced him.

My knees ached and a burning sensation engulfed my legs, but the adrenaline rush shrank both concerns down to nuisance status.

Though I feared what I would see, I forced myself to look to Dr. C. and Aiden again.

To my surprise, Doc C. still wore a necklace, but the pendant had melted into a blob that resembled a teardrop more than its previous design. Leaning down, she kissed Aiden's cheek and cupped his chin with her right hand. Then, she raised her arms in the universal sign of surrender and stood up.

Two soldiers wasted no time in securing her hands behind her back with a long zip tie and pulling her away from Aiden. She didn't speak until another guy approached Aiden.

"It's done and can't be undone."

"What's done?" The soldier standing near Aiden voiced the question, but it was repeated in nearly everybody's expression.

"The pendants on our necklaces had an encryption key that would have made sense of information related to the research data concerning these children. Without them, the notes will remain sealed." The finality in her tone added the word *forever*.

Mulligan shook like a kettle about to explode. I fully expected his next words to be a kill order against everybody.

Nadia chose that moment to make her grand entrance. Her ghostly figure appeared near Dr. P. and Michio. She wore the same clothes she'd had on before, which consisted of blue jeans and a black turtleneck that emphasized her fair hair. The blue-white light that surrounded her translucent figure gave her an other-worldly air.

Michio perked up and waved wildly.

"Hi, Nadia!"

"Hello, Michio." Nadia returned the kid's wave before addressing Mulligan. "Please allow the captives to stand. They are uncomfortable."

Mulligan didn't appear overly moved by the request, but he didn't protest as the men surrounding us helped Mrs. B., Mrs. D., and me to our feet. They took advantage of the moment to apply zip ties, but my legs were grateful for the change anyway.

"You're not even supposed to be awake right now," Mulligan noted. "How did you manage that?"

"The question you really want answered concerns what happens next." The figure of Nadia folded her hands serenely in front of her body. "If we reach favorable terms, my siblings and I will lend what aid we can with the nanotechnology research begun by our creators."

"Why should I negotiate? I have your mother here." Mulligan waved casually at Dr. P. who still held Michio. "I don't want to hurt her. I'd like to work with her, but I will do what is necessary, even if that means the world loses one of the finest biochemists it's ever known."

Nadia didn't flinch at the threat, nor did she miss a beat.

"You should negotiate because we have recently dealt with Senator Foster and Senator Santelli." She let the announcement stand on its own for a two-count before continuing, "That means there's a power vacuum waiting to be filled."

If Mulligan's expression could be trusted, the offer genuinely intrigued him.

You want to give this guy more power?

Nadia's plans could never be accused of being predictable or dull, but this one sounded even barmier than usual, as Varick would say.

"What are you asking for, besides the obvious?" Mulligan folded his arms as he waited for Nadia's answer.

"Your resignation."

The surprising request resulted in three seconds of silence.

"How does this benefit me?" Mulligan's puzzlement rang true.

"You'd get to retire wealthy with full knowledge that you

succeeded in leaving a lasting scientific legacy—"

"That I don't even get to be a part of," Mulligan finished. "No deal. I'm not in this for the money. I want to see the impossible become possible. I want to …." The man trailed off like a windup toy that ran out of steam. His head bobbed left, then right. His eyes closed, and he collapsed.

The soldiers tightened their grips on their guns and eyed each other like the confused guards standing over the melted corpse of the Wicked Witch of the West.

"Thank you, Jillian. Please, stand by." Nadia executed a slow circle that commanded everybody's attention. "I understand change can be uncomfortable, but it does not have to be. Your goals and ours concerning the defense of this country are aligned."

"What are you saying?" asked a brave soldier.

"The leaders who overstepped their bounds by large margins have been—or soon will be—replaced." Gravity slowed Nadia's words to a normal pace. "Everybody will be given the chance to transfer to a conventional posting or accept a new assignment within the Guardians, Votive, Katharos, or whatever organization you already agreed to serve."

I mentally tripped over the third name. If Nadia had more to say right then, I completely missed it.

Katharos. Guardians. They're the same?

Naidine answered my frantic question.

Yes. They are separate sides of the same entity. I can explain more later if you wish, but there are many important details to finalize. You should visit your mother. Ethan is watching over her in one of the hotel rooms.

That announcement nearly stopped my heart.

He's there for her protection. I promise.

It better be one heck of a compelling explanation.

It's just as well Naidine didn't have time to elaborate. I doubt I could have processed more information in the moment.

When Dr. P. set Michio loose, he sprinted to Mrs. B. and tackled her with a huge hug. The beautiful sight made me ache for my own family reunion.

The Mentally, Physically, and Emotionally Drained One,
Danielle Matheson.

Chapter 37: Ceremony

ITEM 277: Jillian's 133rd post-kidnapping journal entry
Item Source: Jillian Blairington

I didn't learn the new guy's name until we were tucked up safe in a borrowed SUV headed back to the Skye High Hotel to settle things with Dr. Mulligan and free the rest of our friends and family.

Agent Paul Rydell had about as messy a family history as the rest of us. He and Senator Veronica Santelli are half-siblings, sharing the same momma. Their momma had lost her first husband to cancer when Veronica was still a baby and remarried Senator Orion Foster just before the girl turned four. A year later, they'd welcomed a happy new baby called Paul. The family had deep pockets and old ties to the halls of power in Texas, but Paul didn't wanna walk in his daddy's shadow. He'd changed his name and joined the army.

Nadia reached out and recruited Paul early in his career. She helped him get the right promotions and smoothed much out with his family. I'm not sure if either of them intended for him to be a double agent of sorts, but that's kinda how it stands right now. Senator Foster has overseen a lot of programs through the years. He's good at what he does, but he's also made a big mistake in trying to control us this way. If we can't talk sense into him, we're gonna have to replace him. Not sure what'll be left in terms of functioning programs when this mess gets sorted. That's a headache for Nadia to handle later.

First, we gotta get back to our people. Then, we need to deal with Dr. Mulligan. Third, we would have to decide how best to protect the innocent people like Danielle's family, my other family, and Malia's second family. I asked who would deal with Senator Foster. Varick, Paul, and my Old Daddy were with us, so it couldn't be any of them. They wouldn't tell me who, but they did promise somebody would work on that problem.

I didn't appreciate the cryptic response, but I also didn't have the energy to fight 'em on it. I needed to rest in case I had to work when we confronted Dr. Mulligan.

We were still a few blocks away from the hotel when Nadia showed us what was happening. I dunno what the others saw, but my head filled with some mighty disturbing images. She musta drawn images from multiple people's heads 'cause the angles changed a few times.

Momma, Danielle, and Malia's new momma formed a line half-surrounded by soldiers. My Second Momma leaned over Aiden, trying to shield him from more soldiers. Nadia's momma knelt in front of Michio. Only one man stood near her, but his gun was very close to her head.

A projection of Nadia stood near Dr. Mulligan.

Jillian, the conversation with Dr. Mulligan is a diversion. Please pull him down to sleep. It would be better if we were in the same room together, but Malia and I will help as much as we can.

I did as asked. It took some time for me to locate Dr. Mulligan within the building, but it helped to have Momma and Danielle in the same room with him. I had left very strong marks on both of 'em. Figuring it more likely Nadia asked Danielle to do something, I pulled Momma into a light dozing state, just enough to activate the mark and use it like a homing beacon. After that, finding Dr. Mulligan within the room was very easy, especially with Nadia transferring images from the room directly to my head.

With Dr. Mulligan out of the way, Nadia convinced the soldiers to stand by and wait for new orders.

About this time, we reached the hotel. Agent Rydell zip tied his sister to the seat belt in case she woke up before we got the wider situation sorted. Fear gave me the energy to sprint after Varick and my Old Daddy as they tore through the halls in a hurry. The agent stayed behind me 'cause I was the only one unarmed.

I thought we'd end up where the hostages were being held, but instead, we burst into a small conference room where we found Nadia, Dustin, and Malia. The three guards in the room with 'em did not look happy. I think Malia's Gift held them in place. She did something similar back in the hospital where we fought cancer cells on behalf of Christy's momma.

Varick and my Old Daddy subdued the men and freed my siblings. Then, we went to the gym room holding nearly everybody else we loved. I expected we'd just bust in there like we did in collecting Nadia, Dustin, and Malia, but Varick made us wait.

Nadia and Malia scanned the room for trouble. They identified two people only pretending to accept the orders Nadia gave through her projection and marked 'em for me. I did my thing.

What followed was a beautiful, confusing mess of chaotic reunions.

I wanted to check on Danielle, but somebody had freed Momma. She intercepted me and squeezed me so hard it hurt. I woulda had to wait anyway 'cause Varick got to Danielle first, and they didn't stick around long. Nadia let me know they were going down to meet Danielle's Momma while Ethan fetched Dr. Devya.

When Momma finally let me go, I left her with Mrs. Davidson and went to see if Nadia needed any help.

Our hug was brief 'cause Nadia wanted me to get everybody up to the conference room where we'd been earlier in the day. I guess she coulda left that job to the soldiers, but she sent 'em after the food instead.

I didn't bother asking Nadia about her reasoning 'cause the chance of her explaining more was low. It seemed like busy work to me. Besides, if she took a fancy to the idea, Nadia coulda just blasted the announcement through everybody's head.

My first stop was Momma and Mrs. Davidson 'cause I figured they needed something to do. Next, I headed for my Second Momma and Dr. Paladon. They both nodded like they expected such an announcement. Aiden and Michio wrestled each other on the floor near 'em, so I counted the message delivered to 'em as well. I scanned the room for Dustin and his momma but couldn't find 'em.

They will meet Father and Ethan before joining us for the ceremony.

I sent Nadia the usual questions when one drops surprising information, but she didn't bother explaining further. Guess I coulda refused to help her till she explained, but that woulda frustrated me even more. Getting directions from Nadia, I led the way up to the conference room.

The soldiers had set up several long tables with food and put a few more rows of chairs in place. Memories of what happened before tried to intrude, but the festive atmosphere drove 'em away. Malia calmed the boys enough so Momma, Mrs. Davidson, and Maisha could get 'em to eat. I didn't need any prompting. The smell beckoned me to the table. After piling a plate with heaps of garlic chicken and spaghetti with alfredo sauce, I balanced a roll on top of it and looked around to see who to sit with.

Most of the mommas sat with the boys. Malia sat a short ways away from the others, and Dustin did the same but on the opposite side of the crowd. At first, I didn't know who I should talk to. Figuring I might need the backup anyway, I went to Malia and stood next to her for an awkward few seconds, waiting for her to notice me. Her plate of food was half empty. She sat very still and stared into nothing. Finally, I touched her arm. Malia stirred like someone slowly waking from a nap. When her eyes first fixed on me, they were blank, but they cleared before I could worry about her.

"Sorry, Jillian. I was just resting," said Malia.

"Most people lay down and close their eyes to rest." I sat down next to my sister and looked at the mound of food on the plate.

"It's not that kind of rest." Malia stopped talking but I could tell she had more to say.

Realizing that I'd forgotten to get a fork and knife, I set the food on the empty seat next to me and got up.

Malia held a complete utensil set out to me.

"I helped Michio gather food, but he decided to eat with your mother," she explained.

Somehow the act of standing reminded me of my original plan. I accepted the fork, knife, and spoon but didn't sit.

"Let's check on Dustin."

Malia agreed, gathered the remains of her meal, and followed me. She'd chosen mostly salad options, so her plate was light enough to carry with one hand. The bottle of water she carried reminded me to get a drink. Setting my food beside Dustin, I went to the drinks table to see what they offered. I didn't want to take the time to make some tea, so I grabbed a bottle of water and returned to Malia and Dustin. I thought they'd be mid-conversation, but I found 'em sitting in silence.

"What's wrong?" I handed the bottle of water over to Dustin 'cause he looked like he needed it more than I did. "Hold up. Be right back." I dashed off to get myself a replacement bottle of water. "Now start talking."

My stomach complained about being around so much good food and not getting any, so I ate while I studied Dustin and Malia. I'm used to Malia being crazy calm in almost any situation, but Dustin's usually as energetic as Michio and Aiden. Getting nothing from him, I glanced at Malia for help. She eventually explained.

"Dustin is mourning the partial loss of his Gift, and he has an important decision to make very soon."

"What decision?" I frowned 'cause I don't like being the last to know something.

Nadia came over and rested a hand on Dustin's right shoulder.

"He must decide the fate of our program."

Didn't think I could get more confused, but for once, Nadia's words clarified nothing.

"What's to decide?" I took a large bite of my neglected chicken to keep from shouting the other dozen questions crowding my head.

"The senate subcommittee in charge of our program has agreed to my two proposals, but the decision for which gets enacted rests here." Nadia set her other hand on Dustin's left shoulder.

I slowed my chewing, swallowed, then took a long drink of water to give any of 'em a chance to explain. I think Nadia wanted Dustin to enter the conversation. The waiting time woulda killed me if I didn't have anything to do, but fortunately, eating required some concentration.

"What are ya deciding?" I kept my eyes on Dustin to invite him to speak.

"Accepting a pendant," Dustin answered.

"Taking on great responsibility," said Malia at nearly the same moment.

Nadia launched into the wider explanation that tied their two answers together. I could dream about it to report every word she said, but since I'm not even allowed to write about some parts, I'll summarize.

Dustin's literal answer and Malia's figurative answer both held truth. The six original founders of Votive—that's the public name for the company that made us—each had a necklace with a gold pendant containing a modified version of the Rod of Asclepius. Before I could ask, Nadia showed me an image of one and said it was a symbol for the medical field. I wasn't sure how a snake wrapped around a stick could stand for medicine, so she also gave me a crash course in the mythology behind it.

The pendants' design differed in a few key places. The rod the snake wound around was a bolt of lightning, and the bottom end was a tiny globe. According to Nadia, the symbolism had to do with wielding science to change the world.

Just before Dr. Pauling left the company, Nadia and Dr. Carnasis added nanomachines to each pendant. These machines carried an encryption code to part of the database being stored in Dustin's head. They didn't remember that work 'cause Dr. Devya gave 'em something to push the memories way back out of reach.

The explanation worked for telling me why Nadia had wanted Cora's necklace destroyed. I hadn't noticed that my Second Momma and Dr. Paladon were also missing their necklaces until Nadia caught me up on stuff I'd missed 'cause it happened before we arrived. However, the explanation failed to tell me what weighed so heavily on Dustin. I was about to tell

Nadia this when she finally got to the point.

"The committee wants Dustin to accept one of three remaining pendants. It's more than a symbol now. It carries a key to the research. Bearing it will tie him to the data's fate but allow things to move forward relatively smoothly. Rejecting it will give him his freedom but slow the scientific endeavors significantly."

"Why don't you keep it?" I asked. Part of Nadia's long-winded explanation included some details on her proposal, but I can't say much more about it. I can say that in includes a clause that forces Nadia to stay in a black site or in secret labs under heavy guard until her eighteenth birthday. "You're going places with good security."

Malia placed a hand on my forearm and lent me enough peace to not dwell on that part.

Nadia gave me one of her signature sad smiles.

"The pendant would not be safe with me. Being a Minder comes with its own dangers. It would not do to have extra information fall into our enemies' hands."

I expected a drawn-out ceremony with speeches, but I almost missed it altogether.

While we chatted, Dustin picked his head up and nodded. I caught a glimpse of his eyes. They appeared crystal blue for a moment before flipping back to green. Standing, Dustin marched up to the platform, circled around to the right, and ascended the three steps.

Dr. Devya stood in the center holding a necklace. I couldn't see it well from my position, so Nadia sent me a mental picture of it. The pendant's design matched the others, but the gold chain was significantly thicker than Cora's chain had been. After shaking hands with Dustin, Dr. Devya lifted the chain up and lowered it onto Dustin's neck.

Dr. Paladon, Dr. Carnasis, and Cora stood slightly behind Dr. Devya. Dustin moved down the line and shook each of their hands. Cora pulled him into a long hug.

One brave soul started clapping and everybody joined in. A few cheers mixed in. Dustin looked nervous. Dr. Devya looked relieved.

"Does that mean, he accepts?" I asked, nodding to Dustin.

"It does indeed." The muted satisfaction in Nadia's tone set me at ease but a small sigh had the opposite effect.

My expression demanded she explain the sigh.

"There's more to do. Two more ceremonies must be arranged," Nadia explained.

"Varick and Danielle have accepted the other two necklaces," said Malia.

"Arrangements are being made, but the handoffs will have to wait until we can consult with Dr. Robinson and Senator Pauling. We can meet later tonight to debrief more, but let us spend time with our families." Nadia's smile turned sad again, and this time, I had no trouble interpreting why.

This would likely be the last time these people would ever be in the same place again. Soon, we'd each return to our lives or embark on new journeys.

Chapter 38:
Gift of Freedom

ITEM 278: Nadia's first letter to Danielle
Item Source: Danielle Matheson

Dear Danielle,

I have written many apologies in my life, but few weigh as heavily upon my heart and mind as this one. Should you wish to hear it again think *repeat Nadia's partial list of apologies and rather weighty request.*

Enclosed, you will find separate apologies for each of your family members. They have already been delivered and discussed at length with their respective recipients. You may read them or discard them at will.

Had I more of a Gift for foresight, I would have found a different way to deal with your family. I stumbled upon ATLAS's plan too late to stop it. The best I could do was give the assignment to Ethan and Paul Rydell. I regret that your encounter with him has soured your opinion of Paul. He is a good man who has dedicated himself to our cause. There was legitimate danger because not every man on the retrieval team believes in our cause.

I explained the situation to your sister as soon as possible but not soon enough to prevent trauma. With your parents' permission, I have begun meeting with Katie several nights a week. It will not be forever, but until formal meetings can be arranged with Dr. Sokolowsi, I am obligated to help her. The offer has been extended to the rest of your family, but Katie is the only one to accept thus far.

Be gentle with your mother. She was given a choice to continue her role as Ethan's captive or stay in hiding. She chose to see the event through. Knowing the peril facing you lay outside her control was not an easy burden to bear. Remind your parents that two paths stretch before them. I can pave the way for them to return to the lives they left, or I can create openings and opportunities for them to serve our cause.

Even once Varick, Tyra, Ethan, and Paul accomplished their immediate goals and freed important captives, I let you continue believing your family faced grave danger. I could not let the truth be known or ATLAS would have informed Senator Foster and the danger would have become real again. Your pain, fear, and frustration sold the story to Dr. Mulligan and ATLAS.

For this and many other reasons, I owe you apologies. I have previously confessed that I planned the operation that brought you and Jillian into our fold. Father wanted to take Mrs. Blairington, but I did not think it safe to let her come here while she carried Isaac. The drugs given to you during the initial kidnapping are not approved for use during pregnancy.

Here, I confess that the meddling went much deeper. I arranged for Madeline to take off the day you met Mr. Blairington. I also prompted him to go to the pharmacy where you worked. He had already bought enough vitamins, but I suppressed the memory because I knew you were not scheduled to work again for three days. He also required prompting to bring up babysitting so soon after meeting you.

I am sorry my plans have brought you much pain, but if I could do it again, I would make the same choices. You are resilient, resourceful, and caring beyond description.

Varick, Jillian, and I would not be complete without our interactions with you. We are better because of you.

Thank you for everything you have done for us. I ran hundreds of scenarios and statistically analyzed many plans. The outcome we received should not have been possible. You may not think your presence made a difference, but it did. Dr. Mulligan focused on Cora as the lynchpin, but you were our secret weapon.

In the darkest of moments, your steadfast support and love sustained us.

I do not make my job offer lightly. I shall prepare a more thorough document containing detailed explanations and sample lessons, but for now, the short version will have to suffice. I need a representative. This person will be a proxy, a decoy, a bodyguard, and more.

Once upon a time, Dr. Cliella and I fashioned Grace Carter so I could attend university classes as a small child. The nature of the contract arranged limits my movements until I come of age. It's not much different than life has always been. One day I will take risks for myself, but it was easier to set the senate subcommittee at ease by agreeing to the proposed conditions.

They fear to let my face be known. Minder Gifts are still much sought after, despite the many accomplishments by those possessing other genetic Gifts.

Will you become my representative?

I have no right to ask you to accept more danger on our behalf, yet you are a part of our family. Someday, I hope to call you sister in the formal sense, but for now, I owed you the asking.

You are uniquely suited to working with us. I cannot promise safety, but I dare say you would rarely be bored.

If you wish to finish college, I can rearrange the projects I intend to pursue. There will always be more people to help, and there will always be more work to do. The nature of the work will differ if I have a representative.

You also have my blessing to cut ties with us. Losing your companionship would hurt immensely, but we would survive. My commitment to you is not tied to your decision in these matters. You will always have my love and protection for as long as I am capable of giving such.

We love you, and we need you.

Michio and Aiden send enthusiastic greetings.

Your loving friend,

Nadia Elena Ayers

***

ITEM 279: Danielle's 85th letter
Item Source: Danielle Matheson

Dear Dr. S.,

Two soldiers keeled over like they were struck down by a vengeful deity. Then, Varick, Mr. Antel, Jillian, Nadia, Dustin, Malia, and Agent Rydell hit the room like a hurricane. Nadia must have warned the soldiers that would happen because they took that as the cue to leave in small groups. Their purposeful steps spoke of an unknown mission, but I didn't get long to ponder what it might be.

Varick came up behind me and touched the zip ties around my wrists. They snapped. Whirling, I launched myself at him. Pivoting with the momentum carried me in a half-circle around him. We laughed, cried, hugged hard and long, kissed even longer, and then, settled into a gentler embrace. I broke this one off when an errant thought of my mother struck me. Thankfully, Varick understood my panic and led me to right that massive wrong.

By the time we stood before the right door, I was a mess. My head and heart pounded. My breaths came too fast and weren't nearly as effective as they should be. I would have had a hard time twisting the door handle or taking one more step at that point. The effort to not cry sapped my strength.

Seeing or sensing my state of high emotion, Varick slipped around behind me, looped his arms over my stomach, and drew me back into his chest.

"Steady, Dani," he whispered. "She'll be free in a moment. You can do this. Touch the lock."

Lifting my hand, Varick brought it to hover over the door handle.

Something moved through my hand and entered the lock. I don't even know how I recognized the sensation. The light on the electronic lock flipped from red to green and a faint click confirmed that the lock had surrendered almost without a fight. The sensation of something moved back through my hand in reverse, leaving only the feeling of Varick's warm hand upon mine.

Together, we turned the handle and entered the room holding my mother.

At first, we saw nothing unusual. The room looked identical to the one I'd been given.

Varick slipped around me and stepped forward cautiously.

A defiant cry and a lampshade whipped around the corner as Varick reached it.

Ducking aside, he reached up, caught the body of the lamp, and wrenched it free from the attacker's grasp.

A fist followed.

Leaping forward, I caught the fist.

Varick tossed the lamp aside and caught the figure's other hand before she could spin and continue the fight.

She struggled briefly, then the fight drained out of her.

"Varick! Where's Dani?"

The worry in my mother's tone hit me hard, but I managed to speak.

"Here." The word wasn't loud, but it restored something in my mother.

Her tackle was almost as impressive as my greeting to Varick.

More laughing and crying ensued.

When our emotions settled enough to allow for conversation, Mom asked the key question.

"Is it over?"

"Soon," Varick promised. "Nadia is finalizing the deal with the government, and Dr. Robinson, Agent Landry, and a few others we trust should be rescuing your family now. I need to go witness something. You're welcome to come or wait here. After that, I will see you get home safely."

I don't think my mother was thrilled with the prospect of a delay, but the idea of being alone any longer appealed even less.

We arrived in the conference room in time to watch the project mantle pass to Dustin. I had no idea that's what it was at the time, but Naidine explained sometime during the flight back to New Jersey.

The purpose of that trip was four-fold. First, we met my siblings and father at the Newark airport and escorted them home. Second, we took Jillian's mother to reunite with Mr. Blairington and baby Isaac. Third, we met Dr. Robinson and Senator Jack Pauling and his family in an empty field near an abandoned farm house to conduct a small, private ceremony. Fourth, we checked on Benny Connelly since he has a Gift like Jillian's and Anastasia because she was meant to have Gifts like Nadia's.

When Nadia first asked if I would accept one of the pendants, my instinct was to turn her down flat. The offer came with a disconcerting number of warnings. Hysterical laughter might have filled my head for a while, but eventually, it occurred to me that if I turned it down, she would ask somebody else. The idea made me feel like a coward. That, of course, prompted a long conversation where she assured me I had every right to pass on the responsibility.

I'm not completely sold on the idea of working for Nadia, but as long as Varick's my boyfriend, I'm going to be involved with Jillian and her siblings. I might as well make myself as useful to them as possible.

Only Jillian, Malia, Mrs. Davidson, Mrs. Pauling, and Agent Landry witnessed the commissioning. Dr. Robinson placed her necklace around my neck, and Senator Pauling did the same for Varick. They gave short speeches that boiled down to *good luck, you're gonna need it*.

We only had a few minutes before we needed to get back to the airport to take Malia and Mrs. Davidson home, but I saw Dr. Robinson exchange a few words with Malia. I have no idea what they said, but I noted how much Malia looks like the lady. I think Dr. Robinson and Mrs. Davidson got to talk briefly too. I kind of want to know how that talk went down, but I'm suppressing the nosy side of me. Nadia probably witnessed it, and Jillian could get it from Malia in a dream. It finally sank home why people would work very hard to control these children. Their Gifts aren't just cool tricks. They're insanely invasive and powerful.

The flight to Erie International Airport passed pleasantly, Malia and Jillian had the seats in front of Varick and me. Mrs. B. sat by the window right next to Jillian. Mrs. Davidson had the seat across the aisle from Varick. I spent most of the flight holding Varick's hand and enjoying the novelty of being near him.

Somewhere in the skies over Pennsylvania, I chose the Gift I wanted. Nadia had explained the limitations of the nanomachines I had been injected with. They could mimic one aspect of a Gift, but likely not the whole of it. I picked one of Varick's Gifts.

Specifically, I wished for his ability to beat almost any lock.

There's always the hope that I'll never wear handcuffs, ropes, or zip ties again, but if it happens, I want the ability to break free on my own. Waiting for rescue is a very icky feeling that I would like to never repeat.

Nadia reminded me that training with such an ability would mean a lot of confinement. She knows my distaste for bindings all too well. I told her as long as she or Varick were with me during the training, I'd be okay with it. The idea of being less helpless should be enough to sustain me. The idea of being a better protector to my family is even more attractive.

I'm not naïve enough to think the ability to break out of chains will keep people from trying to put them on me. In fact, the challenge may drive people to get creative, but I refuse to let the idea of increased challenges become an invisible chain.

Dustin's drive to not be a captive drove him to be a captor. Yet, when the chips were down, he proved to be the bravest of them all by accepting his role in the succession of Devya's program. As the keeper of the notes, Dustin is uniquely qualified to keep the various projects on track. He and his siblings effectively removed the traces of their own origins to prevent the history of abuses from repeating. But there are still thousands of promising projects in their infancy that will benefit from his guidance. That's a lot to put on a pre-teen.

The Reflective One,
Danielle Matheson.

Chapter 39:
Blood Magic

ITEM 280: Jillian's 134th post-kidnapping journal entry
Item Source: Jillian Blairington

My next chance at real sleep happened on the trip from western Pennsylvania back to Las Vegas, Nevada. I guess I coulda slept on the way from Nevada to Newark, New Jersey or from the money sign state to Pennsylvania, but I wanted to spend the time with my sister. I sat in the middle between Momma and Malia on both of those flights.

If I had to pick a favorite seat, the middle one wouldn't be it. Dr. S. said that Momma needs to spend time with me to recover from stressful situations like me getting kidnapped. The middle seat let Momma fulfill that need and let me spend the hours chatting with Malia.

The flight from Pennsylvania back to Nevada wasn't that long, but we also had a few hours of downtime in the airport. Varick and Danielle watched over me while I worked.

Usually, Nadia helped me recap adventures and answered any burning questions, but this time, I found myself back in Varick's game *The Immortal Warrior III: The Path to Truth*. I'd left soon after learning I had earned the Life Giver achievement.

My avatar knelt on the hard stone floor next to the slumbering form of Captain Shamus McKenna. A sound at the dungeon door alerted me to somebody about to enter, so I took my mouse form and ducked into the small space behind Captain McKenna's back.

My hiding spot gave me a good look at the four men entering the hallway outside the line of foul metal cages. The captain and I were in the middle cage.

Two men wore clean Royal Guard uniforms and did their best to blend into the background.

The man in front wore fine, silk robes and a gaudy, gold crown studded with six blue gems.

I couldn't see the back of the crown from my current position, but my character remembered seeing that crown in very different context. The sight made my little mouse heart race faster. I'd last seen that crown on my father's head.

The fancy clothes man—my character's uncle—stared hard at the man who had entered the room a step behind him.

The guy wore dark robes with a cowl that covered his face. The outfit prevented me from recognizing him, but something about his presence felt very dark.

I instinctively flattened my thin mouse body to the ground even though the men shouldn't have been able to see me.

"Does he look like somebody who's been touching the Deep Magic?" demanded my uncle.

"I know what I felt, Lord Caravey." The dark-robed guy sounded miffed. "Magic was used here recently. Strong magic."

"What manner of magic?" Lord Caravey's tone snapped out impatiently.

"Hard to say." The man held out his right hand and bowed his head. The movement caused his cloak to shift and reveal an intricate design underneath. "The currents feel blue, white, and yellow. Healing … and perhaps transformation."

Even the partial view showed me that the man was a sorcerer and part of the Sandrak Order. Dread quickened my heartbeats to a painful point. Although the Order welcomed many kinds of magic users, its most infamous members practiced Blood Magic, which was among the most feared and powerful forms.

A memory cutscene carried my avatar back to a horrible day. I'd been in bird form high up in the ceiling rafters when a man wearing similar dark clothes walked in and struck my mother with a powerful Blood Magic spell that drained much of her life away. He'd given my father an ultimatum from my mother's brother, Uncle Orius Caravey: forfeit the crown or lose your wife. As soon as the man left, my father had summoned me down from the ceiling and had Captain McKenna lock me in the dungeons for my safety. That had been the beginning of the original *The Immortal Warrior* game.

"May I try something, my lord?" asked the sorcerer.

My uncle huffed but granted permission with a nod.

The sorcerer stretched out his arms with his right hand braced behind the left and spoke some words in a language I didn't recognize.

The blood inside my body suddenly felt uncomfortably hot. My mouse form flew back like a ball given a solid kick. I struck the wall and rolled out from behind Captain McKenna. My tiny body flipped end over end three painful times then transformed into my human form. I landed in the corner with my shoulders pressed painfully against stone on my right and metal bars on my left.

The slow smile that formed on my uncle's face spoke of surprise and delight with a broad streak of mocking.

"Princess Annabel, what a pleasant surprise. Your mother will be most pleased to hear you've been found safe and sound."

Surprise struck me on two levels.

One, I don't think I'd ever paid much attention to the character's name before. Sometimes, I get to create the characters myself, but for this one, I'd stepped into her life when I first worked in one of Varick's video game dreams. It's me. Well, sorta. Ashlynn Annabel Ayers was the first name I'd been given by Dr. Devya and Dr. Carnasis.

Two, Princess Annabel had spent almost three very long role-playing games thinking her mother had died in the first few seconds of the first game.

"She's alive!" The soft statement contained my disbelief and hope in almost equal measures.

"Of course, she's alive. I couldn't kill my little sister …" My uncle's grin had a cruel cast to it, "until I found you."

The sorcerer picked up the explanation.

"Doing so would release her remaining magic into you."

"But now that you're here, I can complete the ritual." Uncle Orius waved the Royal Guards forward. Pointing to the taller one, he said, "You, bind her and take her up to Olivia's room." His finger settled in the other guard's direction. "And you, assemble the others and fetch an enchanted collar." His cold, dark eyes slid my direction. "She's too weak to shift right now, but that will not last. I'll not lose her this close to my destiny." Finally, his attention moved to the sorcerer. "Go with them in case she recovers quicker than anticipated."

I looked at my mana bar and desperately wished it was full. The bar glowed brighter for a second, but the game refused to grant the wish.

Whatever the sorcerer did wiped out three quarters of my stamina bar. The Royal Guard assigned to me helped me up and guided me out of the cell.

"I want it done today!"

My uncle's impatient cry caused the guard to straighten. The man told to bind me fetched a length of rough rope and secured my wrists near my waist. At least he chose to leave my hands in front of my body. As we exited that portion of the dungeon, he beckoned two more soldiers and had them half-carry me through the halls. Gradually, the crude, rough stones of the dungeons gave way to nicer stones and wooden walls as we entered the palace proper.

Driven by my uncle's will, the guards hustled me up several familiar flights of stairs and down a long hallway to my mother's room. I remembered the way well. Before we could enter the room, the sorcerer halted our progress.

The guards obeyed, but even I could tell they wanted to be done with this job.

"We must wait for the collar to control her magic," said the sorcerer. "It's unlikely the queen will be well enough to willingly transfer her magic to the princess, but we should proceed with caution."

We didn't have to wait long.

A servant flanked by two guards sprinted down the hall carrying a large pillow with a fancy necklace on it.

When my uncle had said *collar*, I expected something simple and crude. This looked expensive.

Without much ceremony, the sorcerer picked up the necklace and moved to put it around my neck.

I retreated, but that only placed my back against the wall and made it easy for the soldiers to pin me in place. I felt the exact moment the clasp closed because it changed the necklace. Instead of a thin, gold chain, something thick and strong settled high on my neck and tightened to a point just shy of painful.

By the time we entered the room, quite the crowd had gathered around the large bed. A combination of candlelight and magic orbs placed in glass containers lent gentle light to the place. Royal Guards lined the perimeter. Two of 'em propped up Captain McKenna near the foot of the bed.

The guards with me brought me around to the bed's right side if you're standing at the foot. Spotting the lady on the bed, I ran the last few steps, but the guards stopped me before I could touch her. The new position let me see that the woman had features very similar to my Second Momma.

"That's close enough." My uncle spoke from the semi darkness across from me. "We wouldn't want any unauthorized magic transfers to happen."

When I looked toward the voice, I paid more attention to three figures lined up opposite me. Although outfitted in fancy fantasy dresses or robes, the ladies had familiar faces. Left to right from my point of view stood Cora, Dr. Paladon, and Dr. Robinson. My avatar recognized the women as The Gray Lady, The Alchemist, and The Warrior, respectively. I'd met 'em throughout my travels through Terabane. Each lady wore a ruby-red amulet that radiated dark magic as it suppressed their powers. Wrist bindings like mine magnified their helpless states, but their defiant expressions said they were not beaten yet.

My uncle circled the bed with slow purpose. He stopped behind me and laid heavy hands upon my shoulders.

My mother's eyes followed his progress, but she didn't move much. Her position spoke of an unnatural weariness.

"And now, dear sister, we shall return to our previous discussion about the magic you wield." Uncle Orius's pleasant and jovial words did not match his actions. His left arm pulled me close, and his right hand brought a shiny dagger mighty close to my neck. "Release it to your daughter, so I may claim the magic. Do it now, and the boy will live."

At my uncle's gesture, the men holding Captain McKenna changed positions. One man moved behind him, put one arm around his center, and used his other hand to draw his head back. The other man drew a short sword and pressed the tip to the captain's exposed neck.

"Refuse, and I will destroy them both."

My mother blinked slowly, like she needed the extra second to gather strength enough to speak.

"You misunderstand the magic."

Sonia's disembodied voice spoke.

"Chosen One, now is your moment to set things right. Act or perish."

I had no idea what she was talking about. With a blade at my throat and no way to access my magic, only the *perish* part seemed doable. I glanced in despair at my mana bar. It was still blue, which confused me 'cause I thought the collar prevented me from doing magic.

"The enchanted collar prevents you from transforming. It has no other ill effects," said Sonia.

Since nobody else reacted to the sound of her voice, I figured she was still speaking directly to me, but it wasn't a thought in my head like a conversation with the real Nadia.

Her words got me thinking almost as fast as my sister speaks. Not much time had passed in the game, but the few delays had allowed my mana bar to fill a little over the halfway mark. My red health bar held steady at full power, and my yellow stamina bar was almost full. Remembering a power I'd picked by accident when I was still learning the game, I tapped into my health bar and moved an equal measure of points from the red bar to the blue bar. When my blue bar hit full, I reached for the three women across from me, my mother, and Captain McKenna.

Heat sprang up in my chest and filled my body. It got uncomfortably hot under that enchanted collar, but I pressed on and bid the magic to do its thing. Being more specific is preferrable but wasn't really an option for me.

All five of my targets turned into mice. The necklaces bearing the amulets that prevented them from accessing their Gifts did not change with 'em. A second later, I let 'em return to normal form. Almost in sync, they closed their eyes and turned their right palms up.

Pushing me away, my uncle shrieked.

I spun in time to see him clutch at his crown. The blue gems popped off the crown and flew past me at dangerous speeds. I whirled again in time to see them land in the outstretched hands and return to their usual colors. The lady representing Cora held a brown gem that sometimes changed to yellow and then to pink. Dr. Paladon clutched a dark green jewel that sometimes turned purple. Dr. Robinson cradled a multicolored gem that sometimes turned a deep, smoky gray color. I knew my mother would have a crystal that was brilliant red, then a bold blue color and sometimes completely clear.

Nadia and her blasted gems again.

A girl's light laughter pulled me from the game.

"You are correct, Jillian. The magic gems represent each of us, and one truth is that our Gifts will always be stronger together. Congratulations on beating the game. Ask your questions, then return to the dream to enjoy the fruits of your labors and decide the fate of Terabane."

The jolt of the plane landing interrupted before I could take Nadia up on that offer, but that didn't bother me. The hard part was over. I knew that my return to that world would be triumphant.

Chapter 40:
My Boys Number Four

ITEM 281: Allison's ninth letter to Dr. Sokolowski
Item Source: Allison and Jeffrey Blairington

Dear Dr. S.,

I don't even know where to begin.

Jeffrey and I have had a long talk. He's here with me, so ya can take this as being from the both of us.

I've said it before, and I'll say it again. Jeffrey can't take back what was done, and I know it was done to save our son. The hurt is still there, raw as ever, but I honestly can't say I woulda done differently if placed in his shoes. Malia has offered to help us sort our feelings. Eventually, I may take her up on that offer, but for now, I am trying to deal with the emotions myself.

In a way, the inner turmoil is providing a necessary counterpoint to the uncertainties facing us. I am mighty proud of Jillian, but it breaks my heart to feel this distance between us. I love her with everything I am, but I can't give her what she needs and that Dr. Devya man can. He can help her strengthen her Dream Shaping Gift. She's always gonna face danger, and if this man can help her survive, I gotta let her work with him.

It makes perfect sense in my head, but the crushing pain is still pounding my heart to powder.

I'm told she'll be able to visit from time to time, but our lives won't ever be the same. She won't be sitting at her desk pretending to do math homework or chasing TJ through the back yard. I feel like she grew up in a second and the unfairness of that hurts something awful. Still, she's alive, and she seems comfortable with the young woman she's becoming.

In happier news, my boys number four now: Michio, Aiden, Isaac, and TJ. We picked Theo up from Pastor Carl's house soon after meeting Jeffrey and Isaac at the Newark airport.

Michio and Aiden did some subtle work on the pastor's wife, Tammy. She should recover from the pneumonia in a few days. The boys were cautioned not to do a complete healing 'cause we can't risk exposing their Gifts to the public.

We didn't even go home. Nadia has some contacts who will sell the house on our behalf. The proceeds will be funneled through some companies to make it untraceable. New accounts will be set up for us. I don't know if we'll be getting different names or just disappearing. I don't mind. Momma's about the only person who I'd really like to keep in contact with, and she's gonna come stay with us on the farm.

Never saw myself as a farmer or a gardener, but I do love pretty flowers.

Jeffrey and I have agreed to work with Maisha to take care of the boys. We'll live wherever they live. For now, that means a remote farmstead somewhere. Nadia hasn't told us yet. I thought I'd care more about not knowing where we're going, but everybody I love is here, except Jillian. Not sure who's gonna come train the boys. I thought it might be their mommas, but the lady scientists are slated to work elsewhere. I'm sure they'll visit, but that doesn't answer the question about a teacher for the boys. Guess I'll find out later.

I wanna clarify that I don't feel qualified to raise my boys, but I can love 'em well.

Don't worry if ya don't hear from me for a while. Part of the plan to safeguard the children involves secrecy and silence, but after all you've done for us, you deserved as formal a thank you and farewell as I could muster on short notice.

Thank you for everything you've done for me, for Jillian, and my whole family.

Sincerely,
Allison and Jeffrey

Chapter 41:
Fates and Futures

ITEM 282: Danielle's 86th letter
Item Source: Danielle Matheson

Dear Dr. S.,

I think I can finally answer that question I asked you ages ago. I wanted to know if recording enough of my strange adventures would let me get rid of them and become normal again. The answer is no.

Try as I might, I cannot picture a return to college life. I can't imagine a career in psychology either lecturing future generations about the topic or even doing what you do and helping people work through difficult times in their lives. No offense to you. If you couldn't tell by the eighty-something letters I've bombarded you with over the past fear years, I'm a big believer in the work you do, but I can't do it myself. I've seen too much.

Never thought I'd be a college dropout. I haven't found a way to spring that announcement on the parents yet. If any ideas occur to you, please share.

The idea of working with Nadia is exciting and terrifying in multiple ways. The training document she sent me is over three hundred pages. She assured me that we would tackle it topic by topic over time. I skimmed the table of contents to get a feel for the lessons she had in mind. Her curriculum would put most five-year masters programs to shame. She intends to cover politics, science, history, English composition, reading comprehension, memorization, hostage negotiation, cooking, survival, Spanish, French, Latin, and Chinese.

Varick's slated to be my physical trainer. I thought it would be for simple self-defense like he'd been teaching me before, but the subsection on physical training spanned twenty pages.

College would be worlds easier, but I've given the matter a lot of thought and hit the same conclusion every single time. Becoming Nadia's public face will be the most challenging, noble, and reckless thing I've ever set my mind to doing.

Now that my future is relatively certain, perhaps you'd like to hear about some of the others' fates. Skip this part if you must, but I shall provide a faithful record of what I know.

The original plan for Cora and Dr. C. will move forward. They're officially retiring from service to the United States government and starting new careers with Turner Imports, the company owned by Cora's family. Since Dr. C. knows a lot about the nanotechnology program, she has agreed to do some consulting. Aside from running the import-export business, Cora and Dr. C. will help Nadia establish networks of supporters and safehouses for genetically Gifted people. It's sadly ironic that the most powerful people need the most protection.

Now free of the need to prove himself, Devya will return to his first love: research. It's probably a kinder fate than the man deserves, but I think getting shot by Mulligan and healed by the boys softened his spirit a bit.

To me, the most surprising decision is Dr. Paladon's one to officially return. She's been working for various private labs and taking Guardian contracts for years, but this time, Dr. P. will be a few rooms down from Devya.

Dustin informed us that Edward wants to work with Devya and Dr. P. His decision to let his siblings cripple his Gift became the turning point that ultimately saved us. It wouldn't surprise me if Cora agreed to consult via phone or video conference.

Another strange pairing is Dr. Robinson and Agent Rydell. Both have expressed an interest in seeing the nanotechnology project succeed in an ethically sound manner. I don't know where their lab will be

Senator Sean Pauling, formerly Sean Jackson Pauling who

helped found Votive, will continue his political career. When asked, he readily relinquished control—and responsibility—for one of the last three pendants. I even got to meet his wife and three children.

There's a chance Anastasia and her adoptive family will be threatened due to their connection to Devya's children, but for now, Varick and Rydell believe minimal supervision is required.

Ethan, Tyra, Dee, and Varick will work with Rydell and Dr. Robinson. The first two are almost done their detoxification programs to rid their systems of the growth serum Dr. Lanier forced them to take.

Agent Kanter and most of her misfit crew plan to run a training ground for Gifted people. Those slated to stay with her are Que, Tae, and Kay who have technical, emotional, and mental Gifts respectively. If Kay gets his way, he'll receive direct training with Nadia.

I think that covers the scientists and the acquaintances I'm aware of. Let's move on to villains. Not sure I like the word because it makes them seem like cartoon bad guys ready to entertain small children on a Saturday morning.

Senator Orion Foster officially retired from both public office and several secret appointment positions. I said good riddance, but Nadia reminded me that he did some good over the years. The story the media will run with cites health reasons, but really it came down to the simple fact that somebody had to take the fall for such a spectacular misuse of government property.

Senator Veronica Santelli will keep her public positions and remain on the subcommittee in charge of the Guardians, but she'll be reporting directly to her brother instead of her father.

I hesitate to list ATLAS's fate here because it's a program, not a person. It's a terrifying, horribly invasive program that nearly got us all killed recently, but Malia assures me the worst parts have been crippled or are being carefully monitored. I believe Kay's brother, Que, will work to ensure it stays that way.

While I'm talking about entities rather than people, I'll happily report that Katharos is no longer a threat. Acting upon a recommendation from ATLAS, Senator Foster had directed funds to Katharos in exchange for their help stress testing Nadia and the others in Devya's labs. That boils down to setting fanatics and would-be assassins against them to see how they would fare. Not exactly the most responsible way to stress test your people, but nobody asked me how to run the program. Anyway, the removal of funds and the arrest of several key individuals has effectively hobbled the organization.

Surprisingly, Mulligan wasn't working directly with or for ATLAS. His overreaches came from accidentally impressing the right people and being launched through the ranks too quickly. Essentially, he's a science nerd who got pressed into being an administrator without much of a talent for the work. That led to a bevy of poor decisions. Nadia thinks ATLAS may have played him like a musical instrument to get him to do the heavy lifting in terms of people gathering. His power base has been decimated, but he'll be allowed to pursue some research opportunities as long as he stays very far away from Dr. Paladon, Dr. Carnasis, and pretty much anybody connected to Devya's program. Since Nadia will now take a direct hand in his lab assignment, it's safe to say he may never walk in the same state as her mother.

Dr. Kayla Burrel and Dr. Francis DeLuca will be allowed to continue their research. Kay has agreed to work with them.

That should do it for this batch of psychos.

I shall now palate cleanse my head by talking about some of my favorite people.

Nadia tells me she'll split her time between London and the States. I assume that means she'll spend some time with Dr. C. and Cora, but with her, it could mean anything. She knows more people on a deeper level than I've laid eyes upon in my life, so it's entirely possible she could be dealing with people I've never met.

I should probably clarify that she's not physically going anywhere. I wanted to blame Devya for that, but Nadia claims she's okay with the contract clause. The senate subcommittee demanded she stay in a secure site until her eighteenth birthday. The idea of that being a few years away struck me as odd, but that's entirely a perception thing on my part. I've gotten so used to talking with Queen Elena and Naidine that I forget that Nadia's a teenager. It's sad and infuriating but not much of a change from life as she's always known it. As a Minder, she can do most of her work without physical travel, but it's still unfair.

Jillian's folks and Maisha will live somewhere remote and share responsibility for raising Michio and Aiden. For all intents and purposes, that means Isaac will be raised with two older brothers. Malia and Nadia scouted locations in Pennsylvania, Kentucky, and Texas, but I don't know if they chose something yet.

I also don't know what was said, but Jillian and I watched Isaac for a few hours while her parents had a heart-to-heart chat. When they returned to pick Isaac up, there was definitely less tension between them. What went down isn't the sort of thing you can brush off easily, but I do know that Mr. B. plans on quitting his job as manager of Charlie's Chocolates and moving wherever Nadia ultimately places them.

In a strange twist of fate, I think Jillian's old daddy, Jason Antel, will be doing some work on the facilities slated to hold Maisha, the boys, and the Blairingtons. He's worked for Devya since being swept up with Jillian during that second kidnapping I helped plan so she could get to Nadia. A small, drama-loving part of me wants to see what'll happen if Mr. Antel ends up staying at the same location as his ex and her husband.

The fairy tale ending goes to Malia and the Davidsons. I think there's even a twice-postponed wedding happening soon. Malia might switch over to a homeschooling program so she can train with her Gifts more often and accept odd jobs from Nadia. If she stays involved in the public school system, her work for Nadia will be more like science version of the National Guard—several weekends a month and a few weeks during the summer.

The Matheson family is runner up for the fairy tale award. At the risk of sounding self-absorbed, my absence takes us out of the running for picture perfect finish. Nadia and Varick both concluded that the future risks to my family are minimal now that we essentially control ATLAS.

My parents get to return to their normal lives. My siblings get to return to school. They're thrilled about that part. The only one not picking up to the point before life chucked us collectively off a cliff is me. I have a lot of work to do and attending college would only interfere. See above for the partial list of stuff to cram into my poor head and beat into my muscle memory.

Mom said Katie wants to start meeting with you. She's working on Dylan, but he's harder to read. Like me, Dylan inherited a powerful protective street from Mom. He also picked up on Dad's ability to function through personal stuff that's not okay. I'm worried about him. Dad too if I'm being completely honest. They both internalize stuff, but the difference is that Dad has a lot more life experience to ground him. Malia promised to monitor their emotional states for me.

Nadia assures me that I'll still get to see my family, but the break's a lot more thorough than I expected a few months ago when I headed off to college. I'll miss my roommate, Karen, and my old friend, Christy Roman, but since I don't know exactly what manner of beasts my work with Nadia will unleash, I think a clean break with them is the safest option for now.

This representative work is temporary, but the skills involved in the training process are useful ones. Who knows what I'll be doing in five years.

Jillian hasn't told me where they're sending her. She might have been able to return home if the Blairingtons chose to also return. Since they're headed for parts unknown, she has the option to go with them, but knowing her, I doubt she'll take it. Like Nadia, Jillian can work from almost anywhere. She has developed her Dream Shaper Gifts well to this point, but the recent events have highlighted the weaknesses and limitations. Thus, the idea of formal training has more appeal.

The idea of Jillian training directly with Devya still puts a sour expression on my face, yet I can't deny that he's likely the best suited to the task. Dr. Carnasis did a lot of work with Jillian, but it was Devya's passion and vision that launched the work in the first place. The man is still a massive jerk to whom I still owe several punches for the way he treats people. Still, if training with Devya will make Jillian's job easier, safer, or more effective, I am for it.

I'm excited to have Varick as a combat instructor, but I understand he'll still be running off here and there without much rhyme or reason. I don't like that part, but I'm slowly warming to the idea of accepting it. Even if our relationship morphs into a long distance one, I have Jillian, Nadia, and Malia to help me keep tabs on him. I love Varick. I've said the words to him before this but writing it out lends a sense of permanency.

Domestic bliss may never be an option for us, but I can't just flip a switch and stop loving him. Always thought planning things out far into the future would be best, but in this matter, I instinctively know day to day is the best we can hope for.

This may be the last letter you receive from me for a long time, maybe forever. You already know my level of correspondence is boom or bust. It's not solely the possibility of life getting busy soon. You have risked much to help us thus far. Some distance now may keep you safer, freeing you to help my family and those like us.

I must end with a huge thank you. Sharing my thoughts with you and learning from your thoughtful questions has helped me process a lot. Continue using those gifts. You have no idea how many lives are made better for it.

Nadia's Representative (Part Spy. Part Diplomat. Part Gopher.),

Danielle Matheson.

Chapter 42: The Lost Prince

ITEM 283: Jillian's 135th post-kidnapping journal entry
Item Source: Jillian Blairington

This is gonna be my last journal entry for Dr. S. 'cause Nadia says the government people don't want records of my training. I'll probably continue writing 'em. I just won't be able to send 'em. Guess I could just write for me, but I first started journaling 'cause Dr. Wittier said it'd be good for me. Dr. S. said almost the same thing. It's gonna be odd not to have an audience of one, but government agents get mighty ornery about the idea of their secrecy rules being broken. Maybe they'll let me write journals for Danielle. She's gonna be in a different program but probably one with a similar security setup.

Nadia told me about the stipulation—that means something like stuffy requirement—as I climbed into the SUV to head back to the Skye High Hotel. It's my temporary home until they finish arguing about where to send me. It's kinda a big jigsaw puzzle 'cause they need to find secret labs for a lot of people, some of whom can't be mixed. Secret labs are the only ones with the right security for our project.

Danielle and Varick got to come with me on the ride to the hotel, but they didn't stay. Not sure where they're headed, but I think they might already have an assigned training location. My goodbye with each of 'em consisted of a long embrace. I hope I didn't seem cold and unfeeling, but I also couldn't let my guard down and cry.

I don't mind my own company, but the time with my family had spoiled me. Despite having wall-to-wall meetings scheduled till late in the evening, Nadia made sure I got assigned the same room Danielle had stayed in. Nobody had cleaned it yet, so it still had the duffle bag of clothes left for her. She's a lot taller than me, but I found enough clean things in the bag to arrange a suitable outfit to sleep in.

Since there wasn't much to do and I'd traveled most of the day, I showered, changed, and climbed into bed. I didn't even need to use my Gift. Sleep came naturally. I let normal dreams happen for a few hours before returning to Terabane.

The scene moved forward without missing a beat.

The color-shifting gems landed in the hands of the characters with features like our collective mommas. They didn't waste any time.

My mother held her hands out toward me. The collar around my neck snapped and tumbled to the ground.

The Warrior leapt across the room and held my uncle's blade hand long enough for me to twist free.

The Alchemist tossed me a Mana Restoration potion.

I downed the potion in a series of frantic, unladylike gulps. My blue bar filled beautifully.

As Uncle Orius recovered from his shock, my Woodland Creature spell hit him square in the chest and turned him into a baby deer. The sorcerer waved in my direction, but my spell was faster. He yowled as my thought won and turned him into a cat.

Meanwhile, the Gray Lady stretched her free hand toward Captain McKenna and removed the enchantment surrounding him.

Bright light filled the room and lifted the captain up.

The guards with him stumbled back and covered their eyes. One fell. He sat up quickly but stayed on the ground shielding his eyes.

The captain's body rotated three times, and his features changed. The beard disappeared. The hair became wavier and changed shades from red brown to gold brown to a mixture of blond and brown. His cheekbones changed angles. His features looked like Edward for a moment before they shifted some more, aging him backwards until Dustin hovered in the light a foot off the ground.

The light gently lowered Dustin until his feet touched the ground. When that happened, he opened his eyes and stared around.

The baby deer stamped in frustration then stumbled, jumped, and landed awkwardly.

A handful of the soldiers dropped to a knee and bowed their heads. The rest gripped their sword handles hard and warily eyed everybody in the room.

I prepared to turn the lot of 'em into more woodland creatures. It would tax my mana bar but that would be the least of my problems if I missed any soldiers.

The Alchemist circled the bed and helped my mother drink a new potion. It didn't resemble the normal Health Restoration Elixirs, but I remembered that the Alchemist made her own potions. I'd even experienced one during a particularly tough level of *The Immortal Warrior II: Quest for the Lost Heirs*.

I waited with everybody else, eager to see what effect the potion would have upon the queen. She looked more alert but didn't exactly leap out of bed.

"The king is dead, and the usurper is vanquished," said one of the kneeling guards. "Who shall rule in his stead, Your Majesty?"

"That is up to the Chosen One."

My mother's announcement startled me.

"Why me? Why not you?"

"I am not an heir of this kingdom. You and your brother may split the power, you can take it for yourself, or you can grant him the right to rule."

Despite Nadia's earlier words about beating the game, I felt like this was a test and guessing wrong would have some serious consequences.

"What happens in each situation?" I didn't think the question made much sense, but the game characters followed the sentiment well enough.

The Gray Lady answered the question.

"All paths carry risks. Splitting the power may lead to future strife should the two of you disagree. It will also complicate succession beyond your generation. Both seizing power for yourself and giving it up come with the threat of rebellion."

I stared hard at my brother. His game name of Edward floated to the top of my memories. I remembered holding him as a baby, chasing him through the palace, and teaching him how to hold a sword as Captain McKenna had taught me.

"What happened to Captain McKenna?" I blurted the question.

The soldier who'd spoken before answered.

"He perished."

At a gesture from my mother, the man rose and continued his tale.

"The captain rode out with Prince Edward to see if the nearby village of Aleron needed aid from the recent flooding. That's when the prince vanished. I know nothing more."

The Gray Lady stepped forward and continued the story.

"They were ambushed by Kyrus and Maolik." She nodded toward the black cat I'd just formed from the sorcerer. "They killed the captain before Kyrus used one of my enchantment scrolls to transform the prince into the captain."

"Why?" I didn't like feeling so lost or having to ask that question a dozen times, but they weren't exactly laser focused in their explanations.

"The Deep Magic," answered my brother. As with the other familiar faces, his voice fit Dustin.

"Had your father ordered his death, our gifts would have been corrupted," explained my mother. "Such a taint would have let Orius seize it without my cooperation."

"But he forgave the captain who lost his son," I finished. The memory dutifully played for me, but I halted it. I'd review it later, but the decision could wait no longer. "What do you wanna do?" I directed the question to my brother.

He returned my gaze and answered with wisdom beyond his years. Given the wording, my guess is Sonia spoke to him.

"Ruling is a privilege and a burden. I cannot do what you can, nor can you do what I can." He grinned at me. "You would hate the details of running a kingdom. Besides, I am but a child surrounded by more experienced rulers. I will yet grow into the role."

Once I untangled the meaning, I agreed and let his decision stand. The game title came to mind. It wasn't called *The Immortal Ruler*. I was a warrior, a dragon tamer, and a protector.

As soon as I registered my decision, a new title popped up with the triumphant chime of an unlocked achievement. It read: Wise One.

Another cutscene started and words scrolled across my vision. It yammered on for some time about how Terabane enjoyed a long and semi-peaceful reign of King Edward Ayers, mostly thanks to the protection of his sister, the Immortal Warrior.

Soothing music played as pictures of idyllic scenes faded in and out. I only caught some of 'em. Villagers danced under fairy lights. Long tables held nearly endless varieties of food. King Edward sat on his throne surrounded by our mother, the Alchemist, the Warrior, and the Gray Lady.

I watched the rolling credits for a few minutes before withdrawing from the dream. The peaceful feeling followed me.

The game wasn't a perfect analogy, but it reminded me of my purpose. Dustin's cooperation meant the programs would continue in some way. I would learn my Gift well so I could protect my family.

Epilogue:

ITEM 284: Carla Wittier's tenth letter
Item Source: Dr. Carla M. Wittier

To Dr. Stephanie Sokolowski:

I have received your latest batch of correspondence with Jillian and Danielle, and I share your concerns over their intentions to withdraw. While I can understand their reasoning, both young ladies have many troubles to work through. It sounds like they are headed into situations requiring more support, not less. I suppose one of Nadia's personalities could provide such mental support, but she should not have to bear that responsibility. Likewise, Malia could provide adequate emotional care, but she will have her own troubles.

In many ways, this is a bittersweet end with numerous sacrifices being made by these children. Perhaps Nadia will keep us informed.

I would like to establish a relationship with Dustin. His desire to be a hero has been fulfilled, but as with Nadia, such a weighty decision should not have to rest upon his young shoulders. The boy should be navigating the preteen perils of middle school, not bargaining with his personal freedom.

Despite Allison's doubts, the Blairingtons are uniquely suited to raising Michio, Aiden, and Isaac well. I wonder what will become of young Isaac. It is never easy to live in someone's shadow, but he will only know of life among the Gifted. I suspect he will rise to the occasion as Danielle has done but much about the future is uncertain.

I have enjoyed getting to know you through your work with Jillian and Danielle. If you hear anything further, please keep me apprised of their situations. I will do the same. I am immensely curious to know their fates, but a small part of me wishes to hear no more so the fantasy that they live happily ever after will never be broken.

Kind regards,
Carla M. Wittier, PhD.

Thank You for Reading:

Thank you for sharing in this science fiction adventure. This is the end of Devya's Children, but I will be continuing to work with some of the characters in The Minder Project.

If you'd like to try a different flavor of scifi or another genre, check out my website (juliecgilbert.com). Many stories can be experienced in ebook, paperback, or audiobook. I highly recommend the audiobooks, as I've worked very hard to hire talented people to bring these stories to life.

Hop on the newsletter (https://www.subscribepage.com/n7e8l8) if you want to keep up with life and new release news. Plus, subscribers get the first crack at exclusive giveaways.

Please consider leaving a review at your favorite retailer. Your opinion matters, and it will help other readers find this series.

Everybody has gifts. Use them well.

Sincerely,

Julie C. Gilbert

www.ingramcontent.com/pod-product-compliance
Lightning Source LLC
Chambersburg PA
CBHW070858180626
46817CB00003B/823

* 9 7 8 1 9 4 2 9 2 1 6 1 5 *